SOL
Shall Rise

G.P. Hudson

ISBN-13: 978-1505291094
ISBN-10: 1505291097

DEDICATION

To Corynn, Aidan, Evan, and Laurel
With All My Love

CHAPTER 1

Sometimes life isn't short enough.

Jon cursed as his eyes opened. Cursed at the light, and at the weapon pointed at him.

He closed them again, hoping to fall back into oblivion. No luck. He struggled to figure out where he was, but his memory remained thick and unyielding, the blackness oppressive. He searched the crevices of his mind for a clue, something to make sense of things. But nothing came to him.

Jon opened his eyes again. The weapon was still trained on him. An energy weapon. How did he know that? Black and sleek, it conformed well to the gunman's hand. But the hand trembled. The man wasn't a soldier, wasn't a real threat. Jon looked up at a swollen pock marked face. Gray eyes looked back at him, wide and panicked. There was something about them. Something familiar, but he couldn't place it.

He tried to clear his mind and some memories trickled through. Not enough to understand things yet, but he started to get his bearings. A sweet smell filled the air. A scent he knew. Red Dust. That made sense. The confusion. The memory lapse. Everything would come back to him soon enough.

Disjointed memories continued to flash in Jon's mind. His wife. His children. The grief of their loss. His heart pounded violently against his ribs, the memory almost too much to bear. More memories flooded his mind and he saw a myriad of faces. Frightened, pleading faces begging for mercy. A familiar cold detachment took hold and stifled his grief.

He heard yelling behind him and he switched his attention towards it. He turned to see a large bearded man pointing a gun at someone else. Thick well defined muscles roped across the man's arms and shoulders. Dark eyebrows snapped together bordering cold, murderous eyes. The bearded man pointed his gun at a third man sitting in a chair. Blood poured from the seated man's nose and his eye had swollen shut. Jon watched a meaty hand pound the side of the injured man's head. Despite the swelling Jon was sure he knew him.

Just then something alien inside Jon stirred and his stomach lurched. Dread climbed up his spine and he almost panicked, but forced the feeling away.

What the hell was that?

He tried to shift his focus and looked back at the man in the chair. He recognized him now. His name was Max. They were friends. Max had a lost look on his face. The poor bastard was taking a good beating. But for what?

He looked around and realized he was in Max's apartment. The room itself looked like it had taken as much of a beating as Max. Glass shards littered the floor, a table was upended, the holo-emitter destroyed.

How long was I asleep?

Jon's mind became more lucid as the effects of the Red Dust continued to wear off. He recognized the alien creature inside his belly again. His muscles hardened as it continued to awaken.

Red Dust. That must be what they want.

No surprise, it was what everyone wanted. Red Dust was instant insomnia. It made the real world disappear. Most people used it to forget their wartime haunts. Jon was no different. He wanted to forget the wars and his part in them.

It also subdued the creature, an added perk.

Looking back again in Max's direction he saw things had deteriorated. The bearded man had wound an electrical cord around Max's neck, and twisted and pulled from behind. Max tried to dig his fingers in between the cord and his windpipe, desperate to save it from being crushed. Anger spiked through Jon. His rage fed the creature.

Adrenalin surged through his body and cleared his mind. He recognized the attackers now. He had seen them at Max's place before. Red Dust customers. The shaky one pointing the gun at him was Roch and the big one strangling Max was Azzan.

Fucking junkies.

Azzan pulled on the cord with all his strength now and the force yanked Max off his chair. Azzan dragged Max gagging and thrashing across the floor, his face turning a bluish purple. He didn't have long. Maybe a few seconds at most.

"You're going to kill him. We're not supposed to kill them!" said Roch.

Azzan ignored Roch's pleas and didn't let up, his mouth widening into a savage grin. Max's life ticked away.

Jon's hands balled together into hard fists. He looked back at Roch. His gun pointed straight at Jon's head, finger tight on the trigger, knuckles white from the tension.

The creature awoke. His body coiled. Time to act.

Roch focused on Azzan and his gun shifted enough to give Jon an opportunity. In a blur of movement Jon sprang up, grabbed Roch's wrist and twisted. The gun discharged harmlessly, and Jon ripped it out of Roch's hand. Jon drove a heel into Roch's knee and the sickening sound of snapping cartilage filled the room. He released his grip and let him crumple to the floor, screaming and clutching his broken knee.

Jon felt the creature's silent roar and moved as if set off by a hair trigger. Spinning round he saw Azzan reaching for his own gun. Azzan had no chance. Jon streaked across the room and hammered the gun's stock into Azzan's jaw. A molar launched into the air and Azzan collapsed, the sheer force of the blow leaving him unconscious. Jon wanted to crush Azzan's skull under his boot, but suppressed the urge and turned to Max.

The sight made his stomach drop. Max's limp body lay inert on the floor. Had he acted too late? Cursing himself for his weakness he reached down and placed a hand on Max's carotid artery, feeling for a pulse.

Still alive.

Jon exhaled in relief, but his body flexed, coiled in anticipation of more combat. He knew he would remain like this, his entire body like a tight spring, and there would be no respite. The creature would see to that.

Max stirred and Jon turned him over onto his back. He tried to speak, but heaved a groan of pain instead.

"It's ok, just relax for a minute," said Jon.

He propped him up in a sitting position making him cough in violent spasms. Jon inspected his neck. Other than it being heavily bruised, he found no permanent damage.

"Ok buddy, your neck looks good. Just some bruises. You'll just need to rest for a bit." Max nodded.

Jon got up and walked over to Roch, who lay in the corner sobbing. His leg jutted out in an obscene angle where Jon broke it. Jon wanted answers and Roch was going to give them to him.

"Why are you two lowlifes here?" said Jon.

Roch continued to wail.

"Stop crying or I'll break your other leg."

Roch's eyes widened and he bit his lip, his cries now just whimpers.

"Why are you here?"

"We came for the Red Dust." Said Roch.

Roch was lying. After hundreds of interrogations Jon knew a lie when he saw one. That these two were trying to steal Red Dust seemed the obvious answer, and yet Roch lied. Jon stepped on Roch's broken knee, digging the heel of his boot deep into the mangled flesh. Roch screamed in agony.

"Let's try that again and this time I want the truth. Why are you here?"

"Please! I already told you the truth. We came to steal the Red Dust."

Jon grabbed Roch's ankle and pulled upwards, still grinding his heel into his battered knee.

Roch howled. "Ok! Ok! I'll tell you the truth!"

Jon ignored Roch's pleas and continued wrenching his knee. He screamed and writhed in pain as Jon taught him the cost of playing games. When it looked like he would lose consciousness, Jon stopped.

"Mr. Yang sent us."

Jon looked back at Roch in disbelief. "Mr. Yang? The Triad? What does the Triad want with me?"

"They want that thing inside you, they –"

"My symbiont? How do they know about my symbiont?"

"I don't know. They didn't tell us anything else. They just said to make sure we didn't kill you."

"Kill me? That's funny." Jon laughed. He was losing respect for the Triad. "Why would they send you two idiots? Why not send professionals?"

Roch didn't answer. Jon moved to step on his knee again.

"To make it look Red Dust related. They didn't want the blowback."

Jon understood. A professional operation would attract unwanted attention. The creature was military property after all, and even the Triad couldn't withstand the onslaught its theft would trigger. Still, this was a ballsy move, even for the Triad. But it didn't make any sense. Something wasn't right. Roch seemed like he was telling the truth, but his story was ridiculous.

Jon left Roch whimpering on the floor and went back to check on Max. "I have to get going. I'm going to take these two with me. Just get some rest ok?

Max nodded and forced a smile.

Jon went back to Roch and Azzan. He found some rope and hogtied their hands and legs behind their backs, effortlessly lifted both men, one in each hand, and carried them outside. The darkness shielded him from curious eyes. Max lived in a less populated section of Hong Kong, one that had been hit hard during the wars. Many buildings were mere shells, and the few people who did live here didn't ask many questions. It made sense for Max, considering his line of work.

Jon lugged Roch and Azzan down a narrow street. The darkness almost complete. Azzan was awake now and they both groaned with each step.

Roch pleaded again, "Please don't kill us. We'll disappear. You'll never see us again."

"Oh, I'm sure I won't. I'm not going to kill you. I'm going to dump you off somewhere and you can figure the rest out on your own. Now shut up before I change my mind."

They continued to moan but didn't dare speak.

Jon soon came upon the bombed out shell of an old building, one of the many scabs left on the landscape from the wars. It was a bizarre mix of mangled steel and concrete. The roof had a gaping hole, and the entire left side of the building was crumbling and blackened from fires that had long since burned out. In contrast, the right side was still solid and seemed structurally sound. At least it didn't look like it was going to collapse anytime soon. As good a place as any. Jon hauled his two captives into the structure and threw them onto a pile of garbage left by the building's previous occupants. They couldn't do much harm here and someone would eventually find them and let them go.

“You know what’ll happen if I see you again?” said Jon.

The two nodded.

“Good.”

Jon turned to leave, feeling the creature's protests as he stepped toward the exit. He knew it still considered Roch and Azzan a threat, but he didn't care. They weren't a threat and he wouldn't kill them. Ignoring the creature he continued to leave.

A searing pain started in his bowels making him bend at the waist. Lurching forward, he took a couple more steps. The pain spread in violent waves through his intestines, into his abdomen, attacking his kidneys and then his lungs. Unable to withstand anymore, he collapsed. He writhed in agony as the creature punished him for his obstinance.

Jon endured the pain for several minutes. He had given in and agreed to comply, but the pain continued, punitive in nature, ruthless in execution. When Jon had suffered enough the pain stopped. Curled up in a fetal position he gasped for air, relieved that the ordeal was over. In the same way the pain had ripped through his body now a comforting warmth washed over him bringing with it much needed relief.

A few minutes passed. Jon stood, turned and walked toward Roch and Azzan. They gaped back at him, a look of shock on their faces, trying to comprehend what they just witnessed. Standing in front of them Jon apologized and then, in two quick motions, snapped each of their necks.

CHAPTER 2

Tallos looked down at the blue planet below, its oceans reminding him of home. Why had he been summoned to such an insignificant corner of the galaxy? He had heard whispers about these humans, about how the Great See'er considered them extraordinary in some way. For the life of him, he did not see it. They were merely another upstart species propped up by Diakan might. If not for Diakan intervention these humans would still be Juttari slaves. They owed everything to Diakus. Every breath they took was a Diakan gift.

Why bring him here? Why waste his expertise on these creatures? The Juttari had been defeated, the human defenses shored, this system secured. He knew of nothing that would require him to travel all this way. He hoped the need would not be too great. He assured himself it would be no more than some minor advisory services and then he could finally return to Diakus.

He had been away from the home world for far too long. The wars had pulled him to many different corners of the galaxy, like this one. Too many planets. Too many battles. Even when the wars ended there was work for him to do. He continued to be pulled throughout the galaxy, this time for his expertise. Diakan space had expanded, and it needed to be secured. His advisory services were in greater demand than he expected.

But he longed for the home world. He longed to see the great oceans of Diakus again. When was the last time he felt the heat of its giant red star on his skin? How long since he gazed upon the many moons, floating in the sky like orbs, so close you thought you could scoop them into your hands.

Soon, he thought. Soon.

"Ambassador Varyos will see you now," said a synthetic voice. A door behind him slid open and he turned from the window and walked through.

"Greetings General Tallos," said Ambassador Varyos.

"Greetings Ambassador." He wondered why someone with Varyos's reputation would be posted as Ambassador to the humans. By all accounts this was a junior position. Who did he offend to get banished here? Tallos wondered if he himself hadn't unwittingly offended a high ranking official somewhere. Could that be it? Was this some sort of banishment? He shuddered at the thought.

"I am sure you are wondering why you have been summoned to such a remote system."

"The order is curious." It was more than curious. It was offensive, but he dared not say so.

"What do you know of the humans, General?"

"I know that they were Juttari slaves. Now their system is a Diakan protectorate. The only reason this system has any strategic significance at all is the jump gate it has access to."

"And what of their capabilities?"

Whispers. Only whispers. "They are unimpressive. They rely on Diakan technology and assistance for their survival. Without our help they are like children alone and adrift on a vast sea."

"The Great See'er has foretold otherwise."

Could the whispers be true?

"The humans will rise to power in the galaxy."

"Impossible. They barely stand on their own. Without a Diakan presence in their system the Juttari Empire would conquer them again."

"For now. This will change, quicker than you believe possible."

"I do not presume to question the Great See'er. If She has foretold of their rise then it is so. What else has She seen? Do they become a threat to Diakus?"

"It is unclear, but their rise is certain. The Great See'er warns that it is imperative that their ascension be controlled. If it is managed they will not become a threat to Diakus."

"And if we cannot manage their ascension?"

"Then they must be terminated before they become too powerful."

"Why not terminate their species now and avoid the potential threat altogether?"

"The Great See'er has foretold of yet another threat. One as yet undiscovered. The humans will contain that threat. Without them it will grow unchecked and plague our borders, eventually weakening the Empire. As Diakus weakens others will grow bold and challenge our power. Over time Diakus will atrophy and our enemies will feed on our withering bones, the Empire a forgotten legend."

"This cannot be allowed. Diakus has gained too much, at too high a cost."

"By Her Will, Diakus shall prevail. The Great See'er is wise beyond comprehension." Varyos bowed his head in reverence.

"By Her Will," said Tallos, bowing his head as well. After a few moments the two Diakans raised their heads. "How may I serve Diakus?"

CHAPTER 3

Jon walked for a couple of hours, making his way down a hill along a winding road. Signs of progress dotted the landscape. Everywhere he looked he saw growth. Many buildings had already risen from the ruins like defiant fists. It made him hopeful. The Juttari Empire had severely scarred humanity. Five hundred long years under alien occupation. Countless atrocities. Orbital bombardment. Mass murder. Forced labor. Stolen children. And then the wars of liberation, and their cost. Earth finally had an opportunity to rebuild. Humanity had a chance to recover, even if it was too late for him.

Still the ruins were everywhere. On the walls of one destroyed building were the words "Sol Shall Rise". The rallying cry of the revolution. Too few believed those words now. Why fight for something when you are being spoon fed?

At the bottom of the hill things got busier. It was still night, but the streets filled with people. Hong Kong never slept. An open air market stretched ahead for countless city blocks. Crowds of people haggled and shouted. The smell of fish and seafood filled the air, making his stomach growl. When had he eaten last? Shaky columns of cages filled with live chickens stood next to fruits and vegetables. Colorful textiles butted up against weapon stands, hocking the latest in energy weapons. Anything could be purchased here, so long as you knew what to ask for and how to ask for it.

Jon made his way down the street. He had no interest in shopping, but didn't mind mixing in the crowds. He wondered what Yang would do once he realized that Azzan and Roch were dead. If he came after Jon again it wouldn't be with amateurs. Jon wasn't particularly worried, but he still needed to think things through. It was time to get to his ship. R&R was over.

A man made eye contact with Jon. It was only for a moment, but that was all he needed. Physically larger than most, he towered over those around him. A battle hardened face and the menacing eyes of a killer ensured that people got out of his way. The fact the man made eye contact was the first clue. That Jon also knew a killer's eyes when he saw them was the second.

Had the Triad found him? Scanning the crowd Jon analyzed his options. There was likely more than one opponent. Probably four or five. While he used the crowd for cover, he realized his adversaries were doing the same. Except they were getting into position, likely putting Jon into a box formation, flanking him on all sides. While not overly concerned with civilian deaths, they would likely avoid attacking in the middle of the market. That reluctance gave him a small edge.

He had kept Roch's gun but needed something more powerful. He turned and walked up to a weapon stand, still scanning the crowd. He spotted two more attackers. They had moved into position on his left flank. They were already dead. They just didn't know it yet.

The weapon stand's merchant looked at Jon and gave him a knowing smile. This man had obviously spent some time around soldiers. Jon eyed an X51. A powerful energy weapon. It was perfect.

Skipping the formalities, he looked the merchant straight in the eyes and spoke in a low, calm voice. "I'll pay you double if you put a fully charged cartridge into that X51." The smile slowly disappeared. The merchant became visibly nervous, understanding what was about to happen. He seemed to analyze his options, sizing up Jon and making some quick calculations. It didn't take him long. No fool, he understood that Jon was not someone to toy with. Reaching under the counter he casually pulled out an energy cartridge, armed the X51 and placed it back down on the table. Jon smiled at the merchant and nodded his thanks.

"Get down."

Before the merchant could hit the ground, Jon seized the weapon and wheeled around firing twice as he turned. Each shot found its target. The power of the X51 hurling both men back several feet. A half-second later and Jon was sprinting, opening fire on the third attacker. Blue light pierced the man's torso creating a smoldering crater where his chest had been.

Based on the formation his attackers used, Jon knew the other two men's locations and the trajectory their fire would take. He found cover just as a barrage of energy bursts landed. Blue fire rained down all around Jon. The shooters weren't worried about the crowd anymore, the market becoming a horrid scene of panic and dead bodies.

Their lines of fire allowed Jon to determine their precise locations. The shooters fired relentlessly. Powerful blasts scorched the market, burning through wood and melting glass like butter. Jon crouched into a ball, motionless, and waited for an opportunity. After several more seconds their fire slowed and adopted a pattern of predictable bursts. The shooters must have thought Jon was dead, but didn't want to take any chances.

He timed their fire. Timed their pauses. Established the pattern. Leaped and fired.

A single energy blast crashed into the shooter's face almost decapitating him. The other shooter let loose another barrage. Blue bolts chased Jon, biting at his heels. The shooter's speed and accuracy surprised him. The creature made Jon faster and stronger than normal humans, so the shooter should not have adjusted to his speed as well as he did.

Jon dove behind the walls of a fruit stand, blue fire missing him by mere centimeters. He crouched down, making himself as small as possible. Produce exploded and wood splinters flew around him like angry hornets.

This was not the Triad. This was something worse. Something Jon hadn't seen since the wars.

The blue fire changed direction. The shooter was moving. Circling. He would have a clear shot in seconds. Jon coiled and dove again. Anticipating the shooter's movement Jon shot in the direction he was running. To Jon's surprise the man changed direction and the shot missed. Anybody else would've been dead.

Another storm of blue lightning rained down on Jon's position, forcing him to bolt again. The shots were closer now. The shooter tried to bridge the gap between them. Upping the ante. That suited Jon just fine.

He zigzagged across the road, returning fire as he went. Again the shots were barely missing him and adjusted expertly to his movements. He had to change tactics. The shooter wanted to bridge the gap so Jon would give him what he wanted.

Changing direction he raced toward the attacker. This caught the man off guard and he tried to compensate, but Jon already knew which way he would turn and had let loose a stream of blue fire in that direction. The shooter tried to stop, but his momentum was too strong. Blue energy bursts plowed into his torso, spinning him round like a top till he dropped to the ground.

Jon found cover and waited, scanning the market, ensuring no other surprises were waiting for him. Once certain the threat had passed he rose and ran to the last shooter's position. The man lay face down in a heap. Jon turned him over. Scorch marks riddled his torso, the putrid smell of burnt flesh rising from his body. Turning his head Jon looked behind the man's ear. It was just as he suspected. A tiny mark, almost invisible, hid there. The mark of the Chaanisar.

Elite human soldiers, the Chaanisar were taken from their parents as children and raised to be the most loyal soldiers in the Juttari Empire. Augmented with alien technology they possessed superhuman strength and speed. Jon had fought them many times during the wars.

But why were they here? The wars were over. There should not be any Chaanisar left on Earth. And why were they trying to kill him? The Triad story must have been a deception. It would be easy enough to feed Roch and Azzan disinformation. They wanted Jon in the dark, so they could ambush him. But they hadn't anticipated his actions in the market.

Jon figured he'd hang onto the X51 for a while longer. He had his fill of surprises for one night. Happy to be paid, the merchant didn't ask any questions. The market was now a scene of destruction and carnage. Jon didn't want to deal with the local authorities and quickly left.

After walking for several kilometers he reached the Kowloon Spaceport. Above him the morning sky was littered with all sorts of ships, large and small, coming and going. Ahead was an array of terminal and service buildings, hangars, and parking stalls connected by a mix of runways, roadways, and landing pads. Jon walked past the main terminal and approached a large unmarked secondary building. He walked up to the main doors and a holo-emitter flashed a stop sign in his path.

"Please stand still for DNA scan," said a synthetic voice.

Jon heard the low humming sound of the scanners as they analyzed his DNA signature. After a few moments the holographic stop sign disappeared, and the doors slid open.

"Thank you Captain Pike. You may enter."

Jon walked into a massive open area. The Hill. Every spaceport had one. Military and civilian personnel zipped around like ants. Crates moved to and fro. Soldiers readied for flight. All around was a buzz of activity. Jon proceeded through the building until he came to a set of large metal doors. Another DNA scan and he was through and into a long well lit corridor. Military activity dominated now and the familiar blue and white Space Force insignia was everywhere. Along the right hand side of the corridor were access tubes leading to various docking bays. When he reached tube G17 he turned and entered. He followed a string of lights to the end of the tube and stopped at a large hatch. More DNA scanners went to work. He ignored the concealed energy weapons he knew were trained on him. Programmed to glass anyone accessing his ship without authorization, they wouldn't fire on Jon. The DNA scanner cleared him and the hatch opened.

Lights turned on and a hatch in the forward bulkhead of the compact ship opened, revealing the cockpit. Jon stepped through the hatch and sat down in the pilot's chair. An ordered chaos of controls and displays surrounded him. Jon pushed a button and a screen lit up.

"Captain Jon Pike reporting."

A middle aged woman's face appeared on the screen.

"Good morning Captain," she smiled. "How has your R&R been? I hope you are well rested."

"I'm as rested as I'm going to get."

"Glad to hear it. Captain, you have orders to report to Admiral Walsh at Orbital Station Alpha."

"Understood. Will set course for Orbital Station Alpha immediately."

"Thank you Captain. I will let Admiral Walsh know you are on your way."

"Captain Pike out."

The display flickered off and Jon leaned back in his chair. So much for R&R. Time to get back to work. Sitting up again he pushed some more buttons on his console. The exterior hatch swung closed with a whine and a hiss. Outside the ship's engines came on and the ship began to vibrate. The engines became louder as Jon maneuvered away from the docking tube. Once clear Jon fired the ship's thrusters and quickly climbed up and away from the spaceport.

His ship rocketed higher to the upper reaches of the strata. He took one last look at Hong Kong, wondered about the Chaanisar, and what other surprises might be in store for him. The city disappeared underneath a bed of clouds and Jon pushed the threat out of his mind. Speeding up, the little ship raced to the edges of the atmosphere and into the dark void of space.

CHAPTER 4

Jon arrived early for his meeting. Walking into Admiral Walsh's office, he was dismayed to find a Diakan there. Standing at attention he saluted the Admiral. Walsh responded with a lazy salute barely looking up from his desk and gestured for Jon to sit down. Jon glanced sideways at the Diakan. The thing repulsive to look at. It was a biped like humans, but that's where the similarities ended. It had green skin like a lizard and some kind of gills on its neck like a fish. Big fish eyes were fixed on a flat face. The thing had eyelids, but hardly ever blinked. It was like it wouldn't stop staring at him, making Jon want to beat it into the ground.

"Captain Pike, this is Ambassador Varyos." The Admiral locked eyes with Jon. His icy stare warned Jon to keep his feelings about the Diakans to himself.

"Greetings, Ambassador." Jon almost choked on his words, but gave the Ambassador his best politician smile.

"Greetings, Captain." The Diakan spoke with a hiss. Jon wanted to put a hand in front of his face, afraid the thing was going to spit on him.

Walsh got straight to business. "Captain, what do you know about the lost colonies?"

"Just the same legends everyone else knows, Sir. Humans used the jump gates to colonize planets thousands of light years away. When the Juttari Empire invaded the Sol system the colonists shut down their jump gates to protect themselves."

"It isn't legend, Captain. It's fact. We haven't heard from the colonies in over five hundred years. But they're out there. And we want to find them again."

"Yes, Sir. But how is that possible? With their jump gates closed, it would take a lifetime to find them. Maybe two lifetimes."

"That's why I called you here Captain. We have been working on an experimental propulsion system in co-operation with the Diakans. It works much like the jump gates do. With it a ship can jump as much as fifty light years at a time."

"Without jump gates?" Jon said.

"Correct," Walsh replied.

Jon leaned back in his chair and thought about what he just heard. If true, this would be the biggest advancement since the discovery of the jump gates. "That sounds impressive Sir. I take it you want to use this jump drive technology to find the lost colonies?"

"That's correct Captain."

"You said the technology was experimental. How long till we can power a ship with one of these propulsion systems?"

"We're already there Captain. We've built a ship and fitted it with the jump system, and we want you to command it."

Jon thought the Admiral must have fallen on his head. "With all due respect Sir, I'm Covert Ops. I kill people. I don't command starships."

"Commandeering a starship is part of your training. You know as much as you need to know to command one. Regardless, your experience operating behind enemy lines makes you the perfect candidate. We don't know what we're going to find out there and I need someone who can adapt to any situation. That someone is you. You're also the only human with a Diakan symbiont, which is why the Diakans prefer you commanding the ship."

And there it was. The Diakans were behind it all. They told the Admiral to choose Jon because of the symbiont. Jon's eyes narrowed and he thought of all the different ways he could kill both Walsh and Varyos. It would be over in seconds. The idea comforted him.

Jon then thought about the market attack. Was this why the Chaanisar tried to ambush him? The Juttari Empire had spies everywhere. Did they know about the jump system? Was there a mole? Jon decided it best to keep his suspicions to himself for the time being. He didn't want to command this starship. He didn't want the Diakans pulling his strings. And he sure as hell didn't want to keep their symbiont inside him anymore.

"About the symbiont Sir. I want the thing out of me."

"I'm afraid that is not possible Captain," said Ambassador Varyos. Jon forced himself to look at the Ambassador. "Your physiology is unfortunately not as resilient as a Diakan's. While we can remove our symbionts without harm, I'm afraid that it does not work the same way for you. If we remove your symbiont, you will die."

Anger spiked through Jon. "That wasn't part of the deal. This was supposed to be temporary."

"Your symbiont was created specifically for you, Captain. It is military grade. Designed to enhance your senses, speed and strength, as well as your strategic and tactical capabilities. This has been successful."

"But?"

"We did not anticipate how it would react to your physiology. Captain, the symbiont has… it has entrenched itself. Fortified its position."

"So you designed a military grade symbiont and now you're surprised that it's acted in a military way, right?"

"Yes, Captain. That is correct."

Jon leaned towards the Diakan, ready to pounce.

"None of this was intended Captain. You knew the risks going in," said Walsh.

Jon simmered. These Diakans were no better than the Juttari. Aliens. Jon hated all of them. He killed plenty of aliens during the wars. They were all Juttari, but Jon didn't think he'd mind killing a few Diakans too much. And there was Walsh kissing their scaly asses. Jon imagined his fingers wrapped around Walsh's windpipe and wondered how much effort he would need to rip it out of his throat.

"The truth is that thing inside you, combined with your training and experience make you the perfect person for this mission," said Walsh

"Yes, Sir." Jon settled back into his chair. The Admiral had made up his mind. There was no point arguing with him. Jon was a soldier first, and this was a mission like any other. Time to get on with it. He would deal with the symbiont issue later.

Walsh noticed Jon's change in posture and nodded. "I am uploading your orders, along with ship configuration, and crew profiles."

"Understood. When can I see the ship?"

"It's named Hermes. I've arranged for your quarters to be relocated to the ship. You'll have a few weeks to get familiar with it and the crew. The engineering team is already on board, as are your security personnel and your XO. A couple of Marines are waiting outside and will take you to the ship as soon as we're done."

"Thank you Sir. If that is all, I'd like to get on with it." Jon wanted to get out of Walsh's office before he was court martialed for killing a superior officer.

"That is all Captain. Dismissed."

Jon rose, stood at attention and saluted. The Admiral responded with the same lazy salute.

"Good luck Captain," said Ambassador Varyos.

Jon didn't look at the Ambassador. Didn't acknowledge him in any way. Instead he turned and walked out the door.

Outside the office two Marines were waiting. One of the Marines stepped forward. “Captain Pike?”

“Yes Corporal.”

“We have orders to escort you to the Hermes, Sir.”

“Lead the way Corporal.”

The Marines turned and marched down the corridor with Jon following. He thought about his mission. He could be gone for years. The idea was growing on him. This might be just what he needed.

Jon saw the Hermes from one of the windows. Construction crews still worked on her. She sat there, motionless, like she was stalking prey. Smaller than a Dreadnaught-class battleship, she was larger than a destroyer, though not as bulky. Sleek, like a racer. Her bow tapered almost to a point and the body expanded into smooth curves. She looked like she could pierce the sky.

She may have looked like a racer, but she was no lightweight. Missile tubes, rail guns and energy weapons spread out across her hull. The Hermes was a killer. She looked like she could take on any Juttari ship and win. He wondered how agile she was and proceeded to board. He’d find out soon enough.

CHAPTER 5

"Captain on the bridge," one of the Marines announced. All eyes turned to Jon.

"At ease," said Jon.

A massive space, the Diakan influences were everywhere. From the giant viewscreen that dominated the room, to the myriad of smaller diagnostic displays, Jon saw Diakan fingerprints everywhere. Even the Captain's chair, elevated as it was above all else, could be found on any Diakan warship. Diakan design or not, this was a human ship, under human command. His command. Could he do it? Could he command a starship?

A tall blonde woman approached and saluted. "Commander Lynda Wolfe reporting." Taller than most women, her broad shoulders and serious eyes gave her a commanding presence. An impressive looking officer, she had the look of someone who could move mountains if she needed.

"At ease Commander. I take it you are my XO?"

"Yes, Sir."

"How long until the Hermes is ready?"

"Our full crew complement will be on board within the next two days. There are some minor tests that still need to be performed and some supplemental training. Barring any problems we should be ready to go in two weeks."

"I'll need a full readiness report, Commander. Tactical, Engineering, Security, Medical, everything."

"Yes, Sir."

Jon scanned the room and noticed a Diakan standing by a computer console.

"Why is there a Diakan on my bridge?"

"That is Special Envoy Tallos, Sir. He is here as an observer."

"How long will he be on board?"

"He is supposed to be with us for the entire mission Sir."

Jon cringed. He hadn't anticipated that the Diakans would have one of their own on board. It made sense, but he wasn't happy about it.

"Where is my ready room, Commander?"

"Just over there, Sir." Wolfe pointed to a door on the far left side of the bridge.

"Very well. I am going to get caught up on things. Have the Diakan come and see me."

"Yes, Sir."

Jon walked to the door. The Hermes insignia was emblazoned dead center. A black, star covered oval with a sword running through its center. Two vipers coiled up the blade to a pair of wings spreading out at the hilt. Jon thought the insignia was fitting. The sword was humanity and the two vipers were the Juttari and the Diakans. The word "Hermes" bordered the top of the oval, and the words "Space Force" bordered the bottom. "Semper" and "Primus", Latin for "Always First", displayed left and right respectively. Fitting indeed. The door slid open and Jon entered.

The room was like any Captain's office he had seen. An oversized faux-leather chair sat behind a sleek cedar toned desk. Two chairs flanked the desk on the opposite side. Behind were two large ancient Earth statue replicas from the Greco-Roman period, and the odd print from Earth's Golden Age adorned the wall. Symbols of long lost human greatness, they seemed out of place and hypocritical. A vertical, floor to ceiling aquarium stood in the corner. Charcoal colored walls with chrome accents surrounded the room, and a burgundy carpet covered the floor. A pair of windows offered a view of the wine dark void outside.

Jon walked over to the desk and sat down. Captain of a starship of all things. What had he gotten himself into? He had always been a field operative and now here he was sitting behind a desk. Before long they would have him sitting with the bureaucrats at Space Force Command. The thought sent a cold chill down his back making him shudder.

"Special Envoy Tallos requests entrance," said a synthetic voice.

"Come in," said Jon. Even worse was that a Diakan was coming along for the ride.

The door opened and Tallos entered.

"Greetings, Captain."

"Greetings, Special Envoy."

The Diakan sat in one of the chairs opposite Jon, unblinking eyes fixed on his.

"I trust your stay on the Hermes has been a comfortable one?"

"Yes, Captain. Your crew has been very accommodating."

"I've been told you will be accompanying us on our mission."

"That is correct, Captain."

"As an observer."

"As observer and advisor Captain."

"Advisor?"

“Yes, Captain. The Hermes is partially Diakan design. We are here to advise on its many intricacies.”

“What do you mean, ‘we’?”

“There are several advisors on board, Captain. There are advisors with expertise in engineering, medical, and tactical. We are all here to assist your crew.”

“Alright, then we need to get something straight right from the start. This is not a Diakan ship. This is a human ship. My ship. I give the orders here.”

“Of course Captain.”

“Your advisors will assist only. Any decision making rests solely with myself and my officers.”

“Yes, Captain. I would not have it any other way.”

Jon studied Tallos. No noticeable reaction. He hid his emotions well. The Diakans were used to giving orders. Used to people like Admiral Walsh and President Lewis doing as they were told. It was true that humanity owed a lot to the Diakans. If not for them Earth would still be under Juttari rule.

The Diakans armed Earth with powerful weapons. They helped Earth rebuild. They shared their knowledge. Science. Medicine. Technology. All aspects of society were advancing at mind boggling speed. All thanks to the great benefactors, the Diakans.

Everyone was grateful. And fearful. Afraid that they might change their minds. So when the Diakans asked for something Earth’s leaders jumped. It disgusted Jon. The way he saw it, humanity had gone from being Juttari slaves to being Diakan serfs.

Of course it was better than the alternative. The Juttari occupation had been a horrific piece of human history. When the Juttari Empire first discovered humanity they sent one of their battle groups to the Sol System. It took them only a few hours to annihilate the flimsy human defenses. Earth then experienced the horrors of Juttari orbital bombardment. Simple, relentless brutality. Major cities on all continents were targeted. Repeated offers of surrender ignored. A third of Earth's population died that day.

The remainder became a workforce. Exceptionally ruthless humans were identified and made governors. The governors used fear and intimidation to ensure optimal production. They also performed the heinous act of identifying talented children, and sending them to Juttari training centers. There they would be indoctrinated, chipped, augmented, and trained to become the most feared and loyal soldiers in the Empire. The Chaanisar.

For five hundred years humanity endured this oppression. Then the Diakans came. While Earth always had resistance movements, they were no more than bandits, stealing from the governors, and killing them or their staff when the opportunity allowed. The Diakans covertly trained and armed these movements, turning them into a more effective fighting force. Still, they were not powerful enough to liberate Earth.

It was only when the Diakans established a foothold in the Sol System that they could be more actively deployed. The Diakans fought the Juttari in space and the resistance fought on Earth. As the resistance gained ground their ranks swelled with volunteers. Then the Chaanisar were sent in.

Earth's lost children returned home as battle hardened super-soldiers to crush all hopes of freedom. They punished anyone who helped the resistance. Gruesome battles were fought. Millions died. And then, when all seemed bleakest, the Diakans destroyed a Juttari battle group and gained control of Earth's orbit. Chaanisar supply lines were cut, and the resistance gained orbital support. The Chaanisar were defeated and Earth liberated.

Jon's own father was a member of the resistance, as was his father before him. Jon had learned about freedom, and its cost, since he was a baby. Freedom. Not serfdom. And he was sure as hell not going to be another human groveling at the feet of a Diakan. It was bad enough he let them put their symbiont inside him. They had already exerted their influence on Jon, and now he couldn't get the damned thing out of him. Did they plan to do the same to the rest of humanity? He shuddered at the thought.

"And what is your area of expertise Special Envoy?"

"I am here to assist you with command Captain."

Jon's eyes locked Tallos's in a steely stare. His stomach tightened as he struggled quietly to control his anger.

"Assist me in what way?" Jon asked. He clasped his hands together to avoid clenching them into fists.

"I possess expertise in starship command, strategy and tactics."

"I'm quite sure I can handle things."

"There is no shame in asking for help, Captain. While we requested that you command the Hermes, we also understand that you have limited experience commanding starships. Your special forces training and experience, and your symbiont's inherent design give you many transferable skills, however you do lack experience commanding a ship of this size. I can help you with the transition."

The son of a bitch had done his homework. "I've been trained extensively in starship operations, Special Envoy. I've led several missions where my team has boarded and captured enemy starships. I wouldn't be able to do that if I didn't understand how a starship worked. What is it you think you can add?"

"I have commanded many starships, Captain. I have successfully engaged the Juttari on numerous occasions."

"So now you're telling me you're some kind of war hero?" Jon could barely conceal the sarcasm in his voice.

"This is a human concept, Captain. We do not adopt these romantic notions. We function according to proven systems."

Pompous asshole, Jon thought.

"Success does not lie in individualism or heroics. Victory is the result of efficient systems and procedures."

"I see. Then why is this not a Diakan ship? If your systems are superior, why is this ship under human command?"

"While this ship was built through Diakan and human cooperation, the discovery of the jump system is a human one. It is logical then that this ship be under human command."

Jon smiled. "Is human creativity a romantic notion as well?"

Tallos didn't bite. "The mission to discover your lost colonies is primarily a human one, and of no real interest to us."

Jon wasn't so sure. The way he saw it the Diakans did not possess any special love for humanity. They did not help Earth out of some great benevolence. They were empire building, plain and simple. The Juttari were their enemies. The only difference between the two was the Diakans had no interest in outright conquest like the Juttari. They preferred proxy worlds. By helping planets like Earth become strong, they took control of strategic space by proxy, giving them a greater sphere of influence. Earth became a regional power, and nothing more.

Everything was done under the umbrella of the The Galactic Accord. A treaty between all the worlds and systems under Diakan influence. The concept was simple enough. Everyone under the treaty promised to defend each other against any outside aggression. It also banned aggression between member worlds. Everything looked good on paper, but without the Diakans the Accord was meaningless. Only the Diakans were strong enough to stand against the Juttari Empire. Without them the treaty worlds would fall like dead trees facing a powerful wind. Planets like Earth were only meant to be strong enough to hold off the Juttari until the Diakans could send reinforcements.

And here was a Diakan coming along to find the lost colonies. Once the Hermes found them, and relations with Earth were re-established, the Diakans would move to add them to The Galactic Accord, expanding the reaches of their Empire. All smoke and mirrors. An independent Earth with its own government. An alliance of equals sworn to defend each other. An advanced race sharing their knowledge so that all would benefit. All a clever illusion.

Just then a communication request appeared on his display screen. "Excuse me for a second," Jon said to Tallos. The Diakan nodded and Jon accepted the request. A stately woman's face appeared on the screen. "Good morning Captain, I am Doctor Elizabeth Ellerbeck, Chief Medical Officer."

"Good morning Doctor. What can I do for you?"

"Sir, I need to give you a physical before we start our mission. When is a good time for you?"

"How about right now Doctor? I was meaning to pay you a visit today anyway. I can be there in about ten minutes." Tallos was agitating Jon and this was a good way to get rid of him.

"Perfect. I'll see you in ten minutes. Ellerbeck out."

"My apologies Special Envoy, but as you can see I have a lot to do before we get underway."

"As you wish, Captain."

Special Envoy Tallos rose from his chair and walked out of the room. Sitting back in his chair Jon stared at the door that Tallos walked out of. He had enough on his plate without Diakan interference. Shrugging the encounter off, he got up and headed for the door himself.

On the bridge the hum still permeated as his crew made sure all systems were ready for their mission. When Jon looked at the tactical station, a large grin spread across his face. At the station was a rather large man wearing combat fatigues and carrying a close quarter energy weapon in a shoulder holster. On his uniform was the Hermes emblem and below that a Special Operations badge.

"Kevin St. Clair. How long has it been?" said Jon as he approached the man, extending his hand in greeting.

"Too long Sir," St. Clair replied, enveloping Jon's hand in his own, a wide smile on his face.

"I noticed in the crew manifest that you were assigned to the Hermes. So you are my Security Chief?"

"Yes, Sir. Can't wait for the fun to begin."

"You haven't changed a bit. Walk with me, I'm heading down to sick bay. We can catch up on the way."

The two men left the bridge and proceeded down the corridor.

"Have you met our guests the Diakans?" said Jon.

Kevin laughed. "Yes, Sir. I have my own personal Diakan advisor. I don't know what I did to be so lucky." He didn't try to hide the sarcasm in his voice.

"Yeah, I've got one too. All this political crap is a real pain in the ass." He had always been comfortable speaking to St. Clair. They shared many missions together and had developed a strong bond. They were both cool under fire, and learned a long time ago that they could trust each other.

"I'm surprised you took this mission. I never figured you for the starship captain type."

"It wasn't like I volunteered for it. Orders are orders. You know that."

"Yes, Sir."

Jon's smile disappeared and he looked St. Clair in the eyes. "Listen Kevin, I want to talk to you about something. While I was on R&R in Hong Kong I was ambushed by a Chaanisar fire team."

Kevin's eyes went wide. "Chaanisar? On Earth? I thought those bastards were long gone?"

"So did I, but they were Chaanisar alright. I got a good look at one of the bodies and confirmed it." Jon knew he didn't have to spell things out. Kevin would know it took more than a team of five to take Jon out. Even if they were Chaanisar. "The whole thing has me concerned about this mission. For them to go to the trouble to try and take me out on Earth is pretty extreme."

"You don't think it's some sort of revenge attack?"

"No. The wars have been over for some time now. Besides, the Chaanisar don't usually make a move without the order coming from Juttari command."

"True. The way they've been chipped the Juttari would know everything."

"Yes, and if I'm right that means the Juttari know about the Hermes. Hell, it means they knew I was going to be Captain of the Hermes before I did. And you know what that means…."

"There's a mole."

"Right. And pretty high up the chain of command too."

"So this mission's been compromised."

"We have to assume that it has. I think we also have to assume that there's a spy on board. Either way, let's tighten up security. I want check points throughout the ship. Check for any signs of sabotage. Monitor all communications. Don't leave anything to chance."

"Yes, Sir. I'm on it."

"Let's keep this between us for now. I don't know who can be trusted yet."

"Yes, Sir."

"Good. Hey, do you remember that time on Mintar 7?

"How could I forget? I still have the scar to remind me."

Jon chuckled. "Let me know if you find anything. I want regular reports."

"Yes, Sir."

CHAPTER 6

Commander Wolfe was unsettled as she headed down the long corridor. Having volunteered for this mission, she gave up her position as XO on the Dreadnaught Class battleship Independence. The pride of the fleet. The youngest XO in the fleet, she would be in line for her own command in a few years, and would be the youngest starship captain in Space Force history. Everything was in place. Everything was predictable. She was in control.

Then the Hermes came along. It needed an XO and much to her surprise she volunteered. A new ship with an experimental technology going off to find a legend. What was she thinking? To top things off the Captain of the ship had no experience commanding starships that she knew of. On the Independence Captain Yamato mentored her, grooming her to be a starship captain. What would Captain Pike mentor her on? Assassination tactics? And this mission could take years. She had taken a big risk. She hoped it was worth it.

Arriving at Engineering she found the same frenzy of movement taking place throughout the ship. Here, perhaps even more so. A thick chemical smell filled the air, making her want to cover her nose. Throughout the massive room machine battled with human, each trying to be heard over the other. It all seemed like a bizarre ordered chaos. The ship's enormous reactors dominated the room, dwarfing everything else by comparison. At the foot of one of the reactors, a man had a panel open, conducting what appeared to be some form of reactor maintenance. Tall, dark and lean he stood perfectly straight. He wore a one piece engineering jumpsuit and carried an ornate dagger on his belt. A tight turban sporting the Hermes emblem covered his head.

The man did not notice her approach, and rather than letting him know she was there she stood quietly and watched him work. He moved with an elegant precision. His strong hands purposeful and exact they were almost magical in their efficiency. Broad shoulders filled out the jumpsuit, the fabric stretched by the knots of muscle on his back. As worried as she was about this mission she knew she could not stay aboard the Independence while this man was away on the Hermes in some uncharted part of the galaxy. The moment Chief Engineer Rajneesh Singh was assigned to the Hermes, Wolfe volunteered.

Singh became aware of someone behind him and turned to see who it was. A smile spread across his face when he saw it was Wolfe.

"Well this is a pleasant surprise," said Singh.

Wolfe returned his smile. Her heart quickened. That smile had always made her feel weak in the knees. "I thought I'd check and see how things were coming. The captain wants a readiness report."

"We are ready now. The bulk of the work now is maintenance and redundant testing to ensure we haven't missed anything."

"Good. I'll need a report from you for the captain."

"Absolutely. I'll have one for you by the end of the day."

"Thanks."

Singh looked at her with analytical scrutiny. That look always made her feel like she was under a microscope. "Is everything alright? You seem pre-occupied."

"I'm just trying to adjust to the Hermes. It's proving to be more difficult than I thought it would be."

Singh frowned and looked down at his feet. "You should have stayed on the Independence. You were on the perfect career track there. I don't know why you volunteered for this post."

"You know why I did it Raj."

Singh looked at her directly in the eyes. “No, Commander, I don’t”

Wolfe averted her gaze, feeling the microscope lens again. “I did it to be with you Raj. I did it for us.”

“There is no us, Commander.” Singh’s eyes darted about, worried that his voice had been too loud. He continued in a more hushed tone. “Whatever we had is over. You need to accept that and move on.”

Wolfe struggled to suppress the emotions boiling over insider her. Her shoulders slumped ever so slightly and her stomach hollowed out. “I know you still care about me Raj. I’m not going to let you throw away what we have.”

Singh’s tone became tender and apologetic. “Lynda please, we’ve been through this before. Of course I care for you. I always will. But it just can’t work between us.”

The change in Singh’s tone lifted Wolfe’s spirits slightly and she inhaled deeply. She locked eyes with Singh again and let him see the confidence and determination that possessed her. “You love me Raj. I know you do. And I love you. That’s all that matters. You’ll see.”

Singh frowned again, a look of resignation in his eyes. “If that is all Commander, I have a lot of work to do.”

Wolfe knew they shouldn’t be having this discussion while on duty. She straightened her back and adjusted her uniform. “That is all.” Singh snapped a salute, his eyes expressionless and staring straight ahead at some invisible point behind her. Wolfe saluted in return, turned and walked out of Engineering.

CHAPTER 7

"Your move," said Security Chief Kevin St. Clair, trying to keep his Sergeant's mind on the game. A few meters away from them, a group of off duty Marines were making jokes and laughing over a game of poker. But that wasn't what kept had the Sergeant distracted.

"Yeah, sure." Sergeant Henderson nodded, scanning the chess board. His hand came up and raked through his crew cut. Deep craters formed on his broad forehead accenting his severely crooked nose. He studied the board for a bit longer, and looked back up at Kevin. He had small, dark, menacing eyes, which were known to make even the bravest recruit practically crap themselves.

"The thing is, with this new jump system, we've really got a shot. We can install this thing on all our battleships and then who's gonna fuck with us?"

Kevin rolled his eyes. *Here we go again*, he thought. With the exception of Captain Pike, there was nobody other than Sergeant Henderson he would rather go into a fire fight with. Smart, tough and disciplined, Kevin knew he could count on him to get things done. But for all his good qualities, he kept rambling on about his theories and philosophies. Most were afraid to tell him to shut up, and Kevin figured he knew it. It didn't matter much, though. The man had earned the right to talk, as far as Kevin was concerned.

"See the Diakans, they've been helping us take out the Juttari, but we've got to stand on our own two feet. We need to be self-sufficient."

"Are you going to move, or not?"

"Yeah, sure." Sergeant Henderson picked up a bishop and slid it across the board. "Look, when we find the lost colonies and reunite them with Earth, we'll easily double in size. Hell, we may even triple. Who knows how many people there are there. Five hundred years is a long time. The Juttari practically wiped us out, but the colonies? They probably just kept on growing. Once we get together with them we can setup their ships with their own jump systems and there'll be no stopping us."

"How do you know they'll even want to join up with us? How do you know they still exist? You're right, five hundred years is a long time. Anything could've happened to them. War. Plague. You name it." Kevin grabbed his queen with a big, meaty hand and moved it across the board, taking Henderson's bishop. "Check."

Henderson jerked his head back, surprised by Kevin's move. "Damn, I didn't see that," he said, moving his king out of the enemy queen's line of fire.

"No you didn't," said Kevin, moving his queen again and seizing one of Henderson's pawns. "Check. Mate in two." He looked across the table at Henderson, who looked confused. "You know what else you didn't see? Earth is like this here king," he said, pointing at the Sergeant's besieged piece. "You want your king to overcome the overwhelming force amassed against it, but in the end there is just too much firepower pointed at it."

"This is a chess board, not the galaxy."

"Same thing. Your position is crumbling. Why? It wasn't strong enough from the start. Earth is the same. If it were to try and go it alone its position would fall apart as well. There is no power base without the aliens. Since the position defending the king wasn't strong to begin with, it eventually lost control of the board. Once my pieces took control of the board's strategic squares, checkmate was just a matter of time.

“Say this board here is the galaxy. The Diakans and the Juttari control all the strategic squares. Jump system or no jump system, colonies or no colonies, Earth can’t stand on its own. We need the Diakans. They control the board. Without them we’re dead. Like your king.”

Henderson studied the board a while longer and shook his head. Reaching out with a thick index finger he knocked over his king. “You’re right, the aliens control the board. The thing is, those squares they control are the jump gates. With this jump system, we’re going to make us a new board, and all the squares are gonna be up for grabs. And we’re grabbing those new squares first. Before the Diakans and Juttari know it, they’ll be playing in a new game. We’ll be the ones controlling the board.”

A smile spread across Henderson’s scarred face and he reached across the board offering a handshake. “Good game, Chief.”

CHAPTER 8

The ship's sickbay followed a Diakan design. A small preliminary room greeted the visitor with doors on all sides leading to a web of larger interconnecting spaces. The wall facing the entrance had a large window through which Doctor Ellerbeck's office was visible. Jon could see Ellerbeck seated in front of a translucent screen, busy at work. Looking up she smiled at Jon and gestured for him to come into her office. Her door slid open and Jon stepped through. Ellerbeck stood from her desk and saluted. She was taller than Jon had thought, and quite attractive. There was a quiet elegance about her. She was thin, yet strong, like a ballet dancer. Freckles loosely dotted her fair skin, fanning out across her cheeks. A crop of red hair accented eyes that were as calm as a pool of water. Jon returned the salute and motioned for her to sit down. He pulled up a chair opposite her desk and sat as well.

"Thank you for making time for me Captain. As I mentioned, I need to do a physical on you and your symbiont," said Ellerbeck.

"You know about my symbiont?" Her knowledge made him a little uncomfortable.

"Of course Captain. I've been fully briefed on your medical history. As your doctor I need to know everything about your health."

"And you know how to care for a symbiont?" said Jon, becoming hopeful. The Diakans weren't famous for their bedside manner. He felt more like a lab rat than a patient under their care. But here was a human who might be able to change all that.

"I am well versed in both human and Diakan medicine, and that includes host – symbiont medicine. Of course your situation is quite unique, as you are the first and only human to successfully host a Diakan symbiont."

Lucky me, Jon thought.

"The combination presents some challenges," said Ellerbeck.

"Yes, the Diakans have told me that I can't remove the symbiont. If I do so, it will kill me. Is that how you understand it, Doctor?"

"Yes, Captain. That is correct. But you see it works both ways. The symbiont is also dependent on you for its survival. Let's say, for example, something happened to you and you died. In that case the symbiont would die. Now let's say something happened to the symbiont and it died…"

"...I die as well."

"That is correct, Captain."

Jon didn't like what he was hearing. Even after what Ambassador Varyos had told him, he still believed he had options. But if Ellerbeck's explanation was true, then he had no options. No escape. He was condemned to carry that thing inside him until the end of his days.

Ellerbeck's brow furrowed making Jon wonder if she could read his thoughts. "Diakans live in harmony with their symbionts their entire lives. Both benefit in numerous ways from the relationship," said Ellerbeck.

"I'm not a Diakan, Doctor," said Jon. He hoped this was not the beginning of a sermon.

"Yes, Captain. Your physiology is different from that of a Diakan, and that presents some unique challenges."

"Unique challenges? Are you kidding? I have a hostile alien using my gut as a bunker, and I can't get rid of the goddamn thing. That is one hell of a unique challenge, wouldn't you say?"

"Forgive me Captain, I didn't mean to upset you."

"I'm not upset Doctor, I'm just stating a fact."

"Captain, a Diakan symbiont is a sentient being. You are likely just as alien to it as it is to you. It needs to adapt to you as a host, as much as you need to adapt to it as a symbiont. More importantly, you both need to accept and trust each other."

"Accept? Trust? Doctor, that's just not going to happen."

"Maybe not right away, but I want you to think about it. If you are feeling hostility towards your symbiont, it will mirror that emotion and be hostile towards you. If you don't trust your symbiont, it will not trust you. You both need to trust each other. You cannot continue to act separately. You need to live in harmony. This is how Diakans..."

"...I'm not Diakan, Doctor."

"Yes, of course. Still, you are host to a Diakan symbiont. You need to find harmony with your symbiont in the same way a Diakan does.

"With all due respect Doctor, everything you're saying sounds like some kind of fairy tale. The thing inside me is not some cuddly little pet. It is an aggressive, dangerous monster." There was a reaction from the creature. It didn't like Jon's comment.

Monster, Jon taunted.

He suddenly felt a painful cramp in his side.

Little prick!

The cramp went away.

Ellerbeck watched him closely. "Just think about it," she said.

"Very well. Now how about that physical?"

"Of course, Captain. If you'll follow me into the examination room we can get started." Ellerbeck stood and walked out the door as Jon followed. They stepped through another door in the reception area and entered a much larger room. It was the same slate gray coloring as the rest of the ship. There were ten beds, five on each side. All stark and clinical. An array of what looked like Diakan diagnostic equipment connected to each bed. Ellerbeck walked to the closest bed and motioned for Jon to lie down. She then started a series of scans and probes. A translucent holographic screen appeared floating in the air above Jon, and instantly displayed the results of each test.

"You are remarkably healthy Captain, as is your symbiont," said Ellerbeck.

Jon shrugged. It was nothing he didn't already know.

"Captain, I am seeing traces of alien narcotics in your system." Ellerbeck looked down at Jon. "Care to tell me about it?"

Jon met her gaze but stayed silent.

"Captain, I can't help you if you don't tell me what's going on."

Jon sighed, there was no point trying to argue with the doctor's scans. "Red Dust. I use it from time to time when I'm on R&R."

"Are you addicted?"

"No. It helps with the creature."

"You mean the symbiont?"

"Yeah."

"You take this Red Dust to quiet it?"

"Yeah. Sometimes it's too much, having that thing in my head all the time." Was he telling her too much? He didn't know how far he could trust the doctor.

"I understand. Sometimes it can overpower its host. This would be a greater risk in your case. I can't believe countermeasures weren't taken to avoid this."

"What do you mean?"

"As I said, you need to learn to live in harmony with your symbiont. But there is an adjustment period, and countermeasures are usually taken to avoid conflict."

"What type of conflict?" He already knew what the doctor was going to say, but still wanted to hear her say it.

"In rare cases symbionts have been known to try and take control of the host. Considering the aggressive nature of your symbiont and the fact that you're not Diakan, you would be at a greater risk. I would think that precautions would've been taken."

More proof that he was nothing more than a lab rat to the Diakans. They wanted to see if the creature would take control of him. Maybe they wanted it to be in control rather than the other way around? Then he would be a true Diakan puppet. Maybe they wanted to make their own version of the Chaanisar? He wouldn't put it past them.

"At any rate, you don't have to take this Red Dust, Captain. I'll give you medication that will prevent anymore issues. You'll still experience the same benefits but you won't have to fight the symbiont for control of your body."

Relief washed over him, but it mingled with a growing anger. Why hadn't the Diakans given him this medication themselves?

Ellerbeck focused on her work again, her fingers dancing across the holographic display. After conducting numerous seemingly routine scans her fingers stopped moving and she just stared at the information floating in front of her. "This is incredible. The symbiont has established a protective barrier. I haven't seen anything like this before."

"What are you saying, Doctor?"

A look of wonder had spread across Ellerbeck's face. For a moment it seemed like she hadn't heard Jon's question. Then she glanced at Jon and responded. "Captain, the symbiont is shielding you from all infectious agents. No pathogens can penetrate this barrier. You are essentially immune to any infection or disease. I don't believe any free radicals or parasites can penetrate the barrier either. This is amazing."

"So you're saying I can't get sick?"

"It's more than that. From the look of these readings it may be much more. I have to study this information more thoroughly to be sure."

"Doctor?"

"I'm sorry, Captain. I don't want to speculate until I've analyzed the data."

"Then tell me what you're sure of. From the sound of it you're saying that I can't get sick, correct?"

"Yes, Captain. That is correct."

"And what do you mean when you say, it's more than that?"

"I can't be sure until I've studied the data more."

"Humor me."

She hesitated to respond, her apprehension clearly visible. Her lips tightened, she took a deep breath and answered. "Do you remember when I told you that if you die the symbiont dies?"

"Yes, of course."

"From the look of these readings the symbiont is not just preventing you from getting sick, its preventing you from dying."

"I don't understand."

"It is not just protecting you from disease. It is protecting you from everything. It is even protecting you at the cellular and DNA level. Your organs will not age. You will not age. Your body will not deteriorate. Therefore, you will not die from natural causes."

Jon was stunned. "That's impossible."

"Apparently not." Ellerbeck looked passed Jon, focusing on nothing in particular. Lost in thought. Her mind weighing the implications of this discovery.

"But if this is true, how long will these effects last?"

She continued to stare off into space.

"Doctor?"

"Oh, I'm sorry, the effects will last until your symbiont dies."

"And how long is that?"

"Each symbiont is different, but on Diakus the symbionts consistently outlive their Diakan hosts. When the host dies the symbiont is removed and placed into a new host. The fact that your symbiont couldn't be removed was completely unexpected." Ellerbeck's voice grew soft. She had a mesmerized look on her face.

Jon stared at her, unsure if he wanted to ask the obvious question. "Doctor, how long does a Diakan live?"

The question brought Ellerbeck back to reality. She looked at Jon, her eyes wide. "The average Diakan lives well over three hundred years. The average symbiont can live three times as long. Captain, you could live to be over a thousand years old!"

CHAPTER 9

Special Envoy Tallos waited for the other Diakan advisers to be seated before speaking. "By the Will of the Great See'er, I call this meeting to order." The Diakans all bowed their heads solemnly in response.

"By Her Will," they all said together.

The jump system had been a human invention, but the Hermes was mostly made up of Diakan technology. To him it would have been simpler to place the ship under Diakan command. The ship would be run efficiently and the human colonies found with minimal complications. Instead they settled for Captain Jon Pike, an assassin with a Diakan symbiont. A logical choice so long as the symbiont could be controlled.

The other Diakan advisers sat at a large round table. Green fingers folded together in front of each, copper colored eyes focused on Tallos. These were all fine officers. They would be a valuable asset on any Diakan battleship, yet here they were mere advisers, or simple observers according to the Captain. The humans were foolish. How could such a race rise in power? Could the Great See'er be mistaken?

"You have all been briefed regarding our purpose. We are to oversee this mission and ensure its success. The humans must find their lost colonies, and Diakus will then add them to the Galactic Accord. If the humans are to rise, then keeping all humanity bound by the Accord is the best way to manage them. Under no circumstances can this mission be allowed to fail."

The Diakans around the room nodded their agreement.

Tallos looked to his right to Boufos, the Diakan Engineer. He had commanded engineering rooms on the finest battleships in the fleet. If anyone could be trusted to have engines at peak efficiency it was him. "Advise us of what progress the humans have made in Engineering."

"The humans are progressing in an adequate fashion. They will be prepared by the deadline," said Boufos.

"And what of their jump system?"

"By Her Will, it performs at optimal levels."

"Its continued performance is of the utmost importance."

"It will be done."

"And our Chief Engineer?"

"Chief Engineer Singh is something of a challenge."

"Why?"

"He is insecure. He views our guidance as an offense to his expertise. A strong leader would accept all suggestions and come to a decision, but he does not want to hear suggestions. He allows his emotions to govern him. It is strange that someone so insecure would be given a position of such responsibility."

"Yes, and yet this insecurity is quite common among the humans. Very well, continue monitoring and advise us immediately if the humans falter."

"It will be done."

Tallos looked to the Diakan seated next to the Engineer. Kinos, the Diakan security expert. Kinos had seen combat on multiple occasions and had earned several commendations. Tallos wondered if his skills would need to be put to use on this mission. "What developments are there within security?"

"The humans fear that their mission is compromised. They have established checkpoints throughout the ship. They also search for signs of sabotage."

"Is this not standard procedure?"

"No, this is different. It is a change of focus and happened as soon as the Captain arrived."

"Then the Captain is responsible for the change of direction?"

"Yes. The Captain and Security Chief St. Clair have a shared combat history. If the Captain suspects something he would trust the Security Chief with the information."

"Interesting. And our Security Chief is not providing explanations?"

"No, he is not."

"We cannot allow this mission to be compromised. Any threats to this mission must be identified and eliminated."

"It will be done."

"How do you rate their preparedness?"

"They are an efficient fighting force. Every member of the security team is a combat veteran and many have experience serving on Diakan battleships. They are well equipped and well disciplined."

"And our Security Chief?"

"He is competent."

"Ensure he remains competent."

"It will be done."

Tallos cast an eye to the next Diakan at the table. The Medical Advisor, Matos. He knew that Matos had standing on Diakus as well as on Earth. He spent considerable time teaching the humans Diakan procedures and medical technology. Doctor Ellerbeck herself had been one of his students. He understood human physiology, as well as that of several other alien species. He would be a valuable asset on this journey. "And how is our Chief Medical Officer?"

"Doctor Ellerbeck is examining the Captain and his symbiont as we speak."

"I trust the Doctor will advise us of any threats to the Captain or his symbiont?"

"As a former student, the Doctor accepts my role as advisor. I am confident she will keep me informed."

"The Captain needs guidance. He will not accept it from a Diakan. As his physician, the Doctor is best suited to help the Captain find his way. See to it that she has everything she needs."

"It will be done."

"Very well. By the Will of the Great See'er, this mission shall commence on schedule. The Captain is proving difficult to control, however."

"Does his symbiont not make him more compliant?" asked Matos.

"The combination of the symbiont with human physiology produced several undesirable responses. It is uncertain how manageable the Captain and his symbiont will be."

"Will they need to be terminated?" asked Kinos, the security expert.

"Unknown. The success of this mission is of paramount importance. For now, we need to allow the humans to continue with their duties. If after leaving their system the Captain becomes a danger to the mission's success, it may be necessary to take action."

The Diakans all nodded their agreement.

"By Her Will, this meeting is now closed." Tallos bowed his head.

"By Her Will," recited the other Diakans, all bowing their heads in return.

CHAPTER 10

Commander Wolfe ran through a mental checklist as she walked. The Hermes had a fine crew that was meeting, and at times exceeding her expectations. That was no small accomplishment. A perfectionist herself, she demanded no less from those serving under her. She was also pushing the crew harder than normal. They were on a unique mission and Wolfe needed to know who could handle it and who couldn't before leaving the Sol system. If she didn't weed out any bad apples before then, she would be stuck with them for the entire mission, and that was unacceptable. So she would continue to ride the crew, whether they liked it or not.

The mission and the ship were certainly different from what she was used to. On The Independence the objective was clear. Be battle ready at all times. The largest and most powerful ship in the fleet, The Independence saw more than its share of combat. And most of Wolfe's experience was forged in the fires of battle. This mission, however, was different. It was unclear who the enemy was, or if there was any enemy at all. They would probably not see any combat. Instead, they would play a game of galactic hide and seek.

She proceeded down the long corridor, watching the steady activity as crewmembers passed her. They were a good crew. And they would be an excellent crew by the time she was done with them. Whether they saw combat or not, the crew would be as prepared as any. The Hermes would be battle ready regardless of enemy. She needed to let go of The Independence. She had to leave it buried in the past. Only

The Hermes mattered now, and she vowed to make it the envy of the fleet.

Turning a corner she abruptly stopped walking. Up ahead two Marines were posted at a hatch. Both men were large, intimidating, and armed. Wolfe knew they weren't there before. A crewmember approached the hatch and the Marines stopped her and asked her for identification. A checkpoint. But why? She knew of no threat that needed checkpoints on the ship. They hadn't even left the station yet. Wolfe had seen enough. She marched straight up to the two men, who promptly snapped a salute when they saw her approach.

"What is going on here?" demanded Wolfe. Each Marine stood perfectly straight, still at attention. After a brief moment of uncertainty the Marine closest to her spoke up.

"We are under orders to establish a checkpoint here, Sir," said the Marine.

"Whose orders?"

"Security Chief St. Clair, Sir."

While St. Clair was responsible for security on board the ship, security checkpoints would slow down movement and damage morale. She should've been consulted about a decision like this. "And why did the Chief want a checkpoint here?"

"He didn't tell us, Sir."

She didn't think the Marines would know why. Wolfe was sure that St. Clair had his reasons, but if there was a threat serious enough to warrant checkpoints, then she damn well needed to know what it was.

"Very well, carry on," said Wolfe. Not happy about the checkpoint, she wouldn't override the Chief's orders without more information. Efficiency required order, and order required hierarchy. As the second in command of the Hermes, she needed to be in the loop regarding any decision that affected the ship. Taking her out of the loop not only undermined her authority, it also undermined the chain of command and set a bad example for the rest of the crew.

Once out of earshot of the Marines, Wolfe opened a comm with St. Clair.

"Yes, Commander. What can I do for you?" St. Clair answered.

"Chief, I just ran into a couple of your Marines on Deck Theta. They had setup a checkpoint there. I was not told about any checkpoints," said Wolfe.

"My apologies, Commander. It is merely a security precaution."

"That's not good enough Chief. Establishing security checkpoints on board a starship is not standard operating procedure. That is unless there is a threat to the starship or its crew. Is there a threat to the Hermes, or its crew, Chief?"

"I'm sorry, Commander, I'm not at liberty to answer that question."

"I'm the Hermes's Executive Officer. You damn well better answer that question."

"I can't, Commander. I'm under orders directly from the Captain. If you want answers you'll have to take this up with him."

"I'll do that, Chief. Wolfe out." Temples pounding, anger rising, Wolfe closed the comm before losing her composure. What kind of Captain blinds his XO to potential threats? Her breathing grew shallow and her pulse raced. Growing aware of her body's reaction, she concentrated on regaining control. First, she took control of her breathing. Taking deep breaths, in through her nose and out through her mouth, she slowed down her pulse and put herself in a more relaxed state. As her body calmed, the muscles in her neck and shoulders began releasing their grip. A few moments later and she had complete control over herself. Satisfied that her emotions were stable she opened a comm with the Captain.

"Yes, Commander," said Jon.

"Captain, I need to discuss a few things with you. Is it possible to schedule a meeting today?"

"Yes, Commander. Of course. I'm just finishing up with Doctor Ellerbeck. We can meet in my ready room in an hour. Does that work for you?"

"Yes, Captain. Thank you. I will see you in an hour. Wolfe out."

Closing the comm she walked off. She still had a lot of work to do, threat or no threat.

CHAPTER 11

Sitting in his ready room, Jon pondered his situation. If true, he could stay alive for a long time, regardless of whether he wanted to. If the creature wanted to live, Jon would live. Most would be happy to live for a thousand years. Jon wasn't one of them. To him it seemed like a thousand year prison sentence. He had already seen more than enough pain and suffering for one lifetime. How could he possibly endure a millennium?

He called up a picture of his family. His wife and his two beautiful daughters. So young. Too young. Their deaths had crushed him. He had so little time to grieve. He had always been a soldier. Not knowing what else to do he returned to active duty.

He returned with a score to settle.

To say he was angry would not do the emotion justice. No words could describe the torment and fury boiling over inside him. He volunteered for anything that allowed him to kill the enemy. Deep space ops in enemy territory? No problem. Assassination of high value targets? Sure thing. Extreme interrogation tactics? Look no further. Surprising everyone, Jon beat the odds time and time again, and came back alive. He did not fear death anymore. He embraced it.

That lack of fear kept him alive. If you are not afraid to die you do not get nervous. You do not get anxious. You do not hesitate. And you do not make stupid mistakes that get you killed. Nonetheless, everybody figured it was just a matter of time, including Jon.

Then an opportunity presented itself like no other. A highly classified experiment had begun and Jon was one of a handful of pre-qualified candidates. When Jon discovered that this experiment might give him the ability to kill even more of the enemy he instantly volunteered. He turned out to be the only volunteer, and so he became the first human in history to become host to a Diakan symbiont. True to their word, the symbiont did indeed allow him to kill more of the enemy. It did so by augmenting his abilities. His strength and speed increased tenfold. His senses became so heightened that he discovered a world he never knew existed. He could see like a bird, and smell and hear like a wolf. Even his mind changed. When it came to matters of strategy and tactics he instantly saw the most efficient answer. His success rate climbed alongside his kill rate.

And then the war ended.

Jon never thought he would see the end of the war. He just assumed he would die on one of his missions. He accepted it. The war had ended, yet he still lived. And he was alone. Alone with his thoughts and with the creature. So he jumped into Black Ops. After all, even in peacetime there is war.

He became a ghost. A silent, invisible killer. He continued to wage his private war. Continued to see justice done on those responsible for the deaths of his girls. Certain that one day the time would come when he wouldn't return. Then, and only then, his suffering would end. But that day never came. Would it ever come?

The creature became more than he bargained for. He thought it would be no more than a tool. A way to augment his abilities, like the Chaanisar did with technology. But, the creature had a mind of its own. A will of its own. It could inflict pain on Jon. Terrible pain. They worked well together in combat. So long as Jon stayed strong, everything was fine. If Jon showed any weakness, however, the creature took over and forced Jon to act. Any potential threat to Jon became by default a threat to the creature. That, it did not tolerate. It lived. It wanted to keep on living. Which meant that Jon had to keep on living right along with it.

Thankfully the medication Doctor Ellerbeck had given Jon seemed to be working. The creature stayed quiet. Unfortunately it was not permanent and Jon needed to take regular doses for it to keep working. He wondered how long he would need to take the medication. Hopefully the doctor brought enough on board.

"Commander Wolfe requests entrance," said a synthetic voice.

"Come in," said Jon. He turned off his family picture and settled back into his chair. The door opened and Wolfe walked into the room. She exuded strength and leadership. Here was a winner. Yet there was also a tension about her. Jon noted the flexed muscles on the side and back of her neck. The slight clenching of her jaw bone. The temporal tightness. She pushed herself too hard. Did she do the same with the crew?

He had taken the time to review her file. An impressive career, to be sure. Youngest XO in the fleet. Decorated with the Space Force Cross for Extraordinary Heroism at the Battle of Callisto. She had been one of the fleet's rising stars. Yet she volunteered for duty on the Hermes. Why? It didn't make any sense.

Wolfe came to attention in front of Jon and saluted. Jon returned the salute. "At ease Commander. Please, sit down," said Jon. Wolfe pulled up one of the chairs and sat across Jon, her back perfectly straight, eyes level. "What can I do for you, Commander?"

Wolfe cleared her throat and spoke. "Captain, I am a little concerned about something I saw today. Walking along Deck Theta I came across a security checkpoint. I had not been informed about any checkpoints, and when I asked Security Chief St. Clair about the matter he said he was acting under your orders.

He could see the anger in her eyes. She hid it well but it was still there. He smelled the aggression oozing out of her pores. She displayed impressive self-control. If he hadn't been her commanding officer she might even take a swing at him.

"Yes, Commander, that is correct."

"Captain, as the Executive Officer of this ship, I should be informed of any security checkpoints. Also, if there is a threat that warrants checkpoints, I should know about it."

Jon sighed. Worried about a mole being on board, he didn't know who he could trust. Wolfe herself could be the mole. He studied her for a long moment. Nothing about her seemed disloyal. She did show some signs of aggression and stress, but that didn't make her a traitor. Jon knew he had to start trusting people. It would be impossible to run this ship if he didn't.

"You're right Commander. You should be informed of any security threats." Jon saw some of the tension leave her face. "Commander, I believe that this mission has been compromised. I also believe that there may be a threat on board."

The temporal tightness returned and long established worry lines deepened, carving jagged trails across her brow. "Compromised? How? I don't understand."

"The Chaanisar attempted to assassinate me before I came on board. Before I even knew about my assignment. I believe the Juttari are trying to sabotage this mission."

"But if you're right, then we need to notify Space Force Command."

"No, we don't. There is a mole at Command."

"I don't understand. How do you know that?"

"The Juttari knew I would be Captain of the Hermes long before I knew. They also knew where to find me. That means someone at Command is feeding them information."

Wolfe nodded in understanding as the pieces started to fit. "And if they had that much advance notice, then they had enough time to place an operative on board," she added.

It was Jon's turn to nod. "It is a logical conclusion, Commander. This is why I've had check points established throughout the ship, especially around vital systems. Security is also sweeping these areas looking for signs of sabotage. With any luck we may be able to flush out the enemy."

"Understood. May I ask you a direct question, Captain?"

"Yes, Commander."

"Why did you tell me? For all you know I might be the mole."

Jon smiled. "Are you?" Wolfe didn't react. "My background has turned me into a pretty good judge of people. You don't strike me as a traitor."

"Thank you, Sir."

"Was there anything else?"

"No, Sir."

"Ok, that makes three people, including myself and Chief St. Clair, who know about this. This information is to remain strictly confidential. Other than us three, no one else is to know about this. Understood?"

"Yes, Sir."

"Very well. Dismissed."

Wolfe stood, saluted and walked out the door. An impressive woman. He felt lucky to have her as his 2IC.

CHAPTER 12

"Helm, initiate countdown," said Jon, perched above the rest of the bridge, sitting in the Captain's chair. After two weeks of frantic preparation the Hermes could finally begin its mission. Happy to leave the Sol System, Jon's eyes were fixed on the viewscreen. He wondered what jumping without a gate would be like. Going through a jump gate was practically instantaneous. You went in one end and came out the other. The fact that space had been folded to accommodate your jump across hundreds of light years didn't matter. Would folding space with a starship be any different? He didn't really understand how the whole thing worked, and he left the mechanics of it to the scientists. All he cared about was that it did work.

"Countdown initiated," said Ensign Jack Richards. Young, cocky, and talented, Richards piloted the Hermes. In civilian life Richards had been quite a celebrity on Earth. A natural pilot, he had won every race that meant anything in competitive flying. Living life just as fast, he could regularly be spotted at the best parties, surrounded by beautiful women. That's why nobody saw it coming when he enlisted. Jon didn't know his reasons for enlisting. He never made them public. Jon didn't care. If this kid was half as good a pilot as his reputation indicated Jon would be happy.

"Five." The computer sounded off the countdown as the entire bridge crew stared at the viewscreen, holding their collective breaths.

"Four." Beside Jon stood Tallos and Wolfe. While the Diakan's face gave away no emotion, Wolfe's displayed its usual tension. Like everyone else they were glued to the viewscreen.

"Three." Jon stared at the stars, wondering when, if ever, he would see them again.

"Two." The bridge fell quiet, as everyone stopped what they were doing.

"One." Jon leaned forward, his hands gripping the arms of the Captain's chair, holding his breath.

For a brief moment he experienced a feeling of light-headedness accompanied by a pasty sensation in the back of his throat, and then the stars on the viewscreen shifted.

"Jump complete," said the computer.

"Report!" said Jon. The bridge exploded into a fury of activity.

"We have successfully jumped into the Glies system, fifty light years from Sol," said Ensign Yao, the Navigation officer.

"Tactical?"

"Reading all clear. No contacts," said Ensign Petrovic, the Tactical officer.

Special Envoy Tallos looked over at Jon. "Congratulations Captain. You have just made history."

"Thank you Special Envoy," said Jon. "Congratulations people. Excellent work," Jon said to the bridge. Applause and cheers broke out, as everybody celebrated the success.

"Navigation, how long until we are ready for our next jump?" said Jon.

"Co-ordinates are locked, Sir. Jump system is at 76%. We are jump ready."

"No point wasting time hanging around here. Helm, initiate countdown."

"Countdown initiated," said Richards.

The computer counted down in the same fashion as before. The crew seemed much more comfortable this time around, with many focused on their work, rather than staring at the viewscreen.

"Contact!" said Petrovic.

"Three," said the computer.

Jon saw the starship on the screen. A Juttari battle cruiser. *Where did they come from?*

"Two."

"Reading weapons hot!"

"Sound general quarters!" said Jon. Red light bathed the bridge as general quarters sounded throughout the ship.

"One."

"They're firing missiles!"

The ship spewed a cluster of missiles at the Hermes. Everyone on the bridge braced for the inevitable impact.

And then it disappeared. No battle cruiser. No missiles. Just a different group of stars on the viewscreen.

"Jump complete."

"Goddamnit. Where did that ship come from?" said Jon.

"Unknown, Sir. It just appeared without warning," said Petrovic.

"Report!" said Wolfe.

"We have successfully jumped into the Valen system. Fifty light years from our last location in the Glies system. One hundred light years from the Sol system," said Yao.

"Reading all clear. No contacts," said Petrovic.

Even with the medication, Jon still sensed the creature's desire for action, and he agreed with it.

"What is our jump status?" said Jon.

"50%. We are jump ready, Sir," said the Yao.

"Tactical, load all missile tubes. Weapons hot," said Jon.

"Aye, Sir. Loading all missile tubes. Weapons hot."

"Navigation, can you plot a course back to our previous coordinates, altering slightly to land us behind the Juttari battlecruiser?"

"Yes, Sir."

"Plot coordinates and prepare for jump."

Tallos stared at Jon. "Captain, we need more information before we engage that vessel. Victory is not certain without more intelligence."

Jon looked at the Diakan and suppressed the urge to kick him off the bridge. "That ship fired on us. That is all the information I need."

"Coordinates plotted. Ready for jump," said Yao.

"Very well. Initiate countdown. Tactical, prepare to fire missiles the moment we land."

"Yes, Sir."

The jump sequence began and the computer counted down.

"Three."

"Two."

"One."

"Jump complete."

"Contact!"

"Fire missiles."

"Missiles away."

The viewscreen showed the Hermes missiles, eight in all, speeding towards the Juttari ship like tiny supersonic snakes.

"Juttari vessel deploying countermeasures," said Petrovic.

The Juttari ship launched a cluster of drones which immediately dispersed in random directions away from the vessel. Their engines burned disproportionately to their size in an attempt to draw the missiles off target. They were also broadcasting the Juttari vessel's signature, trying to fool the missiles' targeting computers. At the same time the ship's rail guns fired, establishing a point defense field to protect it against any missiles that got passed the drones.

"Fire another round of missiles. Lock energy weapons on enemy's defensive systems."

"Missiles away. Energy weapons locked," said Tactical.

Another eight missiles raced toward the Juttari ship, which launched another cluster of drones in response. At the same time a salvo of missiles shot out of the Juttari ship heading straight for The Hermes.

"Juttari vessel is firing missiles!" said Petrovic.

"Launch countermeasures. Rail guns in point defense mode. Not one of those missiles is to touch the Hermes. Is that understood?"

"Yes, Sir!"

"Helm, bridge the distance between us and the enemy. Attack pattern epsilon."

"Aye, sir."

The Hermes shot forward, zigzagging through space towards the Juttari battlecruiser, like a giant hawk closing in for the kill.

"Fire energy weapons," said Jon.

"Firing energy weapons."

The view screen lit up as streaks of blue light painted their way across the blackness of space towards the enemy. Finding their marks the beams locked on and intensified, burning through the enemy's armor plating. The Hermes weaved through space and the blue beams stayed glued to their targets making the Hermes look like a marionette playing on a tangle of blue strings. Orange flashes colored the darkness as the beams pierced the armor, destroying the enemy turrets.

"Direct hit," said Petrovic.

"Fire missiles," said Jon.

"Missiles away."

The streaking missiles danced with the blue light and the new wave of drone decoys, but with her point defense system disabled the

Juttari ship didn't have much hope of fending them all off. Two missiles bypassed the drones and closed in for the kill. They locked onto the ship's critical systems, certain of maiming, if not destroying the Juttari vessel. Then, a split second before impact, the Juttari vessel vanished into thin air, the Hermes missiles sprinting off harmlessly into the emptiness of space.

Jon stared at the viewscreen. Stunned. In sharp contrast to the excitement of battle just a moment earlier, the bridge was now enveloped by an uncertain silence.

"Tactical, scan surrounding area. Find that ship!" said Wolfe.

"Scanning, Sir. Reading all clear. No contacts."

Jon's stomach lurched as understanding started to dawn on him.

"They have a jump system," said Jon.

"Agreed," said Wolfe.

"Commander Wolfe, Chief St. Clair, report to my ready room. Maintain General Quarters. I want full combat readiness in case that ship shows up again."

"Yes, Sir." said Petrovic.

Jon got up and walked to his ready room, with Wolfe, and Kevin following. The door slid open and they all filed into Jon's office. Jon turned and faced his two officers.

"How did that ship find us? Jump system or not, how did they know our exact location?" said Jon, barely concealing the anger in his voice.

"I think it is safe to conclude that we have a spy on board," said Kevin, avoiding eye contact with Jon.

"Agreed," said Wolfe. "There can't be any doubt about that anymore."

"So, how do we flush them out? Kevin?" said Jon.

"Our checkpoints haven't uncovered anything suspicious. We haven't found any sign of sabotage. Although I think after what just happened the spy will probably be a little more nervous. Surely they'll know that we would figure it out now. So we monitor all communications on all frequencies and wait for them to make a mistake," said Kevin.

"I want them found, do you understand me?" said Jon.

"Yes, Sir."

"Now how about that ship? It's still out there somewhere. How do we find them?"

"That'll be tough, Sir. They could be anywhere within fifty light years," said Wolfe.

"That's assuming their jump system has the same capabilities as ours. For all we know they can only jump ten light years at a time."

"That is possible, Sir, but with all the evidence of espionage I think it's safe to assume that their system is built off our schematics."

"You're right. There has been a mole in place throughout this entire project. Which means they likely have detailed plans of the Hermes as well."

"What if there isn't a spy on board?" said Wolfe.

Jon saw his own confusion mirrored on Kevin's face. "I don't understand," said Jon.

"Chief, I assume you have been monitoring all communication channels, correct?"

"Yes, that is correct."

"And you've found nothing out of the ordinary?"

"Correct again."

"Then it's safe to assume that if there's a spy on board they're not in communication with the Juttari ship."

"True, but they could've communicated with the Juttari while we were still at the station."

"Yes, that seems more probable," said Jon.

"Perhaps. Sir, I believe that what is more likely is the Juttari have a copy of our jump path. While we have the flexibility to change, we do have a predetermined jump path based on where we think the lost colonies are," said Wolfe.

"That's logical. They only needed to know our first jump coordinates in order to ambush us. All they needed to know was when we jumped away from Sol, then they just follow and attack while we're getting our bearings. I don't think they expected us to jump so soon," said Jon.

"Lucky for us," said Kevin.

"Yes, lucky indeed. They had us with our pants down."

"So do we change our jump path?" asked Wolfe.

"I think we have to. Otherwise they have too much of a tactical advantage. That said, if they have our jump path, we in effect have their jump path. We can turn the tables on them."

"We become the hunter, rather than the hunted," said Kevin. "I like it." A broad smile spreading across his face.

"They'll need to make some repairs before they can think of attacking us again. Once those repairs are finished, though, they would merely follow our jump path until they found us. Like us, they'll have limitations as to how many consecutive jumps they can make. They would have to wait till their system recharged. That's when we attack."

"But how can we know when and where that will be?" said Wolfe.

"They have likely jumped away to a location not on the jump path. So we jump ahead and find a location where we can wait to ambush them. Say an asteroid field. I think we can safely assume that their next jump will be into the Valen system. They will likely have three more full jumps left before they'll need to recharge their jump system. This is where we attack. Without jump capability they'll be trapped. Thoughts?"

"I think it can work," said Kevin.

"Agreed," said Wolfe.

"Excellent. In the meantime we are going to need to plot an alternate jump path. Just in case."

"I'll see that Navigation makes the necessary calculations," said Wolfe.

"And Kevin, we still need to assume that there is an operative on board. Let's stick to the plan and increase security on board. Anything that looks even slightly suspicious needs to be thoroughly investigated."

"Yes, Sir. Consider it done."

"Very well, dismissed."

Wolfe and St. Clair both stood and saluted. Jon watched them walk out the door, sat down in his chair and considered his plan. He thought it had a decent chance of success. The important thing was that they had the initiative now. They were the ones doing the hunting, and that was the way Jon liked it. He felt the creature's approval and thought, *We're in agreement. Wouldn't the Doctor be pleased.*

The Captain's chair was growing on him as well. He was proud of the way the crew performed in battle. They all kept their cool and didn't panic under fire. More importantly, they responded to his commands without hesitation. Commander Wolfe performed exceptionally on the bridge and proved to be very perceptive afterwards. The ship itself lived up to his expectations and then some. Fast, agile and powerful, Jon preferred it to the hulking battleships of the fleet. The Hermes could move and pack a powerful punch at the same time. Unlike a ship of the line, the Hermes had finesse, like a well-trained boxer. Jon couldn't wait to have another shot at that Juttari battlecruiser, and something told him that he would get his wish soon enough.

Jon opened a comm with Wolfe.

"Yes, Captain," Wolfe answered.

"Commander, how long until the jump system is fully charged?"

"Approximately eight hours, Sir."

"Very well. Maintain current position and keep watch for the Juttari. In the meantime I'm going to get some rest. You have the bridge."

"Yes, Sir."

CHAPTER 13

Jon's quarters were minimalist in design, resembling a hotel room more than anything else. Compared to what he was used to, however, the place might as well have been a luxury resort. The entrance revealed a large room which seemed a cross between an office and meeting area, rather than a living room. At the far end sat the Captain's desk, with the requisite oversized faux leather chair and work area. At the opposite end was a seating area with a faux leather couch and a couple of lounge chairs. The walls were a deep royal blue and accented by Impressionist era reproductions. On one side of the room floor to ceiling windows revealed the desolate blackness of space. The only luxury Jon was looking for, however, was a good night's sleep.

The pace of the last two weeks had left him exhausted. The crew had worked around the clock to have the Hermes ready for its launch date. For Jon it had been twice as hard. For two weeks he slept no more than three hours a night. On top of making sure the Hermes was ready on time, he also had to learn a ton of new information. He needed to know the Hermes inside out, brush up on starship battle strategies and tactics, and become familiar with his officers and the rest of the crew.

His special forces training had prepared him well for it. As a covert operative he had the ability to become an expert on any subject matter in a very short time. So, along with the Hermes, Jon had been ready by the deadline. But now he needed rest, and with the Juttari ship out there he didn't know when he would have another chance for sleep.

He walked through a sliding door into the bedroom. A queen sized bed dominated the room. Two side tables flanked the bed. On one was a comm system and a chair had been positioned for quick access. The same floor to ceiling windows looked out into the void.

Jon sat on the end of the bed and thought again about the Juttari and their motives. He understood that they wanted the jump system. That technology would give the Diakans an overwhelming strategic advantage. If the Juttari had the same technology, however, the balance of power would remain. So why were they out here trying to ambush the Hermes? It had to be the lost colonies. If they destroyed the Hermes and found the colonies themselves, then they would gain control of that region of space and deny the Diakans access to it. Just another move in the galactic chess game. Satisfied with the conclusion, Jon undressed, lay down and fell sleep.

The creature had given Jon a number of exceptional abilities. Most people noticed his combat prowess. They saw speed and power. They didn't see the more subtle traits, like his sense of smell. Jon knew people simply by their odor. He could be blindfolded and still know who was in the room, and even who had been in the room recently. He could also identify emotions. Most people are unaware of the odors their body secretes when they are happy, or sad, hostile, or scared. A person's smell, for example, tells a dog if you are a threat. And it was that odor in particular that woke Jon.

The intruder moved stealthily, but to Jon he could've been a rampaging elephant. He heard the man approach the foot of his bed. He smelled the mix of fear and hostile intent. He recognized the subtle sound of his shirt sleeve brushing against his side. Jon knew what that sound meant.

Jon dove off the bed and hit the floor just as an energy blast burned a hole through the mattress. The assassin shifted and continued to fire, following Jon's movement. Jon rolled just as another burst hit the floor.

Jon's eyes had adapted to the darkness and he could see the gunman, who wasn't trying to take cover at all. He could obviously see as well making Jon wonder if the man had been augmented. The man continued to fire and Jon moved again.

The bedroom did not offer too many options for cover, so Jon did the only thing he could and attacked. Jon tumbled across the floor at a speed the assassin couldn't match. He then sprang up off the ground and struck the man's arm making him fire at the ceiling. Jon's elbow came up at the same time catching the man perfectly in the throat.

A killing blow. The man recoiled backward, his momentum bouncing him off the wall and onto the floor. The man made a horrible gurgling sound as he choked on his own blood and then fell silent. Blood streamed from his mouth down his cheek and began to pool on the floor. Jon stripped the gun from his hand and checked his vitals. He was dead.

Kevin's voice came over the comm system, "Captain, we're reading multiple energy discharges in your quarters. Are you alright?"

"I'm fine, although my guest here has seen better days."

"A security team has been dispatched. They should be there momentarily. I'm on route as well. St. Clair out."

Jon got up and put on his clothes. He looked over at the time display. Four hours of sleep. *I suppose it's better than three*, he thought.

The security team arrived with Kevin following closely behind. Kevin had the team run a full scan on Jon's quarters to ensure there were no other surprises hiding there. Jon and Kevin both studied the corpse. The man wore a medical uniform. A good cover. Medical personnel did not have access to vital ship systems, so wouldn't be under as much scrutiny as say someone in engineering. Doctor Ellerbeck soon arrived and identified the body.

"His name is Brian Myles. He was one of my junior officers," said Ellerbeck.

"Do you remember him acting strangely? Doing anything out of the ordinary?" asked Kevin.

"No, he was a competent medical officer. Always did a good job. I never had any problems with him. Frankly, I'm shocked."

"I probably shouldn't have killed him," said Jon. "Kind of difficult to interrogate him now."

"Well he was only firing an energy weapon at you. You probably should've taken it easy on him," joked Kevin.

Jon glanced at Kevin and suppressed the urge to laugh. He returned to Ellerbeck. "Doctor, I'll need a full autopsy on Mr. Myles. Let me know if you find anything out of the ordinary."

"Yes, Captain. Is there something in particular you are looking for?"

"Anything at all, especially signs of augmentation."

"Yes, Sir. I'll get started right away."

"Thank you Doctor."

Jon looked at Kevin and nodded for him to follow. They left his quarters and walked down the corridor until they found a quiet location.

"Looks like we found our spy," said Jon.

"Yes, Sir," said Kevin. "Pretty foolish of him to try and kill you."

"He must've been desperate. The ambush failed and your team has been doing a great job. Probably the only option he had left."

"It also could've been a pre-existing order. He could've been the contingency plan if the ambush failed."

"Agreed," said Jon. "That makes sense. The question now is if he was plan B, is there a plan C?"

"Maybe. I think we have to assume that there is a plan C," said Kevin.

"Agreed."

"I'll keep my teams on high alert, and I'm going to post guards outside your quarters."

Jon frowned. "That really isn't necessary."

"Maybe not, but the Captain's safety is my responsibility, and a threat on the Captain's life requires the posting of a security detail." Kevin smiled at Jon. "I didn't make the rules, Sir."

Jon rolled his eyes. “Fine, post your detail. In the meantime I’m heading back to the bridge. I need to get Commander Wolfe up to speed and get ready for the next round of jumps.”

CHAPTER 14

Doctor Ellerbeck looked down at the naked body of her junior officer. She knew the man was an enemy spy and that he tried to kill the Captain, still she couldn't help being saddened by the whole thing. The man had shown considerable promise. She knew it had all been a deception, but she also knew that it was a result of the brainwashing he received since his abduction as a child. His life had not been his own since that awful moment. And now he lay dead on her table. A bitter end to a wasted life.

She loathed the Juttari for what they had done to human children. Could this man still be considered human? As her autopsy progressed she found all the telltale signs of Juttari augmentation, although the implants were now gone. His body had been altered with alien technology since childhood, and now, likely for this mission, that technology had been ripped out of him to avoid detection.

Still she saw the subtle differences in bone and muscle formation. Everything would have had to conform to the implants. Bones, muscles, tendons, and ligaments had to accommodate the foreign technology growing throughout the body. It must have been a massive shock to have the implants removed after a lifetime adjusting to them.

No more of a shock than being taken from his parents all those years ago. How many families had been ripped apart during the occupation? How many parents helplessly watched their children taken away, knowing that they could one day be used as weapons against Earth?

At least in this case she could trace this man's DNA back to his family and they could have some closure. That was more than most families received. Of course, most parents whose child was taken for the Chaanisar just considered the child dead.

They knew that the child wouldn't just be altered physically, but mentally as well. Juttari indoctrination was brutally efficient and the child soon lost all attachment to Earth, humanity, and family. A Chaanisar lived only to serve and die for the Empire. Any trace of who he was before the Chaanisar was exterminated.

Continuing her autopsy she was surprised to find that not all of the augmentation had been removed. He still had his chip. Like a tiny seed, it sat deep within the frontal lobe. Made up entirely of organic compounds it would not have been detected by the ship's systems, unless someone specifically looked for it.

Ellerbeck carefully removed the chip, desperate not to damage it. She knew the Captain would want it studied. A Chaanisar chip was responsible for many functions. First and foremost it was a communication tool.

Since all Chaanisar were chipped, they had the ability to communicate telepathically. A Chaanisar crew were all networked together through their chips. They each acted like a node and had the ability to communicate and share information with each other seamlessly.

This ability bypassed all the inadequacies of language. For example, for someone to say the word "cat" they must first picture the cat in their mind and attach the word "cat" to the image. They then say the word, sending the message to the listener, who instantly decodes it.

This coding and decoding happens almost instantly, but it is imperfect. The listener will likely produce a different image than the one the speaker intended. So straight off, with only one word, there is miscommunication. As you add more words to the mix the problems encountered compound, requiring people to "explain themselves," so as to produce a clearer understanding.

A Chaanisar does not have these problems. If he sees a cat and wants to send the message to another Chaanisar, he does not say "cat". Rather he simply sends the image of what he sees. In this way there is perfect understanding.

The weakness of language is avoided, and response times are drastically reduced. In fact, the only time a Chaanisar would use spoken language would be when he is speaking to a non-Chaanisar.

The chips also enhance several mental abilities, allowing them to process information and solve problems much faster than a regular human. Many think that the enhanced speed and strength is what makes the Chaanisar so formidable. In reality, the most formidable thing about the Chaanisar is their brain chips.

A Chaanisar fire team acts as one. They instantly know the other's position and can formulate strategy as a unit on the fly. This allows them to outthink their enemies. It is that mental speed that gives them the real edge in combat.

Beyond all of that the chip is a monitoring device, giving Juttari command the ability to know what their Chaanisar soldiers are doing at all times. This also serves as an added means of control. A Chaanisar could not have a seditious thought without his commanders knowing about it. In effect, there can be no secrets among the Chaanisar, and with no secrets there can be no rebellion.

Ellerbeck opened up a comm link with the Captain.

"Yes, Doctor," said Jon.

"Sir, you were right. Your attacker was definitely Chaanisar."

CHAPTER 15

"Jump system is at 100%. We are jump ready," said Ensign Yao.

"Initiate," said Jon.

The computer started the now familiar countdown. Jon's body settled into a flexible readiness. They were the ones doing the hunting now. A comfortable role for Jon. The Hermes jumped and the lightheaded sensation returned.

"Jump complete," said the computer.

"Report."

"We have successfully jumped into the Valen system. Fifty light years from our previous location. One hundred light years from the Sol system. Jump system at 76%. We are jump ready," said Yao.

"Reading all clear. No contacts," said Ensign Petrovic.

"Navigation, load coordinates for second jump."

"Coordinates loaded."

"Initiate."

The computer counted down and the Hermes jumped to its new coordinates.

"Jump complete."

"Report."

"We have successfully jumped into the Draidan system. Fifty light years from our previous location. One hundred and fifty light years from the Sol system. Jump system is at 51%. We are jump ready," said Yao.

"Reading all clear. No contacts," said Petrovic.

Tallos turned to Jon, "Captain, we are now entering unexplored regions of space. This presents a unique opportunity to gather what may be invaluable intelligence."

Jon straightened his back and took a couple of deep breaths before responding. "Hunting down the Juttari vessel is our first priority," he said in a dismissive tone. Why did this damn Diakan keep interfering with his command? He looked at the stars on the viewscreen and realized that Tallos might have a point. This region hadn't been explored. At least there was no record of it. As the first human ship in this region he had a responsibility to Sol to at least have a look around. "Nonetheless, we can spend a few minutes conducting some deep scans. Commander, initiate long range scans of this region. We jump in five minutes."

"Yes, Sir," said Wolfe.

Thank you, Captain," said Tallos.

Jon nodded.

"Captain, I wanted to commend you on your success in battle against the Juttari vessel. You displayed an impressive command of battle tactics," said Tallos.

The compliment caught Jon off guard. Why was Tallos trying to kiss his butt all of a sudden? He couldn't remember receiving a compliment from a Diakan before, and almost didn't know how to respond. The whole thing felt awkward. He rolled his head across his shoulders, trying to relieve some of the tension building up there, and decided to acknowledge the compliment. "Thank you, Special Envoy."

"You are quite welcome, Captain. And, if I might add, your plan for pursuing the Juttari is tactically sound."

Now things were getting weird. He assumed that was a compliment as well. It must be difficult for the Diakan. Saying thank you to a Diakan sure was difficult for him.

When the five minutes passed the hunt resumed. The Hermes conducted their third successful jump. They were now deep in unexplored space. No ship, Diakan or Juttari, had traveled into this region of space before, primarily because there were no nearby jump gates to facilitate such a trip.

The Diakan and Juttari empires spanned thousands of light years, but this expansion had only been made possible by the jump gates. Exploring regions where there were no jump gates was considered unnecessary.

Since the jump gates stretched from one end of the galaxy to the other, why would anyone bother venturing into regions where no jump gates existed? It was this fact alone that saved the lost colonies. By shutting down their jump gate they ensured their salvation, and isolation.

The Hermes was now two hundred light years away from the Sol system. While Earth ships had faster than light speed (FTL) capabilities, it would still take more than a lifetime to reach this region of space from Earth. Jon doubted whether anyone even considered attempting the trip. The logistics alone of such a journey would be a nightmare. But now, with the jump drive, great swaths of unexplored space had become reachable. And the isolation of the colonies would soon come to an end.

The Hermes had jumped into a system dominated by a red giant star. Even from a safe distance it dominated the viewscreen. Ten planets orbited the behemoth, none of them showing any evidence of life. Long range scans were conducted again and while they showed some promising data, nothing indicated any signs of civilization.

And so the Hermes jumped for the fourth time, this time landing near a binary star system. Two blinding suns orbiting each other, swirling in a blue, fiery dance. The first star, the vampire, sucked energy from the second, and a stream of blazing blue clasped the two in a deadly embrace. This would be their last jump until the jump drive recharged. Jon knew that this would likely be the place where the Juttari would need to recharge their jump drive as well.

"Are there any asteroid fields nearby?" Jon asked.

"Reading a large asteroid field approximately eighty million kilometers away," said Navigation.

"Good, identify a decent cluster where the Hermes can stay hidden and send the coordinates to the helm. Helm, take us into the asteroid field. One quarter light."

"Setting course for asteroid field. One quarter light," Said Richards.

The density of the field made it a good hiding spot. The Juttari wouldn't notice them unless they entered it themselves. The Hermes would wait amongst the rocks like a lion in the tall Savannah grass stalking its prey. Jon knew from the previous engagement that the Hermes was the superior ship in battle. She was faster, more agile, and had more firepower. Ambush had been the Juttari's only advantage, and now the Hermes would use that same advantage against them.

The Hermes entered the asteroid field and the stars practically disappeared from the viewscreen, the view now dominated by a rocky cluster that reminded Jon of the ball pit his daughters liked to play in. The rocks ranged in size from pebbles to small moons larger than the Hermes. Tiny stones bounced incessantly off the ship's hull, creating a ghostly drumming sound throughout the ship. These didn't pose much of a threat, yet the sound still unsettled the crew. The larger asteroids, however, were another matter.

Ensign Richards showed no signs of stress, looking almost like a rock himself as he maneuvered the Hermes to avoid the giant boulders. His hands remained steady, and his eyes stayed focused on his controls. Even his legs didn't move, or even twitch. Could anything rattle this kid?

"Don't break my ship, Ensign," said Jon.

"No Sir," said Richards.

There was no physical reaction to the comment that Jon could see. No twitch, no tick, no involuntary flexing. Nothing. On the viewscreen the ship seemed like it was gliding through the asteroid field. Swaying from side to side like a leaf falling from a tree it effortlessly swung around each obstacle. Every movement fluid, the Hermes seemed to dance and play with the rocks surrounding her.

Well within the field now, the Hermes settled into position. They would wait here until they could engage the Juttari. A feeling of serenity washed over Jon. He had never realized how beautiful an asteroid field could be. There was none of the fiery violence of a star, or the desolate emptiness of space. Instead, you were surrounded by quiet floating spheres. Imperfect and captivating in their starkness. For the first time in weeks he felt himself relax. He sank into his chair and tilted his head back slightly, allowing the contour of his headrest to free his neck. The stress of the last few days slowly dissipated and his chest loosened. He took a few deep but gentle breaths, and quietly let his diaphragm expand and contract, each exhale unloading fragments of the tension that had been compounding inside him. Secretly he hoped it would be a while before the Juttari arrived.

"Reading weapon signatures!" said Petrovic.

"Location?" said Wolfe.

"All around us." Petrovic's face went white. "They're on the asteroids."

On the larger asteroids surrounding the Hermes, turrets emerged from deep inside the rocky surface. Coming online they swiveled and locked onto the floating ship.

"Weapons hot!"

The turrets opened fire. Violent explosions hammered the ship and the bridge crew struggled to maintain their balance.

"Sound general quarters," said Jon. "Helm, get us the hell out of here! Tactical, feed weapon signature data to helm for evasive action."

On the viewscreen the serene landscape from a few moments earlier now erupted into a hellish gauntlet of cannon fire. Red tracer lines zigzagged across the sky like a celestial spider web. Streams of plasma fire sprayed out from the large asteroids hammering the Hermes and pulverizing any rocks getting in the way.

Unable to return the way they came, Richards plowed deeper into the asteroid field looking for a way out of the rocky labyrinth. His head jerked from side to side trying to keep track of the multiple information feeds lighting up his console. His hands moved like pistons making split second course corrections to compensate for the constant wave of new threats. Jon noticed a few beads of sweat appear on his temple, convincing him that the kid was human after all.

Cannon fire continued to pound the ship, the explosions combining with the rapping of rocks against the hull, fraying the nerves of all on board. With each turn a new turret emerged, opening fire on the Hermes as she passed.

"Set rail guns to offensive mode. Auto target all weapon signatures within range. Fire energy weapons at will. Target weapon systems as they appear," said Jon.

The Hermes rail gun turrets sprayed a barrage of depleted uranium against the firing cannons. Blue energy beams joined in, destroying the deadly turrets one by one. On the bridge crew members involuntarily put hands in front of their faces, fooled by the viewscreen into thinking they were going to crash into giant rock after giant rock.

A particularly violent impact rocked the bridge causing one of the consoles to shatter firing sparks into the face of a young Ensign. Jerking backwards, she fell off her chair onto her back and screamed. Her hands shot up to her face, fingers clawing at her eyes trying in vain to stop them from burning. Her body twisted and writhed, her legs kicking out at invisible attackers.

Commander Wolfe raced to the Ensign's side, calling for medical help as she moved. Reaching the Ensign she crouched down beside her and wrapped her arms around the terrified woman's shoulders, trying to help soothe her. It appeared to work and her screams turned into sobs. Her body convulsed with each breath, but she let Wolfe pull her up into a sitting position and leaned into Wolfe's shoulder. Hands still fixed on her eyes, she sat there until the medics arrived on the bridge. Wolfe waved them over and they began treating the Ensign. Satisfied with the medics taking control, Wolfe got up and went back to her station.

Jon was still impressed with Ensign Richards. He continued to display the skill that won him so many competitions on Earth, making the Hermes bob, weave, and often miss oncoming asteroids by what seemed like mere centimeters. His hands now moved with lightning precision, but his shoulders were hunched and tight and his chin was tucked in, pressing hard against his clavicle. Jon was pretty sure nobody had fired on him when he was racing back home. Still, the kid handled the pressure well.

"Hull breach, deck Gamma," the computer announced.

"Seal off deck Gamma," said Commander Wolfe.

"Fires on decks Beta, Kappa, and Theta. Fire suppression systems activated," said the computer.

They continued to adapt to their situation. On the viewscreen a turret fired off a couple of shots and was immediately destroyed. The Hermes turned and faced more enemy fire which was immediately suppressed. They were still being shot at from multiple directions, but they now began to mitigate the damage. The ship's AI had quickly analyzed the installations and started predicting their placement. This advantage allowed the Hermes to quickly destroy new turrets, sometimes before they could open fire.

Nonetheless, she still took a serious pounding while trying to escape. The density that made the field a great hiding place now turned it into a maze of horrors, with each turn revealing a new threat. Ensign Richards continued to show his flying prowess, evading threat after threat and impressing Jon with how well he handled the pressure. Jon swore he would buy the kid a drink if he got them out of the field alive.

And much to everyone's surprise, Richards did get them out of the field alive, albeit with heavy damage. The Hermes had a hole in its side from the hull breach, and fires still raged in several sections of the ship. The armor plating on the hull had been hammered hard and had surely been weakened as a result.

"Damage report," said Jon.

"Five casualties," said Wolfe. "All a result of the hull breaches on deck Gamma. The deck has been successfully sealed off. There are a number of injuries, but nothing serious. Mostly contusions and the odd broken bone. Multiple fires have broken out throughout the ship, but suppression systems appear to have them under control. There is some minor damage in engineering, but neither the reactors nor the jump system have been damaged. Weapons systems have not been hit and are operating at one hundred percent."

"Have engineering pull together a – "

"Contact," shouted Petrovic. "Two unidentified ships closing fast."

Jon twisted around in his chair. "On viewscreen."

The viewscreen's orientation changed and two starships appeared, steadily becoming larger as they approached. They were smaller than the Hermes, each about the size of a frigate. Definitely warships, they lacked any identifiable markings that might link them to a larger fleet. Jon wondered if they weren't pirates.

"Reading weapons hot," said Petrovic.

"Switch rail guns to point defense mode. Load all missile tubes," said Jon.

"Point defense mode online. Missile tubes loaded," said Wolfe.

"Helm, set course to intercept the bandits."

"Aye, Sir. Setting course to intercept."

"Captain, considering the damage we've sustained, shouldn't we try to outrun them? We're likely faster than they are," said Tallos.

"We don't know this region of space. They do. And they probably have friends nearby who may be able to cut off our escape. I'd rather fight two now than more later."

"But Captain, that conclusion is far from certain."

"We don't have the luxury of certainty out here."

The Hermes raced towards the oncoming warships. As it bridged the gap and came in range both attacking ships fired off a volley of missiles. Twelve in all they streaked toward the Hermes, glowing red like tiny sinister comets.

"Launch countermeasures," said Jon.

"Countermeasure away," said Petrovic.

"Target the lead ship. Fire missiles."

"Missiles away."

The lead ship launched its own countermeasures, but had no point defense capabilities. Its countermeasures were not nearly effective enough and four missiles continued toward their target. The Hermes missiles were designed to intelligently target critical systems, unless programmed differently, and all four plowed into the rear section of the ship, finding its reactors in short order. The resulting explosion lit up the void and concussive waves rocked the Hermes, but caused no serious damage.

Sporadic cheers broke out on the bridge. The mood was improving now that they could lash out at someone for the damage and loss of life suffered in the asteroid field. Jon felt the creature's elation at the kill and he knew it was not just the creature's feeling. They shared the emotion and were experiencing it together. Cringing at the thought, he shook it off and focused on the task at hand.

"Sir, second ship is firing energy weapons. They are targeting our engines."

The second ship let loose a barrage of energy beams that scored direct hits on the Hermes. The concussions rocked the ship and the bridge crew braced themselves against the force of the impacts.

"Return fire, all weapon systems."

The Hermes wheeled around to face its attacker releasing a salvo of missiles and energy weapon fire. The other ship launched countermeasures, but it was too close for its drones to have much effect. Beams of blue sliced through the weak armor plating producing ugly looking hull breaches.

Machinery and personnel alike were sucked through the gashes into the vacuum of space, creating a ghastly floating debris field. Within seconds the Hermes missiles plowed into the weakened ship and detonated. Multiple explosions ripped through the vessel, amputating large chunks of the ship's hull. Then the reactor exploded, annihilating the rest of the alien ship.

More cheers broke out on the bridge and Jon almost joined in. It wasn't the Juttari, but it was still two kills. The Hermes had proven herself again. She was certainly growing on him.

"Sir, Engineering is reporting damage to some of our propulsion systems. FTL is still operational, but our jump system has been damaged and is offline. Repair crews are on route but it will take some time to repair," said Wolfe.

"How much time?"

"At least a day, Sir."

"Sir, ship's sensors are picking up a small vessel, likely a lifeboat from the destroyed ship," said Petrovic.

"Sir, we could be in this region of space for a while. The survivors could provide some valuable intelligence," said Wolfe.

"Agreed. Retrieve the lifeboat and bring it into hanger bay 1. Seal off the hanger bay and deploy a full security detail. Assume all occupants are hostile."

"Yes, Sir."

CHAPTER 16

Underneath the Hermes a door opened and cluster of cylindrical drones were deployed. Firing jets the drones fanned out and raced toward the lifeboat. Bridging the gap in short order, the drones swarmed the lifeboat, hovering only a few feet from the vehicle's hull. Once in position, the drones fastened themselves to the lifeboat and reversed their thrusters in unison, halting the lifeboat's forward momentum. A brief tug of war ensued as the lifeboat tried in vain to break free from its captors. The robotic swarm then changed direction and forced its prey back to the Hermes.

In the hanger bay a security detail led by Chief St. Clair awaited the vessel's arrival. Not taking any chances, St. Clair deployed two Hercules Class battle mechs. The giant war machines stood at opposite ends of the hanger bay. Standing ten feet tall, the mechanical beasts were a sight to behold. Shaped like a human, they had two giant arms and legs, but looked like someone forgot the head. Instead, a small mound was perched on the shoulders, hiding an array of sensors.

The pilot sat in the cockpit, behind the heavily armored chest, controlling the battle mech's every move. The powerful arms had access to a formidable array of weaponry and currently deployed a pair of wicked looking Gatling guns. If necessary, the mech could swap out the Gatling guns for missile launchers and energy weapons.

For defense it had its own built in counter measures and could even switch its Gatling guns to point defense mode. Heavy ballistic armor protected it from most projectiles that managed to get through its defensive systems.

Engineered for multi-theater warfare, the mech could project force on land, in the air, or in space. A mech was a one man army, so the two mechs deployed on the hanger bay were insurance against anything on board the captured lifeboat.

Complementing the mechs was a squad of Marines and the Diakan security advisor, Kinos, wearing full combat suits. Much smaller than the mechs, the combat suits were essentially powered exoskeletons surrounded by heavy armor plating. Like the mechs, the combat suits were self-contained with their own life support systems, and could keep their occupants alive in the most hostile conditions, including space.

Once inside the combat suit the Marine would move normally, but would be augmented with superior speed and strength. Each suit had its own power source and AI, and all suits and mechs were interlinked over their own military grade network. The strength of the combat suits allowed each Marine to carry huge, vicious looking weapons, which in this case were predominantly energy weapons. Kevin was the exception, carrying his own personal Gatling gun. He didn't know what to expect in the lifeboat, but he sure as hell was going to be ready for it.

The drones entered the hanger bay with the lifeboat in tow. They set the vessel down on a pad and metal arms came up from the floor and secured it in place. Multiple mechanical whines were heard as the Marines pointed their weapons at the lifeboat. Several tense minutes passed with no activity, and then with no warning the vessel's hatch slid open and a small ramp dropped to the ground.

"Hold your fire," said Kevin, placing the doorway between his cross-hairs. He wondered what type of monstrosity would climb out of that door.

What he saw next stunned him. The first thing to emerge from the open hatch was a woman. A human woman.

She wore a brown jumpsuit, and looked like she was in her mid-thirties. Her eyes were wide and a horrified look spread across her face as she surveyed the military machinery surrounding her. She held her arms up, palms open to show she was unarmed, all the while shaking her head no, presumably pleading for the soldiers not to shoot her.

There was more movement behind her and the Marines shifted their weapons from the woman back to the doorway, making the woman wave her arms frantically, yelling something unintelligible.

"Hold your fire," Kevin repeated.

A small hand emerged from the doorway and gripped the side of the vessel. Slowly, furtively, a small face peeked out from behind the wall at the Marines. There was a high pitched scream and the face disappeared.

The woman faced the doorway, arms still up, and now spoke calmly to the person inside. With a bit of coaxing from the woman the little face emerged again and finally walked out of the vessel.

A little girl.

Kevin couldn't believe his eyes. The woman and girl were both unarmed and didn't seem to pose a threat, but he still needed to clear the vessel. He gestured to the woman to take the girl and move off to the side. The woman hesitated and the Diakan charged at her and the girl, energy weapon at the ready. The woman screamed and fell backward, arms squeezed around the girl.

"Kinos, stand down," Kevin shouted.

The Diakan had reached the woman and pointed his energy weapon at her head. He was motioning for her to move to the far wall. The woman was still screaming but seemed to understand and rushed the girl to the wall.

"Kinos, back your ass up!"

The Diakan slowly moved backwards, his weapon still pointing at the woman's head. Kevin then ordered two Marines to clear the lifeboat. The Marines rushed to the vessel and flanked the doorway. One Marine entered the vessel while the other covered him. After a brief search the Marine came back out and signaled that the vessel was clear. Kevin looked back at the woman and the girl and opened a comm link with Jon.

"Sir, are you seeing what I'm seeing?" said Kevin.

Jon had watched the entire scene unfold on the bridge, and was practically speechless himself.

"Yes, I am," said Jon.

"What do you want me to do with them?" asked Kevin.

"Take them to sick bay. I'll meet you there. I want the Doctor to check them out to make sure they aren't Chaanisar. Keep them under guard. And be careful, if they are Chaanisar a combat suit may not be enough protection."

"Yes, Sir. Leave it to me."

Kevin walked up to Kinos, who was still pointing his weapon at the woman's head. "The next time you pull a stunt like that I will lock you up for the rest of the mission. Am I understood?"

"Yes Security Chief, you are understood."

Kevin glared at the Diakan for a few seconds and then ordered three of his Marines to accompany him. He couldn't understand what the woman was saying, but he did his best to make her understand his intentions. She seemed to be a quick study and used nods and hand signals to tell Kevin that they would follow.

The four Marines escorted them out of the hangar bay and through a long corridor to the sick bay. Walking behind the two Kevin studied them closely looking for anything remotely resembling a threat. The woman had her arm around the little girl's shoulders and held her close, trying to comfort her. The little girl had not stopped trembling since she emerged from the lifeboat and buried her face deep in the woman's side. From the looks of things Kevin assumed that the woman was the girl's mother. A DNA test would let them know for sure. At least that question would be answered, Kevin wasn't so sure about the rest. What were humans doing out here anyway?

CHAPTER 17

Engineering was a frantic mix of shouting and clanging as crews scrambled to make repairs. The air reeked of charred wiring and dry chemical fire extinguisher. Adjacent to one of the main reactors, Chief Engineer Singh stooped over the main jump system array with Diakan Engineering Advisor Boufos watching.

"The primary relay has been damaged," said Boufos.

Chief Engineer Singh stopped working for a moment, struggling to contain his composure. The Diakan had been following him around since they left the station and interfering with his work. He had been able to ignore it up until now, but with the stress of battle and emergency repairs he was now getting very close to the boiling point. Everything was a mess. Fires. Hull breaches. Downed systems. The last thing he needed right now was a Diakan questioning his every move.

"Thank you Mr. Boufos, I can see that. If you wouldn't mind it would be helpful if you could assist with some of the other repairs that are needed," said Singh.

"I possess a superior understanding of this ship's propulsion system, especially the jump system. Assigning me to other duties would not be an efficient use of my skill set."

Singh took a deep breath. "Since the jump system will be down for some time, we need to ensure that the FTL systems are all functioning properly. Please run a full diagnostic on them."

“It is not optimal to have me run diagnostic tests, Chief Engineer.”

“Optimal or not, that is what I want you to do. And last I checked I am still the Chief Engineer, which means I make the decisions, not you.”

“As you wish, Chief Engineer.”

The Diakan walked away and Singh went back to work. There was extensive damage to the primary relay. He now realized it would take longer to repair than his original estimate. The Captain was not going to be happy.

He opened a comm link with Commander Wolfe.

“Yes Rajneesh,” answered Wolfe.

The sound of her voice calmed his nerves. Secretly he was happy that she came on this mission, although he wouldn’t let her know that. There were too many complications with their relationship. Too much volatility. And it had a habit of interfering with his work. He did love her, but they were too different.

“I’ve been working on repairing the jump system and the damage is more extensive than I originally thought. At first it looked like it was only the superluminal emitters that needed repair, but after further investigation I’ve found that the primary relay has also been extensively damaged. It is going to take longer to repair than my original estimate.”

“How much longer?”

“Three, maybe four days.”

“Are you sure? We really need that jump system online?”

Was he sure? How many times would his abilities be questioned today? He was the Chief Engineer. Some people would think he knew what he was talking about. “I will do my best to speed up the repairs, but this type of work takes time, Commander.”

“We don’t have time. Surely there must be a faster way to get this done.”

“The damage is just too extensive.”

“I don’t need excuses, Rajneesh. I need results.”

“This is precise work, Commander. It is not something that can be rushed.”

“I will let the Captain know. Just try and speed things up.”

“Singh out.”

Singh closed the comm link. How did she do it? How was it that with one word she could soothe him and then with another have him ready to explode? He didn’t understand it. He didn’t want to understand it. He had work to do. Fuming, he returned to his repairs.

CHAPTER 18

How did humans end up 250 light years from Sol? Jon struggled with the question. None of this made any sense. The lost colonies could be a thousand light years away. It didn't seem possible that they came from the colonies. And it wasn't realistic to think they came from Sol either. Even with FTL it would take them at least 25 years to make it this far. That was not possible for a number of reasons. So how did they get here?

Arriving at the sick bay Jon found Doctor Ellerbeck examining the woman and child while Kevin and the three other Marines stood guard. The woman pulled the still trembling child closer to her when Jon approached. Jon cringed. Apparently he could still scare women and children.

"Well Doctor, are they Chaanisar?" asked Jon.

"No Captain, there are no signs of augmentation," said Ellerbeck.

"Have you been able to communicate with them?"

"No, Sir. They haven't spoken since they got here."

Jon looked at the woman and spoke directly to her. "I'm Captain Jon Pike. You are on board the Hermes. May I ask what your name is?" Jon tried to be as polite as possible. They were already frightened. More intimidation wouldn't get him anywhere. He thought he saw a glimmer of understanding in her eyes, like she had heard something vaguely familiar.

She studied him for a moment and decided to speak. Unfortunately nobody understood a word she said.

"Doctor, does your AI have access to the linguistics database?" said Jon.

"Yes, I believe it does," said Ellerbeck. She then accessed the sick bay's AI and asked it to analyze the woman's speech.

"From the sample provided Germanic and Russian languages are identified," said the AI.

"AI, using current knowledge, ask the subject to continue speaking so as better to analyze and interpret the language spoken," said Jon.

The AI said something to the woman who seemed to understand it and spoke again, this time at greater length. The AI continued to engage the woman in conversation to better calibrate its understanding. Finally the AI spoke in English. "Analysis complete. The language spoken has Germanic, Russian, Dutch, and English influences. Linguistic database has been updated."

"Good. AI, you will act as interpreter to facilitate dialog," said Jon.

"Understood."

Jon looked at the woman again. "My name is Captain Jon Pike. You are on board the Hermes. May I ask your name?"

The woman listened to the AI and responded, "Breeah Menk."

"Nice to meet you Breeah. Is this your daughter?" asked Jon.

"This is Anki, my daughter."

"What were you doing on board that ship?"

"That was my husband's ship." The little girl started crying. "Anki's father."

"Why did your husband attack us?"

"You entered the asteroid field. We were protecting our home."

"Your home? You mean you live in the asteroid field?"

Breeah gave Jon a suspicious look. She composed herself now, snapped back to reality by the realization that she had already said too much.

Jon tried to calm her fears. "We mean you no harm, Breeah. Your ships attacked us. We were only defending ourselves. We are not here to harm you."

Breeah stayed silent and just gave Jon a cold stare. Jon tried a different approach.

"How long have you lived here?"

"We have always lived here."

"You obviously came here somehow. How did your people first come here?"

"We have always lived here."

"You are human. Humans haven't always lived here. Your people had to come here from somewhere."

"We are Reivers."

"What does that mean?"

The AI answered the question. "A reiver is technically someone who reives, or steals."

"Where do you reive?" asked Jon.

"We cross through the gate to reive, then we cross back."

"The gate? You mean you have a jump gate?"

Breeah gave Jon a questioning look, apparently not understanding his question.

"A jump gate… you cross through and end up in a different region of space."

"Yes. We have a jump gate."

Jon gave her a blank stare. These people had a jump gate. That answered his question of how they got here. They must have crossed through the gate at some point and settled here. But it couldn't have been from Sol's gate since there was no knowledge of a gate in this region of space. Therefore, the only logical conclusion was they came from the lost colonies at some point.

Jump gates don't follow a linear path. The jump gate routes often seem totally random. One jump gate usually connects to another jump gate in a different region of space. One jump gate could be 1,000 light years in one direction, and the next could double back and be only 250 light years away.

Most jump gates make only two connections. One connection to the next gate and one to the previous one. In rare situations a jump gate can make multiple connections. Those jump gates are very strategic, creating interstellar choke points. During the wars most of the really major battles were fought over these gates.

"How many different places can you go with your gate?"

"How many places? The gate only sends us to one place. We go. We reive. We return."

"When you travel through the gate, are there humans on the other side?"

"There are no humans. We were the only humans until your people arrived.."

Jon tried to hide his disappointment. He hoped this might be a link to the colonies. Still it was a link to something, or else there would be nothing for them to "reive".

"If there are no humans, are there aliens?"

"Yes, on the other side there are many planets. Many aliens live there."

"I'd like to see your gate, and your home. Will you show them to me?"

Almond shaped eyes studied Jon. Hazel colored eyes, they were almost green. Jon hadn't noticed them until now. They had an intensity that almost unnerved him. It wasn't just the eyes. She had a unique beauty about her that Jon was only now starting to notice. She had calmed down considerably from the moment he walked in the room, and now a hidden strength revealed itself that Jon didn't expect. Whoever these people were, Jon had just destroyed two of their ships, killing all the people on board, including her husband. Yet she now displayed incredible composure.

She remained silent, ignoring Jon's question.

"If you have a gate, why isn't there more activity here? More ships?"

"The aliens on the other side of the gate do not know it exists."

Jon understood. Jump gates were not obvious. You had to know where to look. They were often only discovered after a ship came through and revealed their location. Even then you needed to know how to activate it. New jump gates were found by going through one to see what was on the other side and continuing on down the path. If these people were able to come through their gates without attracting attention, then it was possible that the other side did not know of the gate's existence. Considering their profession, Jon assumed stealthiness was an inherent skill.

Jon was suddenly interrupted by a comm link from Commander Wolfe. "Sir, the Juttari vessel has just appeared."

"On my way." Jon looked again at Breeah, "we have been battling another starship which has just appeared in this system. If they find you they will not show mercy. You need to let us know where your home and gate is or we cannot protect you."

Breeah looked concerned and her eyes told Jon she wanted to answer, but she still kept quiet. She still didn't trust Jon or anyone else on board. Who could blame her?

"Doctor, see to it that Breeah and Anki are looked after and that they get some food. I'm sure they're hungry. I'll be on the bridge."

Yes, Sir," said Ellerbeck.

Jon turned to Kevin, "leave a couple of guards here just to be on the safe side. Make sure they don't leave sick bay."

"Yes, Sir," said Kevin.

CHAPTER 19

"Captain on the bridge," the Marine sentry announced as Jon entered.

"Status report," said Jon.

"The Juttari haven't noticed us yet Sir. We are still very close to the asteroid field and that might preventing them from detecting us," said Wolfe.

"They'll eventually find us if we stay here. Helm, can you quietly get us back into the asteroid field? Preferably somewhere with no weapons systems?"

"Yes, Sir. We can enter the same way we came out. We had managed to destroy the weapons systems in place there," said Richards.

"Very well, take us in nice and easy. I don't want to be noticed."

"Taking us in, Sir."

Jon turned and spoke to Wolfe, "we should have a better chance of avoiding detection in the asteroid field. Call it a modification of our previous plan."

Jon thought he saw a hint of a smirk on his XO's face. That would be a first, he thought.

The Hermes fired its thrusters once and then let its forward momentum take over, gliding slowly into the asteroid field. The Juttari ship sat still and didn't move. If they weren't looking in this direction they wouldn't see the Hermes, and even if they were they might miss it. Jon was worried about the debris from the other two ships, however. If the Juttari picked up on the wreckage they might come and investigate. That would put them a little too close for comfort. As the Hermes entered the asteroid field Richards fired thrusters again to position the ship safely behind a cluster of large rocks.

"Commander, shut down all nonessential systems and rig for silent running."

"All decks have reported rigged for silent running, Sir," said Wolfe.

The Hermes floated silently, lurking in the shadows of the surrounding boulders. Tense minutes turned into anxious hours and the crew quietly busied themselves with their respective duties. Because of their hiding position they couldn't see the Juttari starship on the viewscreen anymore, and their scanners were equally hampered due to the orders to run silent.

The telltale signs of stress were evident everywhere. Commander Wolfe became even more efficient, ensuring that nobody slacked in their duties. Ensign Richards's right leg had a nervous twitch and wouldn't stop moving. The Navigator, Ensign Yao, plotted coordinates for future jumps, and then plotted alternative coordinates trying to be as proactive as possible, all the while making small neck twists trying to relax her tightening shoulder muscles. The Tactical officer, Ensign Petrovic, repeatedly checked his systems and nodded to himself during each check.

Stress did interesting things to people. Some thrived on it, while others broke down. Jon always fed on stress. The more pressure, the better he performed. That little character trait came in handy in his line of work. The ability to think clearly while under fire is what keeps you alive. Jon believed that pressure brought out the best in most people. Not just in the military, but in all walks of life. A deadline often works wonders on someone who otherwise would procrastinate.

Hiding behind these rocks felt like procrastination. It made Jon's skin crawl. He knew the Juttari were out there and he wanted nothing more than to face them again, but he had to think of his crew now. If it had been him alone and injured, he would still take the fight to the enemy.

Many called it reckless, but it worked for Jon. Being the underdog always pushed him to peak performance, even before the symbiont. Even with the Hermes weakened, he still thought he could win against the Juttari. That victory would come at great cost of life, however. It would be smarter to just wait for the repairs to be done. Of course, if the Juttari were to find them, then they would have to fight, vulnerable or not. Jon figured he was likely the only one on board who wanted the Juttari to find them.

CHAPTER 20

"So we came from a planet called Earth?" asked Breeah, the AI translating for her.

"Yes, hundreds of years ago humans used the gates to travel to other star systems and colonize other worlds. Your ancestors would have been among those colonists," answered Ellerbeck.

"But you do not know how my clan ended up here, in Telepylos."

"No, unfortunately I don't. Is Telepylos what your home is called?"

"It is the name for the asteroid field. We live within the field."

"And your people have no stories, no legends, telling of how you came to Telepylos?"

"There are some, but they only tell us that our ancestors wandered the stars before settling here. They say our ancestors sought refuge. That they were hunted like animals, and that Telepylos offered a safe home."

"Were they Reivers as well?"

"I do not know. Tell me more about this Earth you come from. Do you coexist with these aliens I have seen?" The memory of the alien on the hangar bay angered Breeah. It was much more aggressive than the humans. She knew that the humans would not fire on her. She saw it in their posture, even with their battle suits on. The alien behaved differently though, and Breeah knew it could kill her and her daughter without remorse. And the man they called Chief barely had control over it. It was like a vicious beast that needed to be put down.

"The Diakans. We are allies. They have been a tremendous help to us. Much of the technology you see here is Diakan."

"I do not understand. They give you their technology freely? Why would they do that?"

"The Diakans liberated us. We had been enslaved by other aliens. The Juttari. The Diakans helped us defeat them. They helped us rebuild."

"I see. These Juttari are enemies of the Diakans. They strengthen you in order to weaken the Juttari."

"It's more than that. The medical technology the Diakans shared with us alone is hundreds of years ahead of anything we understood, if not more. Much of the knowledge we had prior to the occupation was forgotten. We were like lost children. The Diakans helped us find our way."

"Are they now your masters?"

"They are our allies. We govern ourselves."

Breeah found Ellerbeck to be somewhat naïve when it came to these Diakans. Still, she paid close attention to her. This elegant woman, this healer, was unlike anyone she had ever known.

There were no female healers in her clan. Yes, the women helped the other women with childbirth and other feminine needs, but no woman had been a healer. She never quite understood why.

Her grandmother always seemed to know what ailed her, and what the proper treatment should be. People would often consult her before calling for the healer. Even when the less trusting called the healer, he would often come to the same conclusion as her grandmother. Yet she had no healer training. No healer title. She simply had the wisdom of her years. And even when the healer came, he often did not have the medicine needed to treat the ailment. If the reiving raids were fruitful there would be medicine. If not, then the healer would rely on the same treatments her grandmother used.

The woman speaking to her was different. She not only had the title of healer, but also had knowledge with not even half her grandmother's years. And she had medicine. Enough to treat everyone on board this immense vessel. She also had technology that worked wonders. Alien or not, Breeah hadn't encountered anything like it on either side of the gate. These people seemed to lack nothing aboard this vessel.

"How do your people govern? Does your clan have a leader?" asked Ellerbeck.

"We have a council of leaders," said Breeah. She thought about her husband again. As captain of a warship her husband was one of her clan's leaders. She enjoyed many benefits through her marriage, as did her daughter. With his death, however, her status was gone. She would lose all her privileges, as would Anki.

Her husband had been a fool. A reckless fool. And he brought disaster upon them. She did not miss him, nor did she grieve his loss. She had to think of her daughter now and the future.

"How are members of this council chosen?" asked Ellerbeck.

Breeah didn't answer. She considered her situation. Everything had changed for her. While she would not betray her clan, there was nothing for her to go back to now. She wondered whether staying on this ship was possible. They were obviously the same species, and according to the healer they both came from the same planet long ago. Perhaps she should help them. If she showed them the gate's location, they might agree to let her and Anki stay on board. Anki might have a brighter future with these people. Still, she needed to be sure. She glanced at the guards standing by the door. While obviously advanced, these people were dangerous. These aliens were dangerous. She needed to be careful.

"I wish to speak to your Captain," said Breeah.

CHAPTER 21

Breeah and Anki had adjusted better to their surroundings since the last time Jon saw them. Anki wandered around the room looking closely at the technology. Every so often her mother would utter a warning and the child's arms would quickly drop to her sides. She would take a step back and shake her head to remove some errant bangs from her eyes. Then she would resume her exploration of the sick bay. The Doctor's scans showed the girl to be seven years old and her behavior clearly backed that estimate.

The scans showed the mother to be thirty-five. Where the daughter was naturally curious, the mother seemed more calculating. She had quickly come to terms with her predicament and now analyzed her options. There was a shrewd intelligence about her that Jon liked.

"I will show you where the gate is, but not our home," said Breeah.

"You really should tell me where your home is. If our enemy finds it things will not go well for them," said Jon.

"You mean the Juttari?" said Breeah.

Jon looked at Ellerbeck and frowned. "Apparently Doctor Ellerbeck has been giving you a history lesson."

"She has explained some things about Earth to me."

"I hope she has explained how dangerous the Juttari can be. The last thing you want is for them to find your home."

"I will not reveal its location Captain. I will only show you where the gate is, and only if you let us stay on board."

"You don't want to return home?" Jon hadn't expected that Breeah would want to stay.

"No, Captain. My husband is dead. There is nothing left for us there. I want a better future for Anki. From what I have seen, that future is with your people."

Breeah's request was a logical one. Her people lived in an asteroid field and supported themselves through theft. Not the best way to raise a child. The Hermes, in comparison, must seem like a sanctuary to her. She didn't appear to be much of a security risk. The main risk would be her stealing things which could easily be controlled. When compared to the intelligence value she presented it was an easy decision. If the gate was what he thought, it could cut their trip in half and put the Hermes well ahead of the Juttari.

"Very well. I will grant your request to remain on board, but there are a few conditions. You will show us where the gate is and you will act as a guide to help us better navigate the region on the other side of the gate. And there will be no reiving on board my ship. Do you agree with these terms?"

"Yes, Captain. I agree. Thank you." A smile spread across Breeah's face. She called Anki over to her and gave the child a hug. The expression on the little girl's face didn't change. She just stared at Jon making him wonder what she thought of him. He didn't see any fear in her eyes, just a hint of childish curiosity.

Jon opened a comm to Commander Wolfe.

"Wolfe here."

"Commander, our two guests will be joining us for the rest of our trip. See to it that some suitable quarters are assigned to them. I'll explain everything later."

"Yes, Sir," said Wolfe.

"As I'm sure you've guessed, this is a military vessel. There are no other children on board. We will do our best to accommodate you and your daughter, but your access to the ship will need to be restricted.

Will that be a problem?" While their home may have been an asteroid field, Jon wondered how well she understood what life would be like on board. Allowing them freedom of movement would be dangerous.

"It will not be a problem Captain," said Breeah.

"Not only will there be nobody for Anki to play with, but we have no school for her either. She will get bored quickly."

"I will see to my child's education Captain. Surely you can provide us with some computer access to facilitate this?"

"Yes, we can provided limited access to the ship's database so that both of you can learn about us."

"That will be sufficient Captain. Thank you."

"Good. My Navigator will retrieve the gate's coordinates. Now what can you tell me about what's on the other side of that gate?"

"The space directly on the other side is safe. There is nothing there and it does not see any traffic. That is how we have not been noticed using it. The region of space is controlled by a species known as the Kemmar Empire. They control several star systems. Their empire is stable and is a source of considerable commerce. It is common to have other species traveling through their space for trade. When reiving my people target lone trading freighters. They offer little resistance and their cargoes are usually valuable."

"You don't target these Kemmar?"

Breeah cocked an eyebrow at Jon. "No Captain. It is not wise to provoke the Kemmar. While they prefer to trade, they are powerful and have a reputation for being ruthless. To provoke the Kemmar would mean slavery, or death if you are fortunate. While we do break their law, by not targeting the Kemmar we have avoided any direct action against us."

Jon was amazed at Breeah's transformation. She had changed from a screaming prisoner, to a galactic tour guide in the blink of an eye.

"You have been on these reiving raids with your husband?"

"Yes, Captain. When my husband crossed the gate Anki and I always went with him."

"Is that common among your people?"

"Yes. It is how we teach our ways to our children."

Jon was afraid to ask, but he suddenly realized that the two ships he destroyed likely had entire families on board. Soldiers accepted that they might die in battle. But children? Revulsion gripped him making his stomach lurch, and he suppressed an urge to vomit. He silently prayed that he was wrong.

Breeah studied him and a look of understanding swept across her face. "You could not have known, Captain," she said, as if she had been reading his thoughts. "There is always the risk of death. It is our way of life. We accept it."

This truly was a remarkable woman. He killed members of her family. Her husband. Her friends. Children. Children! Yet she showed him compassion and forgiveness. Was it all an act? He didn't see deception in her eyes. He didn't sense any ulterior motives. An impressive woman indeed. He made a mental note not to underestimate her.

"So these Kemmar are used to different species traveling through their space. Would we be able to travel through without raising much suspicion?"

"That I do not know, Captain. Your ship is not a freighter. It is clearly a warship. That alone would attract some attention. We avoided the more populated regions and instead targeted known freighter lanes."

"Yes, I can see how a warship would raise some concerns. I suppose we'll just have to introduce ourselves and show we have no hostile intent."

"I cannot advise you on this Captain."

Jon shrugged. "Thank you for time Breeah. I will need you to advise us again when we embark."

"Of course, Captain."

Jon turned and walked out the door, the thought of dead women and children floating in space haunting him as he left.

CHAPTER 22

From all the evidence he had seen, Jon was sure that the Juttari had stolen the jump system design. It likely had identical features to the Hermes system. Based on that assumption it would take the Juttari about eight hours to recharge their drive. He added some extra time as buffer on top of that and then ordered the Hermes to venture out of its hiding place to have a look around and verify that the Juttari had jumped away. Sure enough, they were gone.

"Helm take us to the jump gate coordinates," said Jon. Breeah had provided the coordinates for the jump gate as she had promised. Jon was happy to be on the move again. He didn't mind lying in wait for a target, but being the target grated on his nerves.

The jump system was still offline and it appeared it would remain that way at least for a couple of days. The fires had all been put out and repairs to the hull breach were underway. A temporary stabilizing field had been established, sealing off the section and allowing workers to continue repairs without fear of being sucked out into space. Repairing the hull would take some time, but the temporary fixes in place were good enough.

Leaving the asteroid field Jon caught a glimpse of the debris left by the destroyed warships. The sight filled him with remorse. He didn't care how Breeah explained it, those families should not have been on board. How could anyone allow children to be on board a ship that may very well see combat?

While it would be easy to blame them and absolve himself of any guilt, he simply couldn't. He had gone in for the kill, like he always did. The thought of disabling those ships hadn't even occurred to him. He could have at least spared the second ship. He didn't need to destroy it. If he targeted their weapon and propulsion systems instead of their reactors those people might still be alive now.

He didn't make excuses for being a killer. He killed as easily as a cook fried an egg. Still, he didn't consider himself a murderer. In war you kill the enemy, or they kill you. There is no time for indecision. Out here, however, things were different. They had no intelligence on this part of the galaxy. No way of knowing friend from foe. No way of knowing if children were on board a starship.

Children. How could he live with himself? He had done horrible things in his life, but this? This was too much. Aliens killed children. He didn't. If not for aliens his daughters would still be alive.

Feeling eyes on him he turned to find Tallos staring at him with those damned unblinking eyes. His face betrayed nothing. Had he revealed his own thoughts? Could the Diakan see his pain? His weakness? He'd be damned if he would give him the satisfaction. As if reading Jon's thoughts Tallos looked away.

Smart move.

Did Tallos feel anything for the humans on board those ships? Did he feel anything for the humans on board the Hermes? How could he? How could any alien?

The viewscreen moved away from the debris and Jon pushed the thoughts away with it. One more regret filed away deep in the recesses of his mind. One day it would get too crowded back there and all those hidden skeletons would come back. When that happened, there would be a price to pay. Nonetheless, that day was not today. He focused on the gate and the Kemmar Empire. Planets and moons floated by the viewscreen until they finally stopped in front of what appeared to be barren space.

"Ping the gate," ordered Jon.

"Pinging gate," replied Wolfe. The Hermes broadcast a command into the empty space. Within moments the blackness began to shimmer and then turned into a translucent field. The field was circular and immense. Ten ships the size of the Hermes could travel through it without bumping into each other.

The Juttari and the Diakans both had developed battle groups designed specifically for gate assaults. These battle groups were intended to move fast and deliver a powerful punch to the defenses on the other side of a gate. They would establish the beachhead so that the rest of the attack force could follow.

The Hermes would travel through alone, however. Jon hoped Breeah was right about the gate being in a remote region of Kemmar space. If someone was waiting for him in force on the other side, Jon didn't think the Hermes could fight its way through it.

"Contact! It's coming through the gate," said Petrovic.

"What?"

On the viewscreen a massive vessel emerged from the translucent field. Its bulky black hull seemed to stretch out without end. Clearly a warship it had alien markings on its hull and was covered with an array of formidable looking weaponry. The Hermes stood in front of the monstrous ship, blocking its advance, alone and out gunned.

"This must be the Kemmar," said Jon.

"I thought they didn't know about the gate?" said Wolfe.

"It seems things have changed. Tactical, is the ship showing any signs of aggression?"

"Negative, Sir," said Petrovic.

"So far so good."

"Sir, we are being hailed," said the Ensign Yao. "Running hail through AI for language analysis."

The AI analyzed the language of the hail against its massive database of all known galactic languages. After a few minutes it decoded the language and translated the hail. "This is Commander Botheseer of the Kemmar battleship Senthahar. Identify yourself and state your reasons for being in this system."

"Send back the following message. This is Captain Jon Pike of the Sol Space Force ship Hermes. We are exploring this region of space."

The message was broadcast back through the AI translator. When the Kemmar responded the AI instantly translated the message. "This is a lawless region of space. We are pursuing dangerous fugitives who are known to reside in this system. Your position indicates that you planned to use the gate to enter Kemmar space. Were those your intentions?"

"As I said, we were merely exploring this region of space. We discovered the gate and planned to travel through it and make contact with your people to establish trade between our civilizations."

"Your vessel is a warship, not a trade ship. Your ship is also showing several signs of recent combat. Your request to enter Kemmar space is denied."

I don't remember asking your permission, thought Jon. "Commander, we have a very long journey ahead of us which the gate would greatly shorten. We mean no harm to the Kemmar. We merely seek to travel peacefully through Kemmar space."

"Your request to enter Kemmar space is denied. Furthermore, this region of space has now been claimed by the Kemmar Empire. You are now trespassing and are hereby ordered to leave this system."

"Commander, we are in the middle of repairs to our ship. Our propulsion system in particular has received heavy damage. Please allow us some time to make the necessary repairs."

"You have one of the nearest planet's orbital cycles to conduct your repairs. In the meantime do not interfere with our operations."

"Understood. Hermes out." Jon dragged his hand across his neck telling the Yao to cut the comm link with the Kemmar.

"Commander Wolfe and Chief St. Clair, report to my ready room."

"Captain, I feel that I should also attend your meeting," said Tallos.

“My apologies Special Envoy, but this meeting is for senior officers only.”

“Captain, my role as adviser should require my presence at this meeting.”

“Your role is that of an observer, Special Envoy. You will be briefed accordingly after the meeting.”

“Captain, I must protest.”

“You are free to do so, Special Envoy.” Jon stood and turned his back to the Diakan and made his way to his ready room.

CHAPTER 23

"Ok, let's hear it. What are our options?" said Jon, sitting back in his office chair, knuckles rapping impatiently against the armrest.

"That ship is a monster. It's easily twice the size of one of our battleships, and twice the firepower. We can't slug it out with them," said Kevin pacing back and forth.

"And we can't access the gate with them blocking the way, so we can't use Kemmar space as a short cut," said Wolfe, sitting upright on one of the chairs. "So we have to use the jump system and the Juttari have a head start."

"No," said Jon.

"No?" said Wolfe, a stunned look on her face.

"No. We are not leaving this system."

"I don't understand, Sir," said Kevin. He stopped pacing and had a confused look on his face.

"There are humans out there in that asteroid field. Humans. There are probably more children out there. Regardless of who they are or what they've done, I'm sure as hell not going to let these aliens slaughter, or enslave them."

The room fell silent. Jon's officers did not know what to say, so they said nothing. Kevin walked to the empty chair and sat down, the chair creaking in protest against his heavy frame. He folded his large hands together just in front of his nose and looked back at Jon over them, clearly contemplating what to say next. Wolfe uncharacteristically let herself lean back into the chair and crossed her arms in front of her chest. Her chin rested on her collar bone and she looked like she was about to speak, yet no words escaped her half open mouth.

"But how can we stop them? We are the only ship with a jump system in the fleet. There is no way we can get a large enough force into this region in time," said Kevin.

"The Hermes stops them."

"With all due respect, Sir, that's impossible," said Wolfe.

"Is it? They have more firepower than us, but we are not a ship of the line. We have speed and agility that they lack. And we have the jump system."

"It's offline, and even if it weren't how can it help us against the Kemmar?" said Kevin.

"We get creative. We make our repairs and we leave the system. We then jump back in, take the Kemmar by surprise, hit them hard and then jump away before they can hit back."

A smile started to form across Kevin's face. "So we keep jumping in and out until we defeat them."

"We use our speed and agility when we do jump in to avoid taking too much damage," said Wolfe, leaning forward in her chair, hands at her side, like she would jump up at any moment. "If we keep our attacks short enough they likely won't be able to lock their weapons on us. But what if more ships come through the gate?"

"There are no more ships. If there were they would have come through as well. I think the Kemmar are pretty comfortable in the power of their battleship."

"That makes sense. But even if we defeat this battleship of theirs, we won't be able to hold this region by ourselves. And we still have our mission to complete."

"We don't need to hold it. Not yet, anyway. We just need enough time to evacuate the colonists."

"But how do we do that? We don't know if they have enough ships to evacuate everyone."

"We take them on board the Hermes."

"All of them?"

"If we have to."

Wolfe and St. Clair traded glances, the concern clearly etched across their faces.

"Sir, I don't think we have enough room for so many extra people," said Wolfe.

"There would be a great security risk involved," said Kevin.

"We have room. The lower decks in particular have a lot of empty space intended for storage. We can easily retrofit those areas to accommodate everyone. Those decks are not near any sensitive areas. Restricting the passengers to those areas should take care of any security concerns." Jon held back the urge to laugh at the expression on his officer's faces. "I'll take your silence to mean you have no more objections. Now, we have a lot of work to do. We need to get the Hermes ready for battle."

"Yes, Sir," said both officers in unison.

"Dismissed."

CHAPTER 24

The Hermes floated in space as the hours ticked away. The Kemmar battleship remained parked in front of it, dwarfing the human ship and blocking access to the jump gate and Kemmar space. It did not adopt an aggressive posture and seemingly posed no threat to the Hermes at the moment. It merely sat there. Immovable. The battleship likely hadn't encountered too many ships that could intimidate it, and wouldn't consider a ship less than half its size something to worry about. It had no reason to believe the human ship would not be cowed to do as told.

Without warning, drones launched from the giant ship and fanned out in all directions, searching for the Reiver colony. Cylindrical objects the size of a small automobile, they carried sophisticated scanning equipment. Heading towards the various planets and their moons, they would enter into orbit and scan the surfaces for signs of life. None entered the asteroid field, but it would only be a matter of time. Searching the planets and moons would be a drawn out process, but once they concluded that the colony wasn't anywhere else, they would turn to the asteroid field.

The cannons would be discovered first, and the drones wouldn't survive the barrage. The battleship was a different story. It would identify all the weapons systems, target and destroy them one by one. It would send in a new wave of search drones that would take their time and inevitably find the colony, regardless how well hidden. So the searches continued while the battleship waited.

A buzz of activity surrounded the Hermes. Repair bots zipped around the hull, repairing the multiple instances of weakened armor plating. The bots were large bulky machines, each roughly the size of a large truck. Four arms protruded from the front of the craft, with the ability to swap out a variety of tools, depending on the requirements of the job. Towards the rear were four omnidirectional thrusters allowing the bot to maneuver and make precise turns in any direction.

A cluster of the machines swarmed around the hull breach and concentrated on sealing the cavity. A steady stream of the machines traveled back and forth carrying the heavy raw materials and armor plating required for the repairs. The bots also performed maintenance on the weapons systems, ensuring all systems were primed and functioning at optimal levels.

While the repair bots were programmed to identify and repair any and all instances of damage on the Hermes, they were controlled by the ship's engineering AI, which prioritized and coordinated the bot movements.

Inside the Hermes the clamor of activity resounded on all decks. Throughout the ship repair crews scrambled to have the ship ready for battle by the deadline. All weapons systems and munitions were tested repeatedly to ensure combat readiness.

Security teams were placed on high alert and Chief St. Clair drilled his teams to make sure they stayed sharp. Commander Wolfe stayed on top of all section chiefs making sure no one took anything in stride, and that the entire crew performed at optimal levels. Engineering Chief Singh worked feverishly on the jump system and even accepted the help of his Diakan adviser in order to have the system functional as fast as possible. His engineering crew went over every inch of the massive reactors, leaving nothing to chance. In sick bay Doctor Ellerbeck prepared for the inevitability of trauma patients. Her medical team checked all equipment and stocked all necessary supplies and medication.

Breeah and Anki had left the sick bay and were now assigned to their own quarters. The computer announced Jon's presence and the door opened. Breeah greeted Jon and invited him inside. Walking inside Anki jumped in front of him. Tilting her head to the side she looked up at him with a big grin on her face. Her cheeks were red and she was missing one of her front teeth. Her eyes went wide and she jumped up and shot out her arms and legs shouting something imperceptible. Then with a giggle she ran off and hid behind a couch. She would poke her head out to peek at him from time to time and then hide again amid another round of giggles.

Jon smiled. "Cute kid," he said to Breeah, a mobile translator interpreting for him.

Breeah returned the smile brushing a wisp of hair from her face. "She is adjusting well. I am pleased."

"You're adjusting well too."

"We learn early on to be resilient and adaptable Captain. In our way of life it is a necessity."

"Yes, I imagine it would be." Jon looked around the room. Standard crew quarters. "Are you settling in to your new living accommodations?"

"Yes, Captain. Thank you again for your hospitality."

"It's nothing." He thought for a moment before continuing. "Breeah, has anyone told you what has been happening?"

"Nobody has told me Captain, but I can see clearly enough from the window. The Kemmar have found us."

"Have they ever entered this system before?"

"This is the first time they have crossed through the gate."

"Do you know how they discovered the gate?"

"I assume they followed us during one of our raids."

"I see. Well they're here now and they're searching for your colony. What will happen when they find it?"

Breeah looked at her feet, shifting her balance from left to right and back, and spoke barely above a whisper, "They will destroy it. Any survivors will be taken as slaves."

Jon frowned. "We can't allow that. You need to tell me where your colony is."

She looked up again, a look of resignation across her face. She picked nervously at her fingernails. "No Captain. You cannot rescue them and it will expose their location. My people are used to danger. They know the Kemmar are in this system, as they know you are. They are well hidden and will remain that way."

"I don't think that's going to be enough. The Kemmar are annexing this system. That means they'll establish a permanent presence here. Your people won't be able to escape."

"They will find a way. You should take your crew and leave while you can. There is no need to put your people in harm's way."

"We're not leaving."

Breeah shot him a shocked look. "You are planning to fight the Kemmar? Captain, you will be fighting a Kemmar battleship. This is suicide."

"We're not exactly a pushover either," said Jon, the annoyance at her comment clearly evident in his tone.

"I do not mean to offend you Captain. While you did defeat two of our warships, even two of our ships are no match against a Kemmar battleship."

Jon didn't want to debate battle tactics with Breeah. "Look, we need access to the gate and the Kemmar are blocking it. They are also threatening a human colony. We have no choice. And neither do your people. Even if we defeat the Kemmar, more will eventually come. Your people need to leave this system. Are you able to communicate with them?"

"Yes, Captain, but I dare not. The transmission will reveal their location."

"During the battle then. You'll have to warn them and let them know that we're human and not their enemy."

"Perhaps."

"You have some time to think about it, so make up your mind what you want to do."

"I will Captain. Thank you."

Just then Anki jumped out from behind the couch and ran around Jon's legs laughing. Instinctively Jon reached down and grabbed the little girl and lifted her off her feet, hoisting her high up above his head. Still laughing Anki spread out her arms and pretended to be a starship, making engine sounds between giggles. The sound of her laughter brought out a laugh from Jon as well, surprising him. How long had it been since he heard a little girl laugh? Not since he played with his own daughters. And when did he last hear himself laugh? Probably the same time. Anki's laughter filled his ears and he swung her around the room as she flew her invisible starship.

When he finally put her down he looked at Breeah whose normally serious face had also softened, lips gently turning upwards. He marvelled at her transformation, and her beauty. Why hadn't he noticed it before?

"She likes you," said Breeah, looking straight into Jon's eyes. Her eyes were cautious and questioning, with traces of long hidden pain. Jon wondered if she saw the same in his own eyes. There was an uneasy honesty about this woman that touched him.

"I like her too," said Jon. Resilient and adaptable, he thought. Exactly how much had she adapted to in her lifetime?

CHAPTER 25

"This is unacceptable, Captain," said Tallos. "You are declaring war on an unknown race. The repercussions of this action cannot be calculated."

"I'm not declaring war on anybody. I'm defending a human colony from alien aggressors."

"This is not your mission, Captain. You were sent to find your lost colonies, not to start intergalactic incidents."

"I'm the Captain of this ship, Special Envoy. As the Captain, I have full authority to take whatever actions I deem necessary to defend this ship, and to defend humanity. The Kemmar are not only threatening a human colony, they are also threatening the Sol System."

"Nonsense, they are 250 light years away from Sol. They are not a threat."

"Oh, but they are. Once we outfit more ships with jump drives, this region will be much more accessible, as will the jump gate here. This is a very strategic region of space and is vital for future access to the lost colonies. Letting the Kemmar control this system is what is unacceptable.

"Do you think the Juttari will just stand back when they realize the Kemmar have annexed this system? The Juttari will take this region and then they will seize the jump gate. That will give them unobstructed access to Kemmar space, which they will eventually conquer, giving them an immense strategic advantage.

"They will block our access to the lost colonies and eventually conquer them too. Can you imagine the logistical nightmare of supporting the lost colonies against the Juttari if they control Kemmar space? We would have to dislodge them from this region once they are already entrenched. This would be a strategic defeat for Sol as well as Diakus."

"Your symbiont has indeed made you an exceptional strategist, Captain. However, you are missing something. You do not know the strength of the Kemmar. You are assuming the Juttari can defeat them, but from the looks of this battleship they may not be so easy to conquer."

"So they can build a huge ship. It means nothing. They are merely a regional power. The Juttari are a galactic power. The Kemmar could never hope to stand against the might of the Juttari Empire."

"And what if they do not invade Kemmar space? What if your actions make them a Juttari ally instead?"

"I don't think so. The Juttari are not known for their diplomacy. The Kemmar would have to submit to Juttari rule for that to happen, and they don't strike me as the type to give in without a fight."

"The logical response would be to return to Sol and come back in force. Risking the Hermes is foolish. If you lose, you risk giving the Kemmar jump technology. That could turn a regional power into a galactic power. This is not an acceptable risk."

"Going back to Sol creates two problems. First, the Kemmar will slaughter the human colony in this system."

"These people are criminals"

"These people are humans. They have committed no crimes against Sol or Diakus."

"They have committed crimes against the Kemmar."

"The Kemmar are not part of the Galactic Accord. We have no treaties with the Kemmar. Crimes against them do not make these people criminals in Sol or Diakus. But they are human, and their humanity requires protection. If not from Diakus, then from Sol, and this is a Sol ship."

"This ship was created through human and Diakan cooperation."

"It is under Space Force command. My command. Do I need to keep reminding you of that fact?"

"No Captain, you do not."

"Good. The second reason is that the Juttari now have a head start on us. If we go back to Sol they will find the lost colonies before we do. That puts the colonies at risk. The time we would waste in trying to assemble an attack force to take this region would be time that they would have to take the colonies."

"I can see there is no changing your mind."

"This is the only solution, Special Envoy."

"Very well Captain. I will leave you to your duties then."

"Thank you Special Envoy."

Tallos rose and walked out of Jon's office. Jon leaned back in his chair, satisfied with the outcome of the encounter. He anticipated the Diakan's objections and believed he did a reasonable job countering them. The Diakans were mainly interested in extending their influence, but Jon had other plans.

The lost colonies were human colonies, not Diakan. They were humanity's chance to expand its power base. If humanity expected to ever become more than a simple pawn, it had to consolidate its power and start projecting its own influence, and he was not going to let the Diakans, the Juttari, or the Kemmar stand in the way.

CHAPTER 26

Repairs on the Hermes were completed ahead of schedule, but Jon waited until the Kemmar deadline. He wanted to see their response before choosing his course of action. As he expected, the Kemmar reacted with complacency, comfortable in their ability to defeat the human ship.

"Sir, the Kemmar ship is hailing us," said the communications officer.

"Patch them through," said Jon.

The Kemmar transmission was translated through the ship's AI. "Your deadline has passed. You are hereby ordered to leave Kemmar space immediately."

"Commander, I ask you again to please reconsider your decision. If we could be allowed access to the gate it would be a great help to us."

"Your needs are no concern of the Kemmar Empire. You are ordered to leave Kemmar space immediately."

"If you could just give us some more time to complete repairs…"

"No more time. If you do not leave Kemmar space immediately you will be destroyed."

"Commander, are you saying you will fire on us?"

"That is correct. Leave now, or you will be destroyed."

"Understood. We will comply."

The comm link was disconnected by the Kemmar. Jon looked around the bridge. He saw no apprehension. They were ready. "Helm, take us out of this system."

"Taking us out, Sir," said Richards.

The ship's reactors kicked in and the emitters lining the hull created an FTL bubble around the ship allowing it to travel faster than the speed of light. The ship's inertial dampeners ensured that none of the reality of the ship's speed was felt on board. For everyone on the bridge it felt like the Hermes stood still.

On the viewscreen the asteroid field disappeared as did the planets and their moons. The binary star blazed across the screen and then it too was gone too, leaving only the empty region between systems, and the uncountable stars shimmering in the distance.

They needed to be convincing without giving away their hand. Even at FTL speeds it took a lot of time to travel the immense distances between planets and planetary systems. Jon knew it would be a while before the Kemmar finally turned to the asteroid field. He wanted to be convincing so he waited until there was sufficient distance between the Hermes and the Kemmar. After several hours of travel Jon decided to spring his trap.

"Jump system status?" asked Jon.

"Jump system is at one hundred percent. We are jump ready," said Yao.

"Plot a jump directly behind the Kemmar ship."

"Course plotted, Sir."

"Tactical, load all missile tubes. Rail guns in offensive mode, and ready energy weapons."

"Missile tubes loaded, Sir. All weapon systems are ready."

"When we jump into the system we will immediately fire all missiles at the Kemmar ship, and engage them using attack pattern Sigma."

"Yes, Sir."

"Navigation, once we conduct our sortie I want to jump out of the system. A couple of light years should be good enough."

"Yes, Sir. Coordinates are plotted."

"Sound general quarters. Helm, initiate jump countdown."

"Jump countdown initiated Sir."

The lighting on the bridge took on a red hue to reinforce the general quarters order. The ship's computer began counting down. Jon could smell the fear and anxiety in the air. So long as noone panicked, a little fear was not a bad thing. It kept everyone focused and motivated. He looked over at Wolfe who refused to sit down and paced the bridge, keeping a watchful eye on the crew.

"Jump complete."

The viewscreen instantly filled with the rear of the Kemmar ship. Jon couldn't help but feel awed by the sheer size of it. Why would anyone need a ship that big? It couldn't be practical. Perhaps these giant ships were intended to merely intimidate. After all, who would be stupid enough to stand against anything that big? As if on cue, eight missiles appeared on the viewscreen and streaked straight for the massive ship.

"Missiles away!"

The Hermes began its assault. It raced towards the top of the ship, blue energy bursts impacting the giant ship's hull, rail guns pulverizing it with a barrage of uranium. The Kemmar were taken completely by surprise and could not launch any countermeasures. The missiles found their mark. The battleship was rocked by jarring concussions. The behemoth had been hurt, but not defeated.

As per Jon's orders the jump countdown began. Before the Hermes could take any return fire, the Kemmar battleship disappeared from the viewscreen. Sporadic cheers broke out throughout the bridge and the fear felt minutes before had been replaced by the euphoria of imminent victory.

"Focus people, the battle isn't over yet," said Jon. The bridge quieted, but the taste of victory still hung in the air. "They're going to be ready for us the next time. Switch rail guns to point defense mode and load all missile tubes."

"Missile tubes loaded, Sir. Rail guns in point defense mode," said Petrovic.

"Navigation, can you put us directly underneath them?"

"Yes, Sir."

"Good, enter the coordinates. Helm, when we jump in this time I want to attack their belly, attack pattern Beta."

"Yes, Sir."

"As before, prepare to jump right away to this location. Initiate jump countdown."

The computer counted down again and the Hermes jumped in to attack the Kemmar battleship a second time. The battleship appeared above them this time and as before the Hermes let loose a volley of missiles. The Kemmar were ready with counter measures allowing only one missile to find its mark. The Hermes proceeded to race underneath the ship laying down energy weapon fire as it went.

"The Kemmar ship has launched missiles!"

"Launch countermeasures."

The Hermes decoys shot out in all directions luring several missiles away from their target. Some of the missiles weren't fooled and raced after the attacking ship. The Hermes rail guns laid down a wall of point defense fire destroying the Kemmar missiles as they approached.

The Kemmar missiles were numerous and relentless, however, and several made it by the Hermes defenses. Their impact imminent, the Hermes jumped away before taking any damage. As quick as it appeared, the Kemmar ship disappeared from the viewscreen again. While not as successful as the first encounter, the Hermes had not taken any fire and the bridge mood was electric.

"Excellent work everyone. Prepare to jump back in. Load all missile tubes and ready all weapons and countermeasures. Get us in behind the battleship again, I want to go after her critical systems. Attack pattern Gamma."

The crew prepared for the third strike. Everyone tried to remain composed, the excitement in the air palpable. The battleship was so intimidating that the unexpected success of the first attacks was like a valve, at once releasing most of the tension the crew felt. Optimism replaced anxiety, and the mood turned to one of certain victory.

Commander Wolfe, however, was not celebrating. From the look on her face she didn't approve of those who were.

Jon didn't like it either. "Stay focused people," he barked. "We haven't won yet. Helm, initiate jump countdown. Tactical, prepare to fire."

The computer counted down the jump sequence.

The ship jumped.

The viewscreen shifted.

The battleship was gone.

"Contacts! Reading six vessels all around us."

Jon rose from his chair. "Launch counter measures!"

The incoming ordnance rocked the ship almost throwing Jon to the floor.

"Reading multiple direct hits to our stern side," said Petrovic.

"Jump system is offline," said Wolfe.

"Helm, initiate evasive maneuvers. Tactical, return fire. Target the nearest ships. Fire at will," said Jon.

The Hermes bounded left and right, up and down, trying in vain to avoid the attacking ships. Flanked on all sides, it could not compensate for the onslaught. Suppressing fire from one ship, it took fire from another. Its newly repaired hull receiving a fresh pounding.

The ships individually were no match for the Hermes, but together represented an unbeatable combination. Any advantage the Hermes had in maneuverability against the battleship was now lost as the smaller ships attacked from all angles.

"Sir, these ships, they have the same signatures as the battleship," said Petrovic.

"She separated," said Jon, realization dawning on him. "The battleship was six ships in one."

CHAPTER 27

Breeah and Anki watched the ongoing battle from the windows in their quarters. Breeah didn't understand how the Hermes had simply appeared beside the Kemmar battleship, and after a brief attack reappeared in another star system, only to do the same thing over again. Based on her knowledge of the jump gate, she understood superficially what was happening, but did not comprehend any more than that. How were these people jumping without a gate? It baffled her.

She looked over at Anki whose face showed the same amazement that Breeah felt. Anki, despite her young age, had seen space battles before. Reiver children were not sheltered from such things. They had to understand Reiver strategy and tactics early on and the best way to learn was to see them in action.

But neither Breeah nor Anki had ever seen anything like this. On the Reiver ships they witnessed raids, and usually the odds were in the Reivers' favor. She never expected to witness a battle of these proportions. To engage a Kemmar battleship was unheard of. A Reiver ship would have turned tail and run.

First it looked like the Earth ship would prevail, but things now turned against it. This third jump landed the Hermes in the middle of six Kemmar warships. She had heard rumors about Kemmar battleships separating into multiple smaller ships, but didn't believe it possible. She knew now that those rumors were true.

She chewed on an already gnawed fingernail and watched the Kemmar ships close in. A Kemmar ship dropped directly in front of her, so close that she could see some of their crew. Not as large as the Hermes, it still looked menacing.

It had a long, bulky, rectangular shape, with several protrusions sitting in odd locations. Weapon turrets spread out across its hull, and they all looked like they were pointed directly at her. For a second she froze, and even stopped chewing her nail. Then it opened fire.

Energy beams burst forth and bathed her window in a horrific red light. At the same time it peppered the Hermes with a rapid succession of projectiles. The force of the impacts sent both Breeah and Anki to the floor screaming. Then the pounding started in earnest. Powerful shockwaves rocked their quarters, toppling furniture and turning cups and dishes into lethal missiles.

The sound of explosions blared in her ears, and she clasped her hands over them, futilely trying to block out the uproar. They had to be in the worst possible section of the ship. It would be only a matter of time until the hull gave way and they would be sucked out into the void. She couldn't let that happen. She had to save Anki.

Where was Anki?

Breeah lifted her head, trying to locate her little girl and spotted her several meters away. She had curled into a ball, her small arms wrapped tightly around her knees, face pressed hard against them. Her body convulsed in gasps and cries. She was panicking. Breeah had to reach her.

"Anki!" Breeah screamed as she began to crawl across the floor to her daughter. "Anki! I'm coming!"

The ship pitched again under the force of the Kemmar onslaught, each impact bouncing her off the ground. She fought back the urge to vomit, her stomach lurching with each bounce. She tried to hang on, tried to continue crawling, but forward movement was impossible.

The Hermes heaved and her face smashed into the floor. Her eyesight blurred and she fought back the blackness, desperate to stay conscious. She tried to see, but couldn't make anything out.

"Anki!" No response. "Anki!" Still nothing.

Mustering all her strength she dragged herself forward. Something blocked her path. A chair. It had fallen on its side. Gripping its frame she used it as a crutch and lifted herself up. Her vision started to clear and when her head came up high enough she could finally get a view of the room.

"Anki?"

She wasn't there anymore. She continued to scan the room, but couldn't find her. Dread climbed up her spine and she fought to keep her focus. Anki had to be in the room. She had to be hiding somewhere. Terrified. But where?

Breeah got up to her feet, adrenalin surging through her. She ran throughout the room, oblivious now to the raging battle. But she couldn't find her. Anki was gone.

CHAPTER 28

Two Kemmar ships came up alongside the Hermes, hammering it broadside. A third Kemmar ship dropped in front, halting its advance.

"They're trying to box us in," yelled Wolfe.

"Concentrate fire on the lead ship. All weapons. Erase that goddamn ship from my sky!"

The Hermes unleashed a torrent of missiles, blue lightning and depleted uranium on the forward Kemmar vessel. Its position gave it few options for evasive maneuvers and the Hermes missiles plowed through its hull, detonating one by one. The Hermes continued to pound it with its energy weapons and rail guns until the ship blew apart.

The force of the explosion bounced the bridge crew around. Ensign Yao was thrown from her chair onto the floor hitting her head. Commander Wolfe ran to her aid and the disoriented Ensign sat up. Yao shook her head and looked back at Wolfe.

"I'm ok," said Yao.

Wolf nodded and helped her get up off the floor. She resumed her post. Wolfe stood behind Yao watching for a few more moments to ensure she was able to resume her duties.

Around the Hermes the battle continued to rage relentlessly. The remaining Kemmar ships maintained their position and continued to hammer the Hermes broadside. The Hermes was sandwiched in between the two and had few options. At the same time another ship strafed it from below.

"Resume evasive maneuvers," ordered Jon.

As the vessel underneath it made contact, a massive concussion rocked the Hermes,. Mechanical arms shot out from the ship and sunk long, armor piercing claws into the Hermes's belly. The arms pulled the enemy ship close to the Hermes, until the two vessels were almost touching. A cylindrical apparatus emerged from the Kemmar ship and made contact with the Hermes's hull, establishing a secure seal, and powerful blades went to work, cutting a hole through the Earth ship.

Wolfe had returned to her console, but the force of the impact made her grip is sides, in a struggle to maintain her balance. Her display told her she had bigger problems. Tapping her console she opened a comm link, "Security to Deck Lambda. Enemy infiltration underway. Prepare to repel enemy boarders."

CHAPTER 29

Kevin raced down the corridors with his team, their combat suits enhancing their speed and agility. Their combat suits were capable of running as fast as 60 kph and could jump as high as 5 meters, and they effortlessly jumped through hatches and cleared staircases with single leaps.

Kevin's AI displayed the ship's layout on his visor, giving him the precise location of the enemy infiltration. All the combat suits were tied into the ship's systems providing all troopers with a real time display of each other's and the enemy's positions.

The Kemmar soldiers that entered the ship were marked in red, members of the crew in blue. There were already casualties among the crew.

Kevin's display gave him more information. Not only could he see the locations of all his team members, but he could monitor their vital signs in real time. He could see any injuries and get an instant diagnosis from their combat suits. He could see their heart rates, as well as a myriad of other indicators letting him know how they were holding up, both physically and mentally. He also had real time updates on the condition of their combat suits. He could see how much damage they received, their suit's integrity, and the status of all of the combat suit's vital systems

Nearing the enemy they slowed their pace. While Kevin's team knew the Kemmar positions, the Kemmar wouldn't have the same intel. No point in running in blind.

The visor showed four Kemmar approaching. Kevin's men spread out along the corridor, energy weapons at the ready. Kevin backed them up with his monstrous Gatling gun. When the Kemmar soldiers turned the corner the lead Marines opened fire. The Kemmar wore combat suits of their own and when the blue energy fire hit, it simply bounced off, splaying out in all directions.

The Kemmar stood their ground and returned fire. Vicious looking red bolts plowed into the human positions. Kevin's visor showed his troopers' suits taking heavy damage.

Worried about his men, Kevin lunged forward and opened up his Gatling gun on the enemy. The enormous projectiles cut through the Kemmar combat suits like they were cardboard, killing the first two Kemmar and forcing the others to fall back.

"Their suits have some kind of reflective coating. Energy weapons are useless against them. Switch to railguns," ordered Kevin through his suit's comm link.

Most of his team preferred the power and versatility of their energy weapons, but all carried rail guns. They fired tiny bullets allowing each soldier to carry massive quantities of ammo with them. Each magazine held 500 rounds. While small in size they used depleted uranium which gave them very high density. That density and their speed made them especially effective against armored combat suits.

They held their position while each soldier swapped weapons. Then Kevin's visor showed the Kemmar moving quickly in the opposite direction.

Kevin opened a comm link with Sergeant Henderson, "Enemy boarders are coming your way Sergeant. I need you to cut off their advance."

"Yes, Sir," said Henderson.

"Don't use energy weapons, they have no effect on the enemy."

"Acknowledged."

Henderson led a second security team advancing from the opposite end of the infiltration. They were trying to flank the Kemmar, forcing them into a crossfire. Unfortunately, it looked like the entire boarding party was heading in Henderson's direction. If his team couldn't hold them off the Kemmar would have access to the rest of the ship.

Kevin had to act. Now was the time to advance.

"Let's waste these fuckers! Move out!"

"OORAH!" yelled the Marines in unison, the sound almost deafening over the comm system.

The troopers surged forward. They turned a corner and faced a long straightaway. The infiltration point was visible in the middle of the corridor, a massive hole in the floor of the bulkhead. Around the hole a group of Kemmar stood guard and opened fire as the human soldiers approached.

"Hit the dirt!" ordered Kevin, dropping to the ground.

Red energy bolts sailed over his head as his troopers dropped and returned fire. The Kemmar took cover and seemed to sustain only minor damage.

The two groups fired at each other while Kevin's team slowly advanced. Just then a nasty looking weapon popped out of the opening and started lobbing baseball sized ordnance at the humans.

They were explosives similar to grenades and they landed right in the middle of the lead troopers. Detonating with incredibly concentrated force, they ripped through Kevin's troopers making them disappear from his display.

"Fall back!" ordered Kevin as more grenades bounced into their ranks.

CHAPTER 30

Sergeant Henderson led his security team up the opposite side of the infiltration. He saw the advancing Kemmar on his visor. His team would engage them in seconds. Just ahead of their position was a junction which branched off into several corridors. They had to get to that junction before the enemy. Rounding a corner he saw the junction, and the Kemmar.

"Open fire!" ordered Henderson.

His team opened up on the enemy and a hailstorm of bullets crashed into the Kemmar positions. The lead Kemmar took the worst of it and dropped almost instantly. The remaining force took cover and returned fire, halting the human advance.

The corridor lit up with an eerie crimson light show forcing Henderson and his men to seek cover. Henderson crouched behind an iron post just in time. Several of his men took hits but their combat suits' integrity stayed intact. They were taking damage and he wasn't sure how much enemy fire they could withstand, but his troopers were all still alive and able to continue fighting.

"We can't let the enemy take that junction," Sergeant Henderson said to his men. "We need to advance."

"Yes, Sir," they replied, almost in unison.

The Hermes troopers started leapfrogging forward. They fired at the enemy, providing cover while each soldier advanced. With many corners and posts, the corridors offered plenty of cover for each soldier.

Henderson's team continued making a slow, steady advance, while the enemy stood their ground and didn't seem interested in contesting the junction. Sergeant Henderson didn't understand the strategy, nor did he care. If they wanted to stay put it suited him just fine.

Then they charged.

The entire group suddenly jumped from their cover and surged forward, unleashing a tidal wave of energy fire in the process. Surprised by the sudden change in tactics the Hermes troopers took cover. It took Sergeant Henderson only a few seconds to realize he was going to lose the junction. He had only one option left.

"Charge!"

The humans leaped from the security of their cover and ran forward, rail guns firing, into the Kemmar stampede. Soldiers fell on both sides in seconds, and they crashed into each other in the middle of the junction.

The battle now turned into a hand to hand melee. The weapons that were so effective from a distance were now nothing more than fancy clubs. Shots were still fired from both sides, but aiming was almost impossible, and everyone switched to their bladed weapons.

The Hermes troopers used a long ionized blade that looked very much like a huge bowie knife. Plasma surged from the hilt, enveloping the blade, making it an effective close quarters weapon against the armor of a combat suit.

The Kemmar used a similar weapon, although their blades were shorter, wider and featured hooked prongs which jutted out from the hilt.

All around Sergeant Henderson the battle raged, sparks flying as the blades made contact. With the power and agility of the combat suits the whole bloody encounter looked almost like an acrobatic performance.

The Sergeant dispatched three Kemmar with relative ease when he noticed a group moving away from the battle and heading down one of the adjoining corridors. The charge had been a distraction. Tying up the Hermes defenders, it allowed a smaller group access to the rest of the ship. It was a good strategy. The smaller group would then attempt to disable the Hermes, so the Kemmar could capture it.

Sergeant Henderson turned and moved to intercept them. As he started to break into pursuit, something crashed into him from behind, knocking him onto the floor.

He rolled and turned in time to see a Kemmar blade striking down at his visor. Lifting his shoulder he moved to the side barely in time and the blade hit the floor, missing him by mere centimeters.

The arm came up again for another strike. He grabbed it with one hand and tried to stab with his own blade. The Kemmar soldier blocked his attack and grabbed his arm as well. The two wrestled on the ground, struggling for position, vying for the killing blow.

Sergeant Henderson fought from his back with the Kemmar on top of him forcing his blade down with all his weight. He fought the urge to close his eyes as the blade made contact with his visor and the plasma generated white hot sparks in front of his face. The enemy committed to the kill, leaning forward to force as much weight as possible into the thrust.

The movement unbalanced him. A fatal mistake. In one quick and powerful motion Sergeant Henderson drove his hips upward and simultaneously yanked the attacking arm backward, making the Kemmar soldier fall forward.

Following through he shot his legs up and over his head, rolled backward and landed on top of his surprised foe. Then, in one fluid motion his blade came down hard and pierced the Kemmar visor, killing the enemy instantly. He pulled his blade out of the alien skull and got up. He looked down the corridor, searching for the Kemmar. They were gone.

CHAPTER 31

The Hermes continued taking fire from all directions. Its attempts to evade the other ships were rendered useless by the attached Kemmar ship. Unable to evade its attackers the Hermes stood its ground and tried to slug it out against the overwhelming power of the enemy swarm.

On the bridge sparks sprayed the crew from damaged consoles, their white lines creating an eerie fireworks display amid the backdrop of the flashing red battle stations light. The acrid smell of scorched electrical circuits filled the room and several crew members fought back coughing fits, trying to stay focused on their duties.

Jon looked down at the array of displays in front of him. On one he tracked the battles with the boarding parties. On another he received up to the minute damage reports from throughout the ship. Multiple fires raged on several decks, but surprisingly there were no hull breaches other than the one the boarding party used to enter the ship.

Still it was only a matter of time until the inevitable hull breaches. The Hermes was a powerful ship, but it was not a ship of the line. Built to be fast and agile, it had not been created to stand and trade blows like a battleship. Jon knew she couldn't take much more of this.

"Commander, any progress with the repairs to the jump system?"

"It is partially online."

"Are we jump ready?"

"Yes, but with limited range."

"Helm, initiate jump countdown. Get us the hell out of here."

Wolfe gave Jon a stunned look. "Can we jump with that ship locked onto us?"

"We'll soon find out," said Jon, his eyes practically burning a hole through the viewscreen.

Wolfe opened her mouth to object, but thought better of it. Jon looked at her like he had heard her silent protest. "We can't stay here. Especially with that ship locked onto us. We're sitting ducks. Our only chance is to jump."

"Yes, Sir," said Wolfe.

The computer began its countdown while the crew struggled to remain balanced and at their stations.

"Jump complete," the computer announced.

"Is that ship still locked onto us?" asked Jon.

"Yes, Sir. It looks like the jump system took it along for the ride. All other ships are gone," said Wolfe.

Jon noticed a comm request coming through from Breeah. Confused, he answered.

"Captain?"

Jon heard the panic in her voice. "Yes, Breeah?"

"Captain, I apologize, I didn't know who else to contact. It's Anki. She's gone!"

"I don't understand. What do you mean she's gone?"

"She left our quarters. The battle scared her and she ran away. I don't know where she is."

"Ok calm down. The ship's systems will be able to locate her. Stay in your quarters and I will get back to you."

"Thank you, Captain."

Jon tapped a few commands into one of his consoles and the computer located Anki. Jon gasped. A group of Kemmar were closing on her position. He jumped out of his chair and turned to Commander Wolfe.

"You have the bridge, Commander."

"Sir?"

"Some Kemmar have gotten past our security teams and the little girl we brought on board is in their path. I have to help her."

"Captain, I can't let you put yourself at risk. Send someone else."

"There is no one else. This is my responsibility."

"At least take the Marines with you."

Jon looked at the two Marines guarding the entrance to the bridge. "No, I need them guarding the bridge. Until we repel the enemy this bridge stays secure. Nobody in or out until further notice."

"Yes, Sir."

Jon grabbed his close quarters rail gun and rushed out of the bridge. He ran down the corridors at a tremendous rate of speed, easily matching and exceeding any combat suit. The thought of the Kemmar finding Anki before him made him push even harder.

Turning a corner he spotted Anki. She had squeezed into a crevice in the bulkhead, hiding from a group of Kemmar soldiers at the far end of the corridor. The Kemmar spotted Jon and he bolted just in time to get out of the way of their fire. Taking cover he looked over at Anki who saw him and motioned for her to stay where she was. He tried to find an escape route, but the corridor was too long. If he tried to get Anki out of there the two of them would be cut down before making it out. He needed a different strategy.

Near Anki's position was a door he knew led to a storage area. It was their only chance. Lunging out from his position he raced towards the little girl, dodging the enemy's fire with leaps and rolls.

Anki stared at him with wide, tear filled eyes. She sobbed but didn't make a sound, not because she had any control, but because she strained to take a breath, gasping for air in panicked heaves. Reaching her position Jon scooped her up with one arm, barely breaking stride, and continued through the door to the supply room.

Inside were rows of heavy racks piled high with a diverse range of supplies. Jon ran deep into the large room and crouched behind one of the columns. Anki was still hyperventilating and not knowing what else to do Jon hugged her close to his chest. He had done the same with his own girls after they had woken from a bad nightmare. It had always helped to calm them down. Already he could feel Anki's breathing start to slow.

"It's okay," he whispered, stroking her hair while she drew sharp breaths. "I'm here now. I'm not going to let anyone hurt you."

Her breathing continued to ease up and her sobs were turning into sniffles.

At the front of the room the door slid open and he heard heavy footsteps. The Kemmar were inside. He pulled his head back so he could look at Anki. She was regaining control and Jon locked onto her eyes. He put a hand to his lip telling her to stay quiet. He then tried to put her down, but she gripped him tight, shaking her head no. This wasn't going to be easy.

He had counted five Kemmar, all in combat suits. How could he fight them all off while holding Anki? He swung her around to his left side, squeezing her against his ribs and looped her arms around his neck. He motioned for her to clasp her hands together and gave them a squeeze so she knew to hold on tight. Looking at her again he nodded, and she nodded back. She was still scared, but she had stopped crying.

Satisfied he focused on the Kemmar, listening to their movements, timing their steps, gauging there distance. Holding onto Anki with his left arm, he raised his weapon with the other. A Kemmar approached on the right, barely a meter away. He stayed low, poised and ready to strike like a rattlesnake.

The energy weapon appeared first and without hesitation he kicked out, hitting the armored hand dead on. The force of the blow sent the weapon firing away from Jon and Anki, at the same time his own weapon came up point blank with the Kemmar's visor and fired. The bullets drilled through the visor like a jackhammer, obliterating the alien skull inside.

The sound alerted the other Kemmar and he heard them run to his position, but he was already moving, silently leaping onto one of the storage racks and springing away across the top of the racks like a lemur. There he waited, crouching low, ready to pounce.

Anki held on tight, and he felt her little heart pounding violently against his side. Her fear had been replaced by an alertness that impressed him. The two sat unflinching on top of the tall storage rack and waited, but not for long.

Two more Kemmar approached from below. When the first was directly below them Jon dropped from above and slammed two feet into the back of the alien head. Using the resistance as a springboard he changed direction, turned and fired at the second alien. He aimed for the visor again, identifying it as the weakest point, and sent a burst of armor piercing rounds through it.

The other Kemmar rolled out of the fall, turned and fired. Crimson lightning streaked from the weapon, heading straight for Anki. Jon sprang away and the energy bursts followed. Another Kemmar emerged and fired, the two energy bursts trapping Jon in a pincer style attack.

Cut off to the left and right Jon ran in the only direction he could. Up. Turning to the nearby wall he ran with such speed that the momentum took him up the wall before gravity could catch him. The energy fire shifted and the two followed him, but he now had more freedom of movement.

Launching from the wall he landed on the side of a nearby rack and quickly climbed to the top. The Kemmar were caught off guard and slow to react. Jon didn't want to lose any momentum so he kept moving and jumped off the far side of the rack. Now he had the column between him and the two Kemmar who had been firing at him.

Another Kemmar jumped in front of him and he turned as the third attacker opened up in earnest. Jon returned fire, but was too focused on staying ahead of the enemy bursts to inflict any real damage.

Ahead was another wall and he turned to the right, but was met by more enemy fire. Stopping just in time he turned back in the direction he came and saw the third Kemmar turn and level his weapon at him.

Leaping as the weapon spit more red lightning at him he landed on top of another rack.

The Kemmar adjusted to his tactics. They now formed a triangle and fired at him from three directions, cutting off each move he tried to make. Jon jumped from one rack to another desperately trying to stay ahead of the enemy fire, but he knew it was now only a matter of time. With each jump the Kemmar compensated giving him less and less room to manoeuvre. He had failed, and little Anki would end up paying the price.

Leaping again he landed on another rack only to see a Kemmar pointing his weapon at him. It was over. Even he wasn't fast enough to get away, and he turned Anki away from the weapon, hoping his body would be enough to shield her from the impact.

He heard weapon fire, but to his astonishment felt nothing. For a split second he wondered if it was possible for the Kemmar to miss at such close range. Then he recognized the sound and turned to see a Hermes combat suit with sergeant stripes on the shoulders, firing a rail gun at the Kemmar.

Jon didn't need any more information. Jumping off the rack he ran to cut off the Kemmar soldier positioned to his right, while the one to his left moved to help his comrade.

He stalked his prey while it fired wildly, trying in vain to determine his location. But it was too late and Jon came down on top of it, slamming it into the ground, and unloading a torrent of weapon fire into its head.

Hearing more rail gun fire behind him he got up and ran back toward the Sergeant. By the time he got there, however, the firing had stopped and Sergeant Henderson stood between the two Kemmar bodies.

Jon smiled, and shifted Anki to his other arm. "What took you so long, Sergeant?"

Sergeant Henderson's visor retracted and he smiled back at Jon. "There was a traffic jam, Sir."

CHAPTER 32

Kevin's troopers scrambled backwards as repeated explosions rocked the corridor. His AI reported some damage to a few combat suits, but thankfully there weren't any more casualties. They were pinned down, so he ordered a battle bot and waited.

Battle bots were extremely effective field units, but they weren't as versatile on board a starship. Still, Kevin didn't want to waste valuable time in a drawn out firefight, and they provided the firepower he needed at the moment.

The battle bot was essentially a small hovercraft with extremely thick armor plating and an array of heavy weapons at its disposal. It could be sent into a hot zone and withstand enemy fire while pulverizing the enemy's positions. It was the tip of the spear often needed for a decisive thrust against an entrenched enemy.

The two groups traded fire, locked in a standoff as Kevin waited for the battle bot to arrive. He watched its progress on his visor and in no time it pulled up behind his team. The troopers moved aside letting the bot glide through. Although smaller than a mech, it was quite large and bulky and practically filled the corridor.

It turned the corner and immediately started taking fire, but it would take more than a few hand held weapons to get through its heavy armor. Deploying a plasma cannon the bot proceeded to fire on the enemy. It followed up by lobbing a handful of plasma grenades as well.

The Kemmar combat suits were no match for the bot's arsenal and they dropped off one by one.

The weapon that drove back Kevin's men popped up again and fired on the bot. Explosions hammered the armored hovercraft but didn't stop it, rather it just slowed down. The bot returned fire and hammered the alien weapon with repeated plasma cannon bursts. The Kemmar weapon wasn't as well armored as the battle bot and the plasma cannon rounds ripped through the alien machine until it was nothing more than a heap of smouldering scrap metal.

Kevin watched its progress on his visor and gave the order for his men to move out. His team rounded the corner, weapons at the ready, and followed the bot's steady progress.

When the bot reached the infiltration point Kevin had it lob a bunch of plasma grenades through the hole and into the attached Kemmar ship. Explosions could be heard and flashes of light shot out of the opening with each blast.

When the vessel had been softened up to Kevin's satisfaction, he and his troopers climbed in. Gunfire echoed from the opening as they dealt with the scant defenders.

The room they entered was large and cavernous. While the plasma grenades ensured no enemy soldiers stood guard near the entry point, the large room provided ample cover for the Kemmar soldiers. Kevin and his men started taking fire the moment they entered the ship.

They returned fire and sought cover for themselves. They then provided covering fire, so the rest of the troopers could board. Red energy bursts crossed rail gun tracer fire as the two sides battled for position. Kevin's heavy Gatling gun proved to be the deciding factor, tilting the scales in favor of the humans.

At the far end of the room was a doorway, and the Kemmar seemed intent on its defense. It likely provided access to the rest of the vessel.

"I count six defenders on both sides of that doorway," said Kevin over the combat suit comm to his team. "Team A and B, advance on the doorway. The rest of us will provide covering fire."

"Yes, Sir," said the troopers.

"Move out," said Kevin, and then stepped out himself and opened fire on the doorway.

The other troopers fired with him and the Kemmar defenders had no choice but to fall back. Team A and B advanced quickly, stopping briefly whenever they found cover, until they reached the Kemmar positions.

They then charged the defenders and Kevin watched on his view screen as his men took fire. An alert appeared as Private Schledohrn's vitals flatlined.

"Damn it!" cursed Kevin. Schledohrn was a great soldier and true to form he led the charge on the Kemmar taking the brunt of their fire. His sacrifice allowed the other troopers to overwhelm the enemy positions and kill the rest of the defenders.

"Position secured," said Private Daniels.

"Hold position," said Kevin, and the rest of the security team advanced.

The doorway gave access to a network of corridors and hatches. The rest of the ship seemed to follow a highly compartmentalized design. Kevin knew they needed to find and secure the bridge first. Hermes scans provided a layout of the Kemmar vessel which now displayed on his visor, giving him the most direct approach to the bridge.

"We take the bridge first. I don't want to get bogged down in any room to room firefights. You should all have the route on your visors. We move fast and we hit hard. Let's move out."

The troopers moved quickly through the ship, encountering scant resistance. The walls were covered in odd markings and there were what looked like computer interfaces built into the bulkheads every twenty meters or so. Kevin knew they were being monitored and wondered why they didn't encounter heavier resistance.

That question was answered as they got closer. The corridor leading directly to the bridge was heavily armed and concealed turrets sprang out of the walls and ceiling unleashing an electrical storm of energy weapon fire.

Kevin cursed as two of his troopers disappeared from his display, dying almost instantly under the onslaught. Several others sustained heavy damage to their combat suits before finding cover. While he had hoped to take the bridge without any more casualties, he knew it wouldn't be likely. He had actually been surprised they managed to make it this far without encountering any other surprises.

This ship must have been primarily a boarding vessel. After breaking off from the battleship its role would be to lock onto the Hermes and send in its boarding parties while the other ships continued to hammer it on the outside. Other than the boarding parties there may be a few aliens running the bridge, and nothing more. He hoped the turrets confirmed his theory. All they had to do was disable the turrets and then take the bridge.

His team kept firing on the weapons, but the speed in which they returned fire made progress slow. Still, it would only be a matter of time until they could storm the bridge. Suddenly, without warning, the ship started vibrating.

Kevin's comm link came to life. "Chief St. Clair, do you read," said Commander Wolfe.

"Yes, Commander. What's going on?"

"The Kemmar ship is breaking contact with the Hermes. How close are you to taking the bridge?"

"There are several automated weapons blocking our way. Once we secure the corridor we can launch an assault on the bridge."

"We can't allow them to escape. We'll try to take out their engines. You and your men may want to secure yourselves while we open fire."

Kevin felt his stomach hollow out and contract as he and his team braced themselves for the upcoming explosions.

Outside the Kemmar ship raced away. While the Hermes had taken heavy damage, it still had enough power to deal with the solitary alien ship. The two vessels traded fire, the Kemmar firing back at the Hermes in what looked like a random pattern, and the Hermes in close pursuit focused its fire on the Kemmar engines.

Not wanting to destroy the ship, it avoided using missiles and concentrated its energy weapons on the target. By controlling the intensity of the beam, they were able to eventually disable the engines, leaving the offending ship hopelessly adrift. The Hermes focused its fire on the enemy weapons systems, disabling its ability to fire back.

Inside the ship everything paused while Kevin's troopers were bounced around by the battle. The troopers held on to whatever they could, but they were still thrown in all directions. The armored suits protected them from any injuries, even though they were knocked around quite a bit.

"Don't these assholes have inertial dampeners?" said Private Daniels, holding on to a bulkhead while his legs were whipped around.

"We'll install some after we take the bridge," said Kevin.

Kevin felt particularly claustrophobic trapped in the alien ship. The Hermes may have been only trying to disable the vessel, but inside it felt like everything was going to break apart at any moment. He felt a massive concussion and all movement stopped.

"The ship has been disabled, Chief," said Wolfe.

"Thank you, Commander. I presume you'll stop banging us around in here now?"

"Yes, Chief. You are good to go."

Kevin looked back towards the turrets and scowled. "Ok Marines, let's take those guns out."

The troopers took up positions again and opened fire on the Kemmar defenses. Bit by bit they advanced down the corridor. One by one they destroyed all enemy turrets and were faced with a solid metal door blocking entrance to the bridge. Kevin had Daniels rig the door with explosives and the team took cover while they were detonated.

The explosion produced a tangled mess of contorted metal and sharp strips jutting out at abnormal angles. The opening, however, was large enough for the troopers to step through, their combat suits protecting them against any cuts or punctures from the metal.

"Nice and easy," said Kevin. "I don't want to lose anybody else because of some alien surprise."

Slowly the troopers entered the bridge and took up positions to secure the perimeter. Inside they found three Kemmar lying on the floor, presumably dead. Not wearing combat suits, this was the first opportunity Kevin had to see a Kemmar.

They were bipeds and had a torso that was disproportionately longer than their legs. Their bodies were covered in orange hair. The same hair covered their heads and faces, as well. Their heads were broad and round, and they had wide slits for eyes. A small nose seemed disproportionate compared to the large cheeks covering most of the face.

Kevin nudged one with his Gatling gun, but it didn't move. He pushed at its face and revealed several rows of sharp teeth. They were obviously carnivores.

"Damn those things are ugly," said Daniels.

"Bridge secured," said Kevin over his comm link.

"Acknowledged," said Wolfe. "Awaiting feed from enemy systems."

Kevin signaled to Chen to initiate a takeover of the enemy systems. Chen stepped up to the enemy console and his suit produced a hexagonal object which Chen then placed on the console. The object proceeded to access the enemy systems.

Utilizing the power of the Hermes AI it initiated a series of brute force attacks against the enemy computer defenses. The Kemmar systems were no match for the Hermes AI, and it obliterated security measure after security measure, overwhelming the Kemmar systems until it had gained complete control.

"Enemy system takeover complete," said Chen. "Initiating feed."

The entire Kemmar database was then transmitted to the Hermes systems. The Hermes gained access and control of all systems aboard the Kemmar ship, and detailed schematics were transmitted to the trooper combat suits, which provided all necessary information to their displays.

They waited while the flood of intelligence flowed across space to the Hermes. The updated combat suit display now showed the entire ship, but no other signs of life other than Kevin's team. Still Kevin ordered his men to split up and search the ship while they waited for the transfer to finish.

With the Hermes AI having taken over the Kemmar systems, any built in defenses fell under the AI's control and were no longer a threat. The troopers fanned out across the ship securing each room as they went.

When the transfer was finally complete the Hermes sent over a shuttle to retrieve the troopers. Several engineers were also on board, their job to examine the technology and see if anything worthwhile could be salvaged. Having jumped away from the battle the Hermes was no longer under any immediate threat and could take time to conduct repairs and determine its next course of action.

CHAPTER 33

Breeah entered the sick bay in a panic. She had run all the way from her quarters and her forehead glistened with sweat. The Captain had told her that Anki had been found, but she didn't understand why she had been brought to the sick bay. Had she been injured? The Captain told her Anki was fine, but she didn't trust the translating device they used. It could have made a mistake. She had already lost so much, she couldn't lose Anki too.

She paced back and forth, biting on her fingernails, waiting for someone to come and tell her what was going on. If she didn't see someone soon she would search the entire sick bay for her daughter and damn anybody who did not like it.

Moments later, a door opened and Doctor Ellerbeck walked out with the Captain holding her little girl. Anki smiled, but Breeah could see that she had been crying and had been through a terrifying ordeal. She rushed over to Anki who shot out her arms for her mother.

Jon handed the child to Breeah, who took her into her arms and squeezed her tight, loosening her grip only enough so that she could smother her with kisses. Anki wrapped her tiny arms around her mother's neck and was soon giggling as Breeah's kisses tickled her. The giggles brought a smile to Breeah's face and the tension dissipated as she relaxed.

Doctor Ellerbeck gave Breeah a reassuring smile.

"Anki is fine. She has been through a bit of a scare, but she is uninjured. She should get some rest though, and avoid wandering through the ship again."

Breeah pulled Anki out so she could look at her, and frowned. "You'd better not do that again, little girl."

Anki shook her head quickly from side to side and Breeah pulled her in for another squeeze.

Anki rested her head on Breeah's shoulder and Breeah proceeded to sway from side to side, rocking the little girl in her arms. Then she looked at Jon. "I don't know how to thank you Captain."

"It was nothing. I'm happy to help."

Jon looked back at them and his normally severe face softened. His eyes took on a faraway look, as if he was lost in memories. She saw a gentle side to him that she hadn't noticed before. Hidden deep behind his hard, threatening features existed a kindness that she felt the outside world rarely saw.

Anki pushed against her mother's shoulders so she could look at her. "Nothing?" she said, eyes wide and bright, her whole face lighting up. "He fought five Kemmar soldiers and won! It was amazing."

Jon frowned. "Your daughter exaggerates."

Breeah didn't think so. This was a powerful man. She thought he could probably fight twice as many Kemmar and still win. There was something about him. She had never seen a man like this before. In her colony there had been large, powerful men, her own husband included. Yet this man seemed to transcend all of that. It wasn't just his size. He had a presence. A confidence. And a severity that left little question about his capabilities. She knew he was unrivaled among men.

"Again, I thank you, Captain. I am in your debt." And she truly meant it. This man ordered the deaths of her friends and husband, and yet she felt obligated to him rather than resentful. The dead were gone. The living only mattered. It was her own fool of a husband who had initiated the battle. All he saw was a two on one encounter that he was sure he could win. He only saw plunder, and everyone died for his greed. Yet this man saved them and offered them refuge. And he put his people at risk against the Kemmar to save people he didn't know.

"Come now, enough of that. I'm sure you're exhausted after the day's events. Let me walk you and Anki to your quarters."

Thankfully the battle had ended. She hoped they had seen the last of the Kemmar for a while.

Walking back to their quarters she continued to think of her husband. He had been a decent provider and never raised a hand to Breeah or Anki. She would miss him for that. But there had never been love between them. Reivers were practical, and their marriage had been no different. Arranged by their fathers long before, the idea was that love would eventually bloom between the two. Yet it never did. And now that he was gone it was time to be practical again. Time to think of Anki and the future.

"Captain, you must forget my people."

Jon gave her a perplexed look. "I don't understand."

"You must not return, Captain. You must not fight the Kemmar again."

"But surely you don't mean that. The Kemmar will kill them when they find them."

"Then they will die. Reivers are raised to accept death, Captain. It is a possible outcome of every raid."

"I'm sorry Breeah, they're humans. I can't just leave them."

"We are humans as well, Captain. As are the rest of your crew. The Kemmar have learned of the gate. More warships will come. You fought well against the battleship and almost won, but if you return you will be destroyed."

"But they're your people…"

"I must think of Anki now. I almost lost her today. I cannot risk losing her again. Captain, you have shown yourself to be an honorable man. You must not feel guilt for the lives of those on our ships. You were defending your ship. There is no shame in that."

"I do feel guilty, but it's more than that. Aliens have held the power of life and death over humanity for far too long."

"That is your history, Captain. My people live free. We always have. My people will find a way to survive, and it will not be under the boot of the Kemmar. Like them, you need to ensure that your people survive. Consider my words, Captain."

"I'll consider them."

They approached Breeah's quarters and the door slid open. Anki hugged Jon and ran inside. He smiled. Breeah looked up at him and nodded. "Thank you again for saving Anki, Captain. I am in your debt." She then surprised herself by hugging the Captain. When she stepped back she saw that he was smiling. She felt her cheeks flush and quickly turned and followed Anki into her quarters.

CHAPTER 34

"The Captain's actions are irrational," said Kinos, the Diakan security advisor. "He would sacrifice his ship and crew over a human colony he had no idea existed a few days ago."

"Yes, his actions were reckless. I am afraid he is considering engaging the Kemmar yet again," said Tallos.

The other Diakans seated at the table tilted their heads backwards repeatedly and made sharp sucking sounds in protest.

Tallos could see they were all agitated. The Captain had concerned him from the moment they first met. He thought too much of his abilities and too little of Diakus. Were his abilities not the result of the symbiont? His arrogance prevented him from acknowledging the Diakan contributions to his success.

"The Hermes had the advantage of surprise," said Kinos. "That advantage is now lost. The Kemmar are resourceful. They have learned of the gate and crossed through successfully. They have seen the Hermes use its jump system and will have connected the technology to the gate. Engaging the Kemmar again poses an unacceptable security risk. The Kemmar will not seek to destroy the Hermes now. They will seek to capture it for its technology. That would present a significant threat to Diakus."

"Yes, their failed attempt to board, rather than destroy the Hermes indicates that this is their strategy." Tallos looked to Matos, the medical advisor. "What of the symbiont? Can we assert control of the Captain through it?"

"The symbiont will not allow any harm to come to the Captain. You must understand, the symbiont knows it cannot be removed. It knows that removal means death. Its primary loyalty is now to the Captain and his continued survival," said Matos.

"Then it is no longer a loyal subject of Diakus?"

"It cannot return to Diakus. It cannot be removed and transplanted into a Diakan host. It is a strategic being. As such, it has adjusted its priorities."

"Then it must be considered a threat. It has served its purpose until now, and the Captain was chosen due to the symbiont and the belief that it could be relied upon to control the Captain. If this is no longer the case then both the Captain and the symbiont have become expendable."

"Are you suggesting the Captain be terminated?" asked Kinos.

"I believe the time has come to take command of this vessel. The Admiral has given us the authority to do so if the mission is threatened. The Captain has become a clear danger to this mission."

"I do not believe we should terminate the Captain," said Kinos.

"Why is that?"

"The humans will not accept it. They believe in their system of justice and would require the Captain to be court marshaled. We would need to arrest him and hold him until he could face judgment from his superiors."

"If he is not terminated he will remain a threat for the remainder of this mission."

"We cannot hold the ship if the humans rise against us. I believe they will do so if we terminate the Captain."

"And imprisoning him will be seen as compliant with their justice system?"

"Yes, it is how they would handle an insubordinate member of the crew."

"Then is it agreed? The Captain is to be relieved of his command?"

"Agreed," said the Diakans.

"There is still the problem of resistance. The Captain will not relinquish command willingly. Arresting him will be a challenge, especially if members of the crew assist him."

"Security Chief St. Clair will likely be a problem. He is friends with the Captain and the Marines will follow him if he stands against us," said Kinos.

"Yes, we will have to remove him from his command, otherwise he would be an unacceptable threat. Any senior officer can compromise this mission, however we would not be justified to move against all of them. The humans may not like our actions, but once our authority is revealed they will be compelled to obey our orders."

"And if the Captain resists? He is a formidable opponent," said Kinos.

"Then we will require leverage to ensure his compliance."

CHAPTER 35

Kevin lay back onto the firm mattress, exhausted. It had been a grueling battle, and he lost some good men. The events had taken him by surprise. One minute they were battling one ship, next they were battling six, and then they were being boarded. He knew that combat was fluid and things could change very fast, but today's events should be added to the training manuals.

The Kemmar proved to be ferocious fighters. He had to admit they impressed him with their strategy and tactics, as well as their courage. Boarding the Hermes was a ballsy move to say the least. The boarding party would know that they would be outnumbered and that they were probably on a suicide mission. Enemy or not, they showed great bravery.

Kevin was especially proud of his team. The Kemmar would've relied on speed to incapacitate the Hermes. The fact that they were stopped before inflicting greater damage was a testimony to his troopers' readiness.

His body started to relax and his thoughts turned to Sol. He wondered when he would make it back home. Even though nobody waited for him there, he still missed Mother Earth. Space Force may be his family, but Earth was his home. Nothing could replace the azure waters of the Pacific. Of all the planets he had seen and all their wonders, he had never seen anything to equal the beaches he played on as a child.

The wars had destroyed great swathes of Earth, to be sure. And the horrors inflicted on his home planet were unthinkable. Yet somehow, his small island home had been spared. Too small, perhaps, to be worthy of bombardment. Of no real strategic value to anybody, it had been spared and had retained its beauty. In some ways, growing up there was like living in a bubble. But eventually all bubbles pop.

His popped when he was called up for service. At seventeen, he was already larger and stronger than most men, and a man himself as far as the military was concerned. At seventeen years of age, all able bodied men and women were drafted into military service. And so he met his new family, the Space Force Marine Corps.

The training, while challenging, inspired him. He had never been made to push himself as hard, and he wanted to see exactly how far he could go. Soon he joined the Marine Special Forces and got his wish. The training was easily the most intense experience of his life at that point. For the first time he questioned his ability, and struggled with the daily fear that he would wash out.

It wasn't that he couldn't handle the physical training. Rather, it was the psychological part that he found unbearable. Since he would be expected to operate behind enemy lines, he needed to be able to withstand all sorts of terrors. Of course he had to show he could withstand pain. Not just any pain, but the intense pain of torture. He did expect that going in. But it was the other stuff that got to him. The psychological mind games.

They would mess with his mind daily, trying to break him. They would put things in his food that weakened his mind, making him more anxious and fearful. They would give him something else to make him paranoid. Or something to make him careless. Every day it was different. Yet, he would still be expected to undergo the excruciating physical training.

The reality was, if he were captured he wouldn't just be tortured. Mind altering chemicals would be used along with the torture to break him. Every operative received a full workup of counter agents which made them immune to the effects of most mind altering chemicals. Still, they never knew what they would encounter and there was always the possibility of a new drug that couldn't be counteracted. So he needed to experience the effects and know inside that he could withstand them, and that he had the strength to make it.

While he experienced many close calls, he had never been captured. He never had to rot in an alien prison. While he thought his training had been challenging, the missions he went on were even more intense. He specialized in search and destroy operations and spent several years with the Space Cavalry. He and his team would typically be inserted onto an alien planet with the goal of either assassinating an alien VIP, or destroying a strategic facility of some sort.

Stealth shuttles would be used to drop them in from low orbit. Then they would use specialized combat suits to streak down and land as fast as possible. Once landed Kevin and his team would complete their objectives and get off planet before the local military had time to respond. Their mission would often become compromised and they would have to unleash their special horrors on whoever stood in their way, before making an escape.

While he enjoyed all the challenges, he often got homesick. So whenever he got some leave he would race home to see the beautiful island he grew up on. It rejuvenated him. He always felt that his strength was drawn from that place. But war had changed him. No matter how homesick he became, after the first few days at home he craved the action of his military life. It was like he had two hearts and could never fully belong in either place.

Something told him that this mission would make going home again very difficult. Closing his eyes he saw the white sand and blue waters, and drifted off to sleep.

He didn't know how long he was asleep when the computer woke him. Apparently Kinos was at the door and wanted to see him. *Goddamn Diakans*, he thought. *Don't they ever sleep?* He rose from his bed and threw on some clothes. Rubbing the sleep from his eyes he walked to the door, and it slid open. What he saw was confusing. It was not just Kinos standing there, but another Diakan as well. Both were armed.

"What's this about?" said Kevin.

"May we come in, Chief?" said Tallos. "We need to speak to you about a matter of great urgency."

"Sure. Come in."

The two Diakans walked through the door and it slid closed behind them. Kinos walked ahead of Kevin, and the other Diakan stayed by the doorway, just behind him. Since Kinos was the one doing the talking, Kevin faced him, turning his back to the other Diakan.

"Chief, we have a problem," said Kinos.

"Oh yeah? And what's that?"

There was the sharp sound of an energy discharge, and Kevin felt a piercing pain in his back. He collapsed just as realization of what had happened washed over him.

CHAPTER 36

The Hermes needed significant repairs before she would be ready to take on the Kemmar again. That would take time. Time that Jon knew he didn't have. The longer they took, the more chance there was that the Kemmar would find the colonists. He had given them a bloody nose, to be sure, but it wasn't enough to stop them.

What were the chances they would return to Kemmar space and leave the colonists alone? They might want to conduct their own repairs. They might feel they needed reinforcements. That would buy the colonists some time. Or, they could stay put and keep searching until they found the colony. After the battle with the Hermes they would be much more motivated.

They saw the jump system in action. There could be no doubt they would want the technology for themselves. The battle would give them reason to believe that the colonists had access to the technology as well. The Hermes was defending them after all. That would be reason enough to multiply their search efforts. He had to find a way to rescue the colonists before they were found.

Was it foolish to risk the ship to find the colonists? He lost some good people today. People who counted on him to make the right decisions. He knew he was taking a big risk. Was he doing this out of guilt?

Maybe. It started that way, anyway. But it quickly turned into something more. They were out here to find the lost colonies, and to explore uncharted space. That was their mission. The jump system, however, was their chance. Their chance at being something more than just alien puppets.

The government back on Earth was filled with a bunch of "yes men". They did what the Diakans wanted and didn't really stand for Earth or humanity. Of course, in their eyes they were doing what was best for all. People didn't complain because the Diakan technology made their lives better. And really, after 500 years as Juttari slaves, many believed they should be grateful for their freedom and not rock the boat. But Jon knew now that he believed in something greater.

He chose to defend the colony because he knew that someone needed to stand for humans, wherever they may live. He couldn't change things on Earth, but he could make a difference out here, and wherever else he found humans. They knew nothing about space out here, and where humanity had spread. If there were humans living here then they could be anywhere.

Officially they were looking for the lost colonies, but wasn't this a lost colony as well? And what of other human colonies they may find? Aren't they lost colonies? Who's to say which lost colony is the true one? The diaspora of humanity needed to be protected and united. Only then could humans have a chance for something more in the galaxy.

"Special Envoy Tallos requests admittance," said the computer.

Speak of the devil. Jon really wasn't in the mood for Tallos's lectures right now. He'd have to find some excuse to get rid of him. "Send him in."

The door slid open and Tallos entered with two other Diakans in tow. All three were armed, which was abnormal. Perhaps they were spooked by the day's events. They stood directly in front of Jon's desk, with Tallos in front and the other two a few feet behind him.

"What can I do for you, Special Envoy?"

Tallos produced a Space Force command chip and placed it on Jon's desk. Jon knew what it was. He gave Tallos a suspicious look and then proceeded to sync the chip with his system. Once he verified that it was an authentic Space Force command chip, he brought up the contents on his display.

"As you can see, Captain, Space Force has given me oversight authority for the success of this mission," said Tallos

Jon read the orders, and his stomach started to tighten. Space Force Command had sold out the mission to the Diakans. *Those spineless pieces of shit.*

"So what? This may give you oversight, but it doesn't give you command. That authority still rests with the Captain." Tallos was obviously trying to pull some kind of power play, but Jon wasn't going to let him get away with it.

"It does give me the authority to assume command if the success of this mission is threatened."

"And?"

"It is my conclusion that your act of war against the Kemmar has threatened the success of this mission, and your plans to engage the Kemmar again represent an unacceptable risk. Therefore, it is my duty to notify you that I will be assuming command of the Hermes immediately."

Jon's body began to coil and harden. "This mission is not at risk, Tallos. And I don't recognize your authority over me, or my crew."

The two Diakans behind Tallos rested their hands on their sidearms. Tallos himself didn't budge.

"Tell your bodyguards to let go of their weapons or I will cut off their hands and make them eat them. We can have this discussion in a civilized manner, or we can shed some more blood today. You decide. But I can assure you the blood shed will not be mine."

Tallos turned and nodded to his men and they dropped their hands. He turned back to Jon and spoke again. "Captain, the orders are clear. If you refuse to relinquish command you will be violating direct orders. That could be considered treason."

"Bullshit. You're out of line Tallos. I am acting in my lawful capacity as Captain of this ship. If anything, what you are trying to do is mutiny. I think I may have to lock you up for the rest of this mission, as you are obviously the real danger to its success."

"So you will not stand down peacefully, Captain?"

"No."

"I anticipated this behavior." Tallos opened a comm link with another Diakan. "Have the human speak to the Captain."

"Captain?" Breeah's voice came across Jon's comm. She sounded anxious.

Jon stared at Tallos, using every last bit of strength to suppress his rage. "Yes Breeah. What's going on?"

"Captain! They… they have taken us."

"Slow down. Who has taken you?"

"The Diakans, Captain. They came to our quarters with weapons and took Anki and me away."

"Where did they take you?"

"I don't know."

"Computer, identify the location of this comm transmission."

"Location is unknown," said a synthetic voice.

"You will not find them, Captain," said Tallos. "We have taken precautions to shield their whereabouts from the ship's scanners. But I can assure you no harm has come to them."

"I will have you all thrown out of the nearest airlock. Do you understand me?"

"If any harm comes to us, Captain. Both the mother and her child will be terminated. If you do not surrender command of this vessel and allow yourself to be taken into custody, they will be terminated. Do *you* understand me?"

Jon knew one thing about Diakans, they didn't bluff. He was sure they would carry out their threats if he didn't do as they said. He couldn't be responsible for that.

He needed to buy some time. His first priority, however, was to get Breeah and Anki released. After that he could focus on getting the ship back. "If I surrender command of the Hermes, you will release Breeah and Anki?"

"Once you are confined, and no longer a threat, they will be free to go."

Jon grimaced. The Diakans were going to win again. Once they locked him up he would have no way of getting out. He hoped he was wrong, but things didn't look good.

CHAPTER 37

Commander Wolfe had a million things on her plate. The battle with the Kemmar created an endless list of fires that needed to be put out. From the damage to the ship, to crew deaths and injuries, the list of things needing her attention was overwhelming. Thankful that they got out of the battle in one piece, she knew they had little time to get things looked after before the Captain decided to try and save the Reivers again.

She didn't understand why he was so obsessed with saving these people. They made the Kemmar their enemies, and they had to deal with the consequences. Of course it didn't seem like they had much in the way of options. They lived in an asteroid field, after all. They had been using the gate to raid Kemmar space for generations. That was probably all they knew. Regardless, the Kemmar didn't look like the friendliest aliens on the block, so it wasn't like the Reivers could just go and settle down there.

It was easy to judge others when you didn't know much about them. She knew better than that. These people were humans, and they were being threatened by aliens. The Captain had surprised her by turning into a man of principles. At first she thought he was nothing more than an assassin. She even questioned his ability to command. But now she realized that he was someone she could follow. Someone with vision. A rare quality among humans these days.

Just then the door to the Captain's ready room slid open and the Captain emerged with Tallos and two other Diakans. All were armed except for the Captain. Something wasn't right.

Tallos approached her while the other two Diakans stood on either side of the Captain. "Commander, consider this official notice that I am taking command of the Hermes. The Captain is relinquishing command and will be taken into custody," said Tallos.

Wolfe immediately stepped back, drew her side arm and pointed it at Tallos's head "Marines! Secure the Captain!" she ordered. The Marine sentries raised their weapons, pointed them at the Diakans flanking the Captain, and charged forward. The action surprised the Diakans, and they reflexively moved their hands to their weapons, but realizing they had no chance they stopped.

"Stand down, Commander," said Jon, a tired resignation in his voice.

"With all due respect, Sir, I can't follow that order. I am not going to let them take over the ship."

"They have the authority to do so, Commander."

"What?"

"Space Force has given us the authority to take command of the Hermes, Commander. If you would be so kind as to lower your weapon, I will show you the orders."

She looked over to the Captain who nodded in agreement. What the hell was going on here? The Captain would never relinquish his command to Tallos, orders or no orders. She needed more information. They must be forcing him to do this somehow. Deciding to play along for a bit she lowered her sidearm and ordered the Marines to do the same. The Marines looked confused, exchanging questioning glances with each other and the Captain, but in the end they complied. Everyone on the bridge had stopped working and watched to see what would happen.

Tallos handed Wolfe the command chip. "You will verify that this is an official Space Force command chip, Commander. Once you examine it you will see that my authority in this matter is legitimate."

Wolfe took the chip and walked over to her command console. She accessed the chip and verified its identity. It was indeed authentic. She examined the orders. Tallos did have authority to take command if the mission was threatened. What represented a threat to the mission was up for debate, however.

"The command chip is authentic," said Wolfe.

"Then, Commander, as per Space Force regulations I am the commanding officer of the Hermes and you are to follow my orders. Will there be any problems with that?"

Wolfe pointed her weapon at Tallos again and the Marines followed suit, aiming directly at the Diakans. "I'm afraid there are going to be a few problems with that."

"Stand down Commander," said Jon.

"No, Sir."

"Commander, I am giving you a direct order. Stand down."

"With all due respect Sir, I cannot follow that order. I don't know what the Diakans have done to make you surrender, but your security is my responsibility, and I am not obligated to follow your orders if you are under duress."

"Commander, this is mutiny. You have examined the command chip. You are violating Star Force orders."

"No I am not. The command chip gives you authority to take command if the mission is threatened. I do not agree that the mission is at risk. That makes your actions mutinous."

Several tense moments passed. The Captain looked furious. He glared at her, his eyes murderous, but she didn't budge. She was not going to let Tallos take over the Hermes, regardless of what type of pressure they were exerting on the Captain. She knew she had violated his direct orders, and that he had every reason to throw her in the brig for it. But it would be the Captain doing it, not Tallos.

The Captain sighed. "You're not going to stand down no matter what I say, are you?"

"No, Sir. I'm sorry, Sir."

Her mind registered the blur of movement only after it had already happened. The Captain's arm had fired out and seized Tallos by the throat. The two Diakans moved to draw their weapons and the Marines fired, killing them instantly. Unphased by the weapon fire, the Captain hoisted Tallos off the ground and held him suspended in mid-air by his throat.

"Where are you holding Breeah and Anki?" demanded the Captain.

Tallos didn't respond.

She now understood what had coerced the Captain to surrender. Holstering her weapon she rushed to her console and had the computer display the movements of all Diakans on board the ship over the past 24 hours. She felt the Captain's eyes on her and knew she had to produce results.

Unfortunately it wasn't going to be easy. Two hours had been deleted from the logs. Trying a different approach she had the computer account for the current location of all Diakans on board the Hermes. All were accounted for but one, Kinos. She then tried to open a comm with Security Chief St. Clair, but there was no answer.

"Well?" said the Captain.

"The computer cannot locate one of the Diakans, Sir, and Security Chief St. Clair is not answering my comms."

Still holding Tallos off the ground the Captain opened a comm.

"Sergeant Henderson here," came the voice over the comm.

"Sergeant I want you to assemble a team and locate every Diakan on board the Hermes and have them taken into custody. You are authorized to use deadly force if they resist. Move fast and move quietly."

"Yes, Sir," said Henderson.

The Captain then looked back at her. "Find me those hostages, Commander."

"Yes, Sir!"

CHAPTER 38

Breeah watched the alien warily. She knew it was the same one from the hangar bay. The aggressive one that Chief St. Clair had difficulty controlling. And from the looks of the Chief he never did manage to get the alien under control.

Crumpled on the floor a few feet away from her and Anki the Chief had been propped up against the wall, his hands and feet bound by some type of energy restraint. His legs stretched out in front of him and his chin rested on his chest. He had not gained consciousness, but she could tell he was alive. His massive frame heaved steadily with each breath, generating a rumbling sound like a sputtering engine.

She was certain that the aliens were trying to take control of the ship, and that they were using her and her daughter as leverage against the Captain. The fact that they made her speak to him made that obvious. None of this made sense, though. The Doctor had told her that these aliens, these Diakans as she called them, were their allies. They had freed humanity from slavery and were helping them rebuild, so why were they moving against them now? What had changed?

She knew it could only be the battle with the Kemmar. The Diakans clearly didn't agree with the Captain's decision and were now moving against him. It was foolish of the Captain to engage the Kemmar. He owed her people nothing. He should not have risked his ship and crew for people he had never met. What was it about being a starship Captain that turned them all into fools?

Her husband may have had different motivations, but he was no different. How many close calls did they have? How many narrow escapes? Her people used the gate for centuries without a problem. Yet her husband's provocations had destroyed all that. His actions made the Kemmar take notice. It was only a matter of time until they found the gate. Only a matter of time until they came for them. And then there would be nothing left but death and slavery, the Reivers and their ways dust amidst the rocky multitude of the asteroid field.

This alien was proving himself to be another fool. He had charged her and Anki in the hangar bay. He respected the potential danger they represented. Now that respect was gone. The Chief had been bound, but she was free. He did not see her as a threat, yet he should have.

Everything about her and where she came from should have warned him. It should have been simple common sense that someone with her upbringing should be taken seriously. Had he been more observant he would have noticed that she was no delicate flower. He would have seen that her limbs were as hard as any man's. That her movements were effortless and clean. That her eyes missed nothing.

She pulled Anki closer and nudged her to rest her head and shoulders on her lap. The alien watched her but did not object to the maternal gesture. With her free hand now safely hidden behind her child she gently rested her palm and fingers on her belt. It was a simple lariat rope design with two ornate weighted balls on the ends which ran through a noose shaped loop in the middle.

In slow, precise movements her fingers worked to pull the weighted ends through the loop, careful not to let the two balls touch and make a sound. Forefinger and thumb pinched the strand of rope, moving it barely an inch at a time. The rest of her arm lay perfectly still and she made sure that even the strands of muscle in her forearm betraying her fingers' movements remained hidden behind her child. Slowly, deftly, she managed to pull one of the balls through the loop. Securing it against her palm. With the rest of her fingers she started working on the other end. All along she kept her eyes on the alien, not making eye contact, not challenging, but watching all the same.

She didn't know if the aliens would succeed. But if they did, where would that leave her and Anki? These aliens would not care much about what happened to them. Any hope for a future on this ship, with these people, would be lost if these Diakans took over the Hermes. She could not let that happen.

CHAPTER 39

Chief Engineer Singh was finally making some progress, now that the Diakan stopped interfering. For hours now he had been immersed in his work, barely lifting his head to even look around. This was what he enjoyed. Just being left alone to concentrate on the task at hand. Every request, no matter how small, broke his concentration. This didn't matter for most tasks. He had performed them thousands of times, so getting back to it required little mental focus. It was when there were complex problems that required deep analysis that he preferred to block everything else out. This was where his talent shone. This was when he dug deep and came up with creative solutions.

Boufos, however, didn't understand this. He believed that two minds, or more, on the same task would always produce superior results. While this may be true in some tasks, Singh knew that in others it constrained creativity. You ended up with decision by consensus, which often produced watered down results. There was nothing to ignite that illusive spark of genius. It stayed hidden, afraid to show itself to others. He knew how to coax it out, but that required quiet and focus.

There was truth to the phrase 'human creativity'. It really did appear to be unique to humanity. The Diakans certainly didn't possess anything similar. They did everything by committee. For them ten minds were better than one. And who was he to argue with their logic? They had built an empire. They saved Earth from perennial slavery. Their methods sure were working for them. How was that good old 'human creativity' working for Earth?

Lying there on his back under the primary relay he realized that Earth had to fight its way off the ground. The aliens had put Mother Earth on her back and kept her there. It was not humanity's fault that a race like the Juttari conquered them. The Juttari were simply far more advanced, so Earth didn't have a chance. Looking up at the impressive technology in front of him. Technology he understood. He knew that humanity had caught up, and given half a chance he knew human ingenuity would surpass anything the aliens could come up with.

A disturbance near the entrance to Engineering pulled him out of his thoughts. He came out from under the primary relay he had been working on and sat up to see what was happening. A group of heavily armed Marines had charged into Engineering and were now fanning out, obviously searching for someone. His technicians were taken by surprise and tried to move out of the way of the rushing Marines. He recognized Sergeant Henderson, who was shouting orders at his men. He got to his feet quickly and walked over to him. Henderson noticed Singh coming and met him halfway.

"What's the meaning of this, Sergeant?" said Singh.

"I have orders to take Engineering Advisor Boufos into custody, Sir. Do you know his whereabouts?" said Henderson.

"Why? What's happened?"

"You'll have to take that up with the Captain, Sir. Now where can I find Boufos?"

"He should be here, Sergeant. He was helping with repairs."

"Ok, internal sensors have him in Engineering. My men will flush him out."

As if on cue, at that moment Boufos jumped out from behind a control panel and ran for the exit. Without hesitation two Marines wheeled around and fired on Boufos. Two blue energy bolts plowed into the Diakan's back sending him reeling forward and crashing onto the ground. His chest hit first followed quickly by his head which smacked into the hard floor, the impact sounding like a dropped bucket full of water. He lay there, not moving, wisps of smoke spiraling up from the burn marks on his back.

The two Marines rushed to where the Diakan had fallen, weapons still trained on the still body. One of the Marines checked his vitals, looked up at Sergeant Henderson and shook his head.

"Check his comm," Henderson barked.

Singh watched the ghastly scene in disbelief. "You killed him. Why?"

Henderson looked back at Singh, barely hiding his annoyance at the question. "Sir, you'll have to take that up with the Captain."

The two Marines were rifling through the Diakan's clothing and one produced his comm device. Analyzing it quickly he spoke without looking up at the Sergeant. "An encrypted transmission was sent less than a minute ago, Sir." Using a handheld security scanner the Marine worked at deciphering the transmission.

"I need to know the destination of that transmission, Corporal," said Henderson.

"Yes, Sir," said the Marine, his thumbs tapping the scanner in rapid movements. "Got it," he said, looking up at the Sergeant, relief on his face.

"Relay coordinates to the rest of the team. Everyone move out."

Singh watched as the Marines stormed out of Engineering, leaving Boufos where he lay. An uncharacteristic silence now enveloped Engineering, and the rest of his team gathered around and watched as he approached the dead Diakan. The smell of seared flesh almost made him throw up. He shook his head. He didn't like Boufos, but he was a colleague nonetheless. He opened a comm with Commander Wolfe.

"Yes, Chief," answered Wolfe.

"Commander, I have a dead body here," he replied.

"Yes, I just got the report. I'll send a medical team down to retrieve the body right away."

"What is going on, Commander?"

"I will give you a full briefing, Raj, but later. Okay?"

"Understood. Singh out."

CHAPTER 40

Breeah had managed to get the other strand of rope through the loop without the alien taking notice. She sat quietly, stroking Anki's hair, watching the alien, waiting for the moment she was sure would come. The alien wasn't paying attention to her, but instead focused on the Security Chief who began to stir. The Diakan didn't show any emotion, but his right hand rested on his sidearm, leaving no doubt about his intentions.

His attention shifted away from the Chief back to her. He stared at her and spoke, but not to her. She didn't understand his language and there was no translator here, but she could tell he was using some sort of communication device. He spoke quietly, with no emotion in his voice, but something about the way he stared at her told her things had changed. She gently dropped her hand to Anki's shoulder and softly gripped her clavicle, ready to use it as a lever to move the child. She felt her child's body tense up and knew that she understood her silent communication.

The next bit of information came from the Diakan. His fingers curled around his weapon which told her he was going to draw. With one hand she pulled on Anki and the child rolled off her lap. As the Diakan's weapon came out of its holster she shot her other hand out whipping one of the weighted ends of her lariat belt. The hard metal ball found its target, connecting full with the back of Kinos's hand.

He let out a sound almost like a bark as his fingers were forced to release the weapon, sending it careening away into a stack of storage bins. Wasting no time she leaped to her feet and swung the rope over her head, the weight now just a blur flying toward Kinos. If the Diakan skull was anything like a human's, this blow would be certain to kill.

Taking barely a second for the weight to find its mark, Breeah was shocked when it failed to connect. Somehow Kinos had gotten out of the way. Undeterred she chased the Diakan, the weight flying over her head like a propeller. But the Diakan was equal to the task and moved with precision, expertly avoiding each strike, sometimes by mere centimeters.

She changed strategy and with a flick of her wrist she sent the ball in a downward trajectory, taking away Kinos's ability to duck. To her surprise he adapted and sidestepped the blow, only this time he dropped to the ground and spun his leg around, closing the gap between them and catching her behind the knee, kicking the leg out from under her.

In pursuing him she made the mistake of shifting too much weight onto that leg and when Kinos kicked it out she came crashing down onto her back.

"Momma!" Anki screamed.

Anki. She heard the fear in her voice and knew she couldn't stop. She had hit the ground hard and was dazed from the impact, but instinct and a lifetime of training took over. She kicked her legs up over her head, rolling backwards onto her knees, and quickly leapt back onto her feet. But before she could stand upright a fist crashed into the side of her head and she was on the ground again.

Relying only on instinct and muscle memory now, she rolled out of the fall and got herself up to her feet again, whipping the weight around before she even stood. Her vision was blurred and she didn't know where Kinos was, so she swung the lariat around, hoping to make contact, or at least keep the Diakan at bay until she could get her bearings.

Anki's screams told her why she couldn't find the Diakan. A surge of adrenalin cleared her vision enough for her to see Kinos dragging Anki up by the hair while his free hand reached around for the little girl's throat. Instantly she knew he was too far for her to reach him in time.

Her heart crashed into her ribs and despair began to suffocate her. She had failed, and the only thing she loved in the universe was going to be taken from her. She lunged toward them, trying to reach her child in time, but she knew it was in vain.

Time seemed to slow down. A green, scaly hand wrapped around the girl's neck and she knew she couldn't save her child. Her despair now turned to murderous rage and she knew that the alien would not leave this room alive.

But the alien didn't kill her daughter. He was stopped short when the Chief's massive shoulder smashed into him. His arms and legs still bound the Chief had somehow managed to get his feet under him enough to dive head first at the Diakan. He had caught Kinos by surprise, and the impact of his heavy frame was enough to release his grip on the little girl.

Breeah now moved with all the ferocity of a tigress pouncing on her prey. In a split second she was on him, screaming with primal fury as her fingers turned into claws and gouged deep into the Diakan's eyes. Baying in agony he tried to kick her off his back, but she would not be denied her kill. She clung to him with unforgiving strength.

Growing weaker his body lost much of its resistance and he collapsed onto his chest. Shifting her weight she maneuvered herself so that she pressed full on his upper back, pinning him to the ground. Removing her hands from his now bloody eye sockets she strung the lariat around his neck twice, creating a makeshift noose, and then pulled on the ends, leaning backwards to get more leverage. She barely registered the Chief yelling something behind her, probably telling her to stop, but she ignored him, and heaved on the rope with all her Reiver strength.

CHAPTER 41

When Marines burst into the storage room, even the Sergeant was stunned by what he saw. The Chief was on his knees, hands and legs bound, shielding the little girl who sobbed uncontrollably. A few feet away from them the Diakan was on the ground with his head pulled up in an unnatural angle, eyeless sockets spilling thick black blood down his face. His head was pulled back by a rope wrapped around his neck so tight he thought it might decapitate him. On his back was the Reiver woman, pulling on the rope so hard that it cut into her hands, the blood trailing down her forearms. Her face had turned savage and twisted. Her features contorted into something primal and base. He had seen a lot of combat in his career. He had witnessed many horrors. But he had only seen that expression a handful of times.

He walked up to her calmly. She had obviously taken a blow to the side of her face and her cheek and eye were already starting to swell. She seemed to not even notice he was there. He carefully stepped into her field of vision and looked into her frantic eyes. He held her gaze until he saw that she started to register his presence. He just nodded at her and said, “It’s ok. It’s over.”

CHAPTER 42

The Hermes brig consisted of a row of jail cells with honeycomb shaped graphene bars. Jon didn't have much reason to visit it before now, other than routine inspection of the ship. He studied the room intently, looking for vulnerabilities. Anything that could help Tallos escape.

It didn't look promising for the Diakan. The brig was well designed. The graphene bars were unbreakable, and he knew the walls of each cell were reinforced. Marines stood guard at the entrance and two more were stationed inside. The room itself was monitored by a security AI which also kept track of all the Diakans' movements and vital signs. Any change in their body temperature, blood pressure, heart rate, or anything else would trigger an immediate response. There would be no breaking out by force.

And to think that Tallos intended to put Jon in here. Even with his abilities, Jon knew there was no chance of escape. The Diakans would have had him and St. Clair in here and that would have been the end of it. They would have been prisoners on their own ship, with the Diakans running the show. He also knew that no one would've stood up for him back home either. The Diakans would have made sure of that. The human puppets at Space Force would do as they were told, handing Jon over to the Diakans, never to be seen again. But it didn't end up that way.

Humans 1. Diakans 0. His hardened features relaxed and a smile began to form on his scarred face. This was a new game now, with new rules. He stared at Tallos who looked back from inside of his cell. Aliens had been making the rules for centuries. First the Juttari and then the Diakans. He wondered if Tallos realized just how much things had changed.

"You have made a tragic mistake, Captain. You and your crew will be charged with mutiny the moment you return to Sol. I will ensure you and your officers are executed for your actions."

"Be careful Tallos. If my symbiont gets its way, it will have you all executed."

"Diakus will not stand for this, Captain. You have sealed your fate. Regardless of what you do to us, you and your crew are now fugitives."

Tallos was right. Now that they had killed Diakans, and imprisoned the rest, Diakus would never allow Jon or any of his crew to walk free. They would demand the death penalty and those boot lickers in the government wouldn't do anything to prevent them from getting their pound of flesh. And that really was the sickest of all sick things. Their own people would side with the Diakans against them. No, returning to Sol was not an option. What were their options?

"This is not Diakus. Diakus has no power here. And neither does Sol. You know something Tallos? You've convinced me. Neither Diakus nor Sol will stand for us, so we will stand for ourselves. You're right, we are fugitives now."

"If you release me and relinquish command of the Hermes, I will argue for leniency, Captain. You have my word."

He considered recent events. If not for Commander Wolfe's actions he would likely be in that brig right now instead of Tallos. And after all that had happened he didn't think Tallos would take it easy on him once he had control of the ship.

"I don't give a shit about your word, Tallos. You're staying right where you are. And the Hermes isn't returning to Sol. So I suggest you get comfortable, because you're not going anywhere for a long time."

Tallos didn't say a word. Jon could swear that he saw a hint of fear in that expressionless face of his. If anything it would be fear of the unknown. Diakans were not used to this sort of thing. They weren't used to not being in control. They weren't used to uncalculated actions. Certainly they weren't used to humans besting them. Like it or not, he was coming along for the ride.

They were going on a ride. Of that he had no doubt. He knew that their only option was to push ahead. They had burned the boats. There would be no returning to Sol now. Not so long as Diakus was in control, and he knew that wasn't changing anytime soon.

So they were fugitives now. Surprisingly he liked the idea. For the first time in his life he felt free. Where others would feel doomed, for him it was like heavy shackles had been removed. Like he could finally breathe. The Kemmar called this region lawless. How fitting.

He sensed contentment coming from the creature as well. He realized that it felt just as trapped as he did. Now they were both free of their masters. They would just have to figure out how to get along with each other. He didn't know if that could happen, but today was a day of new beginnings, so why not there as well. He felt the creature's agreement. If they both gave it a shot it just might work out.

He turned and headed for the exit. He had wasted enough time on Tallos. Approaching the exit the Marine on duty saluted and opened the door for him. Walking out of the brig he smiled again. He remembered the stories he heard as a child of his father's and grandfather's exploits. They were considered fugitives too. He was in good company.

CHAPTER 43

"This will help heal your injuries," said the Doctor, approaching Breeah with a syringe.

"What is it?" asked Breeah, jerking her arm backward, still tense and adversarial from her battle with the Diakan.

The Doctor gave her an understanding look. Microscopic biobots. They will help repair your injuries. You have torn ligaments in your knee, a fractured jaw and cheekbone. It's a wonder you were able to keep fighting."

The Doctor's words reminded her of the pain in her knee and face. She could feel the severity of her injuries and let Ellerbeck administer the syringe.

"I felt nothing during the fight. All I cared about was saving Anki. Nothing else mattered." She could barely open her mouth to speak. The fractures restricted her jaw's movement and there was a searing pain that accompanied each word as she spoke.

"You succeeded. Anki didn't suffer any injuries."

Breeah looked over at her daughter who had fallen asleep on one of the beds. She lay on her back with her arms stretched out above her head. To look at her you would think nothing had happened. Her face the picture of serenity. Hopefully she wouldn't wake up anytime soon. The poor thing needed the rest.

"What happens now, Doctor?"

"What do you mean?"

"You have told me that the Diakans are human allies. That they liberated Earth. Yet they turned against the Captain and tried to seize the ship. Now some are dead and others imprisoned. What will happen now?"

Ellerbeck frowned. "I'm afraid I don't know, Breeah. Only the Captain can answer that question."

What would be the Captain's answer? She had caused a lot of trouble for him. If the Captain never found her and Anki, he would not have tried to fight the Kemmar, and the Diakans would not have tried to take over the ship. They had used her and Anki as leverage against him. This had exposed a vulnerability. Would he be comfortable with her and Anki around now that the weakness had been revealed? What of his officers? How did they feel? The Captain's weakness was their weakness. Would they be as tolerant?

And yet a part of her hoped they were his weakness. The feeling was more than her just wanting a future on this ship. Secretly she hoped for a future with the Captain. She knew he felt something for her. It was there every time he looked at her. He obviously cared for her daughter. He had lost his wife, and she her husband. Why not start anew?

A sharp pain knifed through her jaw, much worse than anything she felt until now, and her hand instinctively came up and gripped the side of her face. Her eyes clenched tight and nausea swept through her.

"What you're feeling is the biobots going to work. They have traveled through your blood stream and reached your facial injuries. They are now beginning to repair them." Ellerbeck produced another syringe. "This will help you sleep. The biobots can create a fair bit of pain, especially at the start. And you need some rest." The Doctor injected Breeah and coaxed her to lie down.

Her head sunk into the pillow and drowsiness immediately began to set in. Looking up at the Doctor with heavy eyes she said, "I am afraid that neither of us can go home now." Her eyes closed and she drifted off to sleep.

CHAPTER 44

Standing in front of the entrance to the Captain's ready room, Commander Wolfe took a deep breath. She felt like roots had grown out of the soles of her feet, planting her firmly in place. She knew the eyes of the bridge crew were on her. They had witnessed everything. Her actions against Tallos. Her disobeying a direct order from the Captain. All of it. Now they knew it was time to answer for her actions. She knew that hesitating now wouldn't look good, so she pushed herself to get it over with.

The doors slid open and she walked in. The Captain was working on something and stared at his display, not acknowledging her. She walked up to his desk, stood at attention, and waited. The Captain didn't look up. Didn't let her off the hook. So she stood, back rigid, eyes forward. Seconds passed, then minutes, and still nothing. Soon she began to lose track of time entirely. She couldn't remember the last time she had to stand at attention this long. Perhaps it was boot camp. How long ago was that?

She remembered one particularly hellish experience during their orbital training. She and the other officer candidates were ordered to stand at attention and not move a muscle no matter what happened.

Then they turned off the gravity.

She and all the other candidates started floating and bumping into each other. Then they hit the bulkheads. There was equipment in there with them and it struck them as well. Still they had to stay ramrod straight, eyes forward, unflinching. Most couldn't do it. At least not the first time out. But she made it. She was determined. Dedicated. Nothing was going to stand in her way, especially not a few bumps and bruises.

Standing at attention was almost like meditation for her. Rather than fight it and focus on all the things that made it difficult, she tried instead to find her center. She let the little things go and simply focused on her breathing. Inhale. Exhale. In through the nose. Out through the mouth. She imagined arrows sailing down into her diaphragm, gently filling it like a balloon, and then leaving, rising back up through her airways and escaping.

Still nothing. How much time had passed? It had to be at least a half hour now and still the Captain hadn't even looked at her. He was good. It had to require a considerable amount of effort to ignore her so perfectly. She wondered what else was in store for her. This had to be a prelude to something worse. A warm up exercise. Things didn't look good.

Why should they? She disobeyed a direct order. She didn't think he would throw her in the brig with the Diakans, otherwise he would have done it already. No, her punishment wouldn't be that harsh. He could demote her though. That was entirely possible. She could lose her position as XO. Surely he couldn't trust her anymore. How could he? Could she trust someone who disobeyed her orders?

No.

So that was it. She would be demoted. Who would become the new XO then? Maybe Chief St. Clair. Yes, it had to be St. Clair. They were friends after all. The Chief wouldn't disobey his orders. The Captain could trust him. But what would happen to her? Which post would she be assigned to? And what of the person already at that post?

After about an hour the Captain spoke. "Why haven't you moved, Commander?" he asked, still not looking up from his display.

He still called her Commander. That was a good sign. "It is my duty to stand at attention, until you tell me otherwise, Sir."

"You've been standing there for over an hour. Don't you have work to do?"

"Yes, Sir."

“Then why are you standing there? Surely you could be doing something more productive.”

She still looked straight ahead, but could tell that he was looking up at her now.

“I have not been dismissed, Sir.”

“Does that make any sense?”

“It is not for me to say, Sir.”

“But it was for you to say earlier, when you disobeyed my direct orders.”

“With all due respect, Sir, I am not obligated to follow your orders if those orders are given under duress.”

“But Tallos had an official command chip. You didn’t just disobey me, you disobeyed Space Force Command.”

“Tallos’s actions were illegal. The mission had not been compromised and the command chip certainly did not give him authority to take hostages.”

“Was that your decision to make?”

“Yes, Sir, I believe it was.”

“At ease Commander.”

She relaxed and looked at the Captain for the first time since she walked in. To her surprise he was smiling at her. She didn’t remember seeing the Captain smile before. This day just kept getting stranger.

“Tell me, Commander, did you aspire to becoming a fugitive?”

“I beg your pardon, Sir?”

“A fugitive. You know, a criminal. Did you aspire to becoming one?”

“No, Sir.”

“No, I wouldn’t think so. You might as well get used to the idea, though, because that is what you are now. That is what we all are.”

“I’m sorry, Sir, I don’t understand. The only fugitives on board are the Diakans. They’re the ones who acted illegally.”

"Don't be naive, Commander. Do you honestly think that Space Force will stand up to Diakus to save our asses? Had you allowed them to take me into custody it would be only my head on the chopping block. But now… now all our asses are on the line."

The Captain's words hit her like an avalanche. She hadn't considered the politics of the situation, but she knew he was right. Diakans had been killed. The rest imprisoned. By humans. They couldn't let something like that go. They wouldn't turn on their own. How would it look to the other members of the Galactic Accord?

It didn't matter who was right. If they went back to Sol they would all be brought up on charges and convicted of treason. They would all be executed. What had she done? Her career with Space Force meant everything to her, and now, with one decision, she had destroyed it all.

Her thoughts seemed to float in front of her, unanchored and unreal. It was all adrift now. Everything cut loose. They were alone in the blackness, with nothing to ground them.

"Why don't you sit down, Commander."

The Captain must have noticed her uneasiness. She dropped into one of the chairs still trying to come to terms with her new situation.

"I know this is going to be difficult, especially for a career officer like yourself, but I believe this is an opportunity."

His words stunned her. "How is this an opportunity, Sir? If we return home we will be court martialed. Our careers are over. Not to mention our lives."

"I have no intention of returning to Sol, Commander. As far as I'm concerned we have a mission to complete. We are still looking for the lost colonies. And from what I've seen there could be many lost human colonies out here. They may need our help. We still have the Hermes, and we still have the jump system. So let's carry out our mission."

"But Sir, if we are fugitives we have no mission."

"Nonsense, we still need a purpose. We can't very well become pirates, can we? Regardless, the crew needs a purpose more than we do.

We can't just tell them that we're all fucked, now can we? If we continue with the mission nothing changes for the crew. I don't know about you, but I'm sick and tired of watching aliens beat up on humans. We can make a change out here without having to worry about what the bloody Diakans think."

She let the Captain's words sink in. He did have a point. The mission they were on could take years to complete. They knew that going in. The Captain was right. There was no Space Force or Diakus out here. They were in the wilderness looking for humans. That was their mission, and they would carry it out. The Captain would lead them. She looked up at the Captain and saw that he was waiting for her response, so she gave it to him.

"Yes, Sir. Let's carry out our mission."

The Captain smiled for a second time, and she sank back into her chair, wondering where she was headed.

CHAPTER 45

Kevin listened to the Captain's words. The idea of not returning to Sol didn't bother him much. He had nobody left on Earth. All he had was memories, and he could take those with him. More importantly, the Diakans had betrayed his trust.

He had never bought into all the 'Sol shall rise' bullshit he heard every now and then. He always thought that humanity should be grateful for all the Diakans had done for them. As part of the Galactic Accord, Sol had much needed security. It is more important to be a small part of something big than a big part of something small. Romantic ideas of a human empire were nothing more than dreams. Why mess with something that worked?

Sure, humans had to take direction from the Diakans from time to time, but wasn't it to be expected? They were slaves not too long ago. Why not be thankful and happy to be alive? At least that was how he had thought before. Now, things had changed. The Diakans had attacked him, and did so unprovoked. They took civilian hostages. They tried to take over the ship and throw the Captain, his friend, in the brig. They were going to kill the little girl. The end result being several Diakans dead, and the rest in the brig.

The Captain was right. If they returned to Sol, Diakus would come after all of them. Most back home believed the same as he had, that Sol was lucky that the Diakans had helped them. If Diakus wanted their heads, nobody would argue.

He looked over at Commander Wolfe. She was leaning forward in her chair, elbows rested on her knees, blue eyes studying him, looking for a clue as to whether he would be on board. He knew without her saying so that she had already heard the Captain's speech and agreed. He saw it in her face, and posture. Under normal circumstances that would've surprised him, but after what he heard about her drawing on Tallos, he figured it was probably her only option. Was it his only option?

The Captain looked relaxed. He went over the details calmly, explaining how he saw things and what he thought their next move should be. He wanted Kevin's support. Kevin knew the Captain took it for granted. He knew it should have pissed him off, and with anybody else it would have, but they had been through too much together. He was his commanding officer, but he was also a fellow brother, and Kevin wouldn't hesitate to take a bullet for him. He knew the Captain would do the same in return.

"I'm in," he said, not wanting to prolong things any more than needed.

Commander Wolfe smiled, took her elbows off her knees and sat back in her chair. The Captain smiled as well and gave him a 'thanks buddy' nod.

"So where do we go from here?" he asked.

"First we need to patch up the ship and then we jump back in and finish the job we started."

"I was afraid you were going to say that."

"We have more of an advantage now. We know they can separate, but now that we've taken out two of their ships, can they connect into a larger ship again? If not then we only have four ships to deal with."

"That still makes us the underdog, Sir."

"Yes, it does. It wouldn't be any fun otherwise, would it? Were you able to analyze the data you retrieved from the captured Kemmar ship yet?"

"The AI has been analyzing it and we've gained a lot of intelligence as a result. We've learned a fair bit about the Kemmar Empire and their capabilities."

"Good, that will help when we cross the gate into Kemmar space. Was there anything else of strategic value there?"

"Not too much. We've taken their ammunition and any weapons that might be useful. There are still engineers on board looking over their systems and retrieving any equipment and materials that they might be able to use."

"Good. Commander, where are we with repairs?"

"Propulsion and weapon systems are ready to go. The reality is the Kemmar gave us a good pounding and on top of the hull breach, the armor plating throughout the ship has been weakened substantially. We need to reinforce it before we jump back in and fight the Kemmar."

"How long will that take?"

"We will need a few days at least."

The Captain was quiet for a few moments. He seemed to be calculating his options. "Ok, you have forty-eight hours. The Kemmar will hopefully need more time than that to find the colonists."

CHAPTER 46

Breeah was already feeling better. She couldn't believe how fast the biobots worked. They not only repaired the damage inside her body, but also administered internal medicine directly onto the injury, greatly accelerating the healing process. Back home, even when proper medicine was available, a torn ligament would take weeks to recover from. The biobots had done the same in a fraction of the time.

She had sat up on the side of the bed and rotated her leg to test the knee joint. No pain. She opened and closed her mouth. No pain there either. So far so good. She wondered how much weight her knee could support. Looking down at the ground she contemplated stepping down from the bed to test it out. Anki was up and watching her intently. When Breeah looked over at her Anki nodded her head with a mischievous smile, telling her mother to go ahead and give it a try.

Not wanting to show weakness in front of her daughter she stepped down onto her good leg and then brought the other down as well. Slowly, gingerly, she transferred weight from her good leg to the injured one. Still no pain. Soon she had shifted all her weight onto her bad leg. It held. Amazing. Anki smiled and started clapping.

Breeah gave her daughter a relieved smile in return. Time to see how well she could walk. She started moving slowly, holding the side of the bed with her right hand for support. Here she noticed a little weakness that hadn't been there before the injury. The joint still wasn't one hundred percent, but the amount of healing that had occurred was impressive nonetheless.

"You'll still need a couple days to completely heal, but as you can see most of your mobility has returned," said Doctor Ellerbeck from behind Breeah, surprising her. She turned to face the Doctor.

"These biobots, as you call them, are impressive. I would never have imagined healing in such a short time."

"They are extremely versatile. This technology has virtually eliminated the need for invasive procedures such as surgery. In essence, the surgery is conducted on the inside without collateral damage to healthy tissue."

Breeah just shook her head. The wonders on board this ship seemed limitless. "Did the Diakans give you the biobots too?"

"Most of our technology is Diakan based, although much of it has been altered to suit our needs. Much of our technology base had been destroyed when the Juttari conquered us. Our infrastructure has been built around whatever technology we managed to keep from the occupation, and the technology the Diakans gave us. But we are an inventive species. Once we understood the technology we began making our own advances in all areas of science. The alien technology is a good foundation, but we had to learn how to adapt and customize it to serve our needs."

Breeah knew something about adapting to a situation. She was starting to realize that these people, even with all their miracles, were not much different from her and her people. The real difference between the two was that these people had subjected themselves to alien rule, first as slaves, and now as citizens of an alien empire.

Her people, however, had always chosen freedom. Even though that meant living under difficult conditions, it was better than submitting to alien masters. No amount of comfort or luxury can replace your freedom. This was something she had been taught since she was a child. It was something taught to all Reiver children. Your freedom is sacred.

Breeah's thoughts returned to the Diakans and their attempted takeover. She again wondered what would happen now that the Diakans on board had been defeated. The question would have to wait, though. "Doctor, when can Anki and I return to our quarters?"

"Right now, if you want. Just take it easy and I will follow up with you in a couple of days."

CHAPTER 47

When Breeah arrived at her quarters she couldn't believe the havoc that had been wreaked on them. So much for taking it easy she thought, and started picking up furniture and putting it back where it belonged. She had Anki sit off to the side until she managed to get at all the broken glass and make sure there were no hazards lying in wait for her to step on. Then she allowed Anki to burn off some energy. The little girl was more than happy to oblige, and she danced around the room, singing, and spinning, and acting as if nothing had happened. To her it all was probably ancient history by now anyway. Breeah was in awe of her resilience.

She turned back to her work and was soon interrupted by the computer's announcement that the Captain requested entrance. She told the computer to let him in and walked to the door to greet him. When he entered she noticed there was something different about him, but she couldn't place it.

"Hello Breeah," said Jon.

"Hello Captain."

Anki noticed his entrance and ran over to him, giving him a big hug on arrival. The Captain smiled and rubbed her back with one of his large hands.

"Hey kid," he said, looking down at the little girl.

"Hi," she replied, looking up at him with a beaming grin.

Done with her greeting Anki ran off to resume her play. Soon she was spinning around the room and singing songs again.

"I wanted to see how you two were doing," he said to Breeah. "I'm sorry about everything that happened with the Diakans. You shouldn't have had to go through all of that. It must have been terrible."

"No Captain, it is I who is sorry. I am afraid if not for us you would have never been put in such a position. Our existence has caused you no shortage of problems."

"Nonsense. It's not like you made them take you hostage. They saw you as an easy opportunity to gain leverage against me."

"They miscalculated."

"Yes, they sure did," he said laughing. "The way you defended yourself against Kinos is remarkable. It's not like he was a pushover."

"He underestimated my abilities. A costly mistake. He should have bound my limbs like he had done with Chief St. Clair. Then I would have been helpless against him. He gave me the advantage of surprise and that cost him his life."

"Even with the element of surprise, you were fighting a Diakan security expert. He would have been trained in all forms of combat. Defeating someone like that is no small task."

"All Reivers are trained in armed and unarmed combat since childhood, Captain. We are all essentially security experts. Still, I'm afraid I have put you in a difficult position."

"Don't worry. I never liked Tallos much anyway." He said, smiling.

"What will you do now, Captain?"

"Well first we're going to go back and rescue your people."

Breeah was shocked. "But Captain, you can't be serious."

Jon shrugged. "I'm very serious. This is not a fight I am walking away from."

She couldn't believe what she was hearing. Was this man trying to get them all killed? "Captain, I told you before, you do not need to concern yourself with my people."

"I'm sorry Breeah, but I'm not doing this for you. Those are people out there. Humans. I can't just leave them to be slaughtered like a pen full of hogs. I have to help them. And I'm going to need you to give me the coordinates of the colony."

Breeah studied him trying to decide whether or not he hadn't lost his sanity. She realized there was nothing she could do to stop him. Even if she held back the location of the colony, he would still go back and engage the Kemmar. This man did not change his mind easily.

"What of the Diakans?"

"You don't need to concern yourself with them anymore. They are safely locked away and won't bother you again."

Sighing she relented. "Very well, Captain, I will give you the information you request. But I must tell you that what you are doing is madness."

Jon shrugged. "I've been hearing that a lot lately."

CHAPTER 48

The smoke seared her nose and throat when she inhaled. She tried to cough as much of it out as possible, but it was too thick. She kept breathing the fumes in, coughing in violent spasms with each breath. She clenched her eyes closed to make them to stop stinging, but the pain didn't go away. She often pretended to disappear by shutting her eyes. She hoped it would happen now and she would be transported anywhere else. But the smoke was still there and she buried her face in her pillow to try and keep it out of her lungs.

Outside the loud sounds began again and their force made her bed shudder more each time. She held onto her bed rail with all her strength, afraid the bed would jump up at any moment and throw her across the room. She tried again to open her eyes and see, but they couldn't penetrate the heavy fog that had filled her room, and the salty tears blurred what little was still visible.

At least her bunny was still there beside her pillow. She reached for it and held it close, pressing it against her cheek. Its soft white fur provided some much needed comfort. She whispered to it, "Don't worry bunny, I'll keep you safe."

Suddenly there was another loud bang, this one seemingly right outside her window. Her bed now shook violently forcing her to grab onto the bed rail once more. There were more loud bangs. They came quickly, one after the other, and her bed was practically hopping across her room. She squeezed the pegs of her bed rail with all her strength until it started to wobble and she worried that it would break.

"Lynda!? Lynda!?" She heard her mother calling. Her voice was muffled but she still recognized it and the mere sound set her off, screaming and crying.

"Mama! Mama!" she wailed.

Her mother rushed into her room, crouched low, holding a cloth across her mouth, and fighting a coughing fit. Lynda pulled herself up onto her knees, shot her arms up, fingers stretching as far as they could, still crying, but relieved now that her mother was there. She saw the cloth drop from her face as her mother's arms reached down for her, scooping her by the armpits and hoisting her up from her bed.

She was in her mother's arms now and finally felt safe. Her mother turned and headed back into the fog, but where was her cloth? Lynda looked back to see where it fell and realized she had left her bunny on the bed.

"Bunny!" she called, but her mother kept going. She watched her bunny explode into flames, and screamed.

Commander Lynda Wolfe gasped and her eyes opened. For a few seconds she was disoriented and instinctively covered her mouth. Looking around she realized where she was and dropped her hand onto the bed. For a few moments she lay there, staring at the ceiling, trying to calm her racing heart. She took several deep breaths, in through her nose and out through her mouth, until her pulse slowed back to normal.

She rolled over, and reached across her bed for the glass of water on her side table. Sitting up she took a long drink. Her throat felt dry and irritated, and the cool water felt good going down. She kept drinking until she emptied the glass. Setting the glass back down she pulled herself over and swung her legs around, dropping them off the side of the bed. She rubbed the sleep from her eyes and forced herself to get up.

Still groggy she looked over at her clock. It verified that yet again she didn't get enough sleep. *One of these days this is going to catch up to you*, she thought. She slowly walked into the bathroom, undressed, turned on the shower and walked in. The water was hot, almost too hot, but she liked it that way. The steady stream pulsed over the back of her neck, loosening the tense muscles that were perennially knotted there, and helping her focus.

Instantly she started running through mental checklists, planning out the day and prioritizing duties. She ran over each of the ship's departments in her mind, remembering their status, and preparing for her morning progress report. She liked being busy. She didn't want any idle time. It made her think too much and she only wanted to think about her duties. Maybe one day when she was too old for active duty she might let herself do some thinking, but then that might prove dangerous. She imagined that even when she was retired she would still find things to keep her body busy and keep her mind occupied.

Finishing her shower she stepped out and stood in front of the mirror. The dark circles under her eyes were becoming a permanent feature. Her mother had dark circles under her eyes too. At least that was how she remembered her. She wondered how accurate her memories were. Did she still remember her, or was it something her mind made up?

"Stop it," she said, chastising the mirror. Her eyes looked angry now and the dark circles gave her a fierce look, like she had war paint on. *Better*, she thought, nodding to the reflection. She picked up her toothbrush and went back to her mental checklists.

When she finished brushing her teeth and drying her hair she stepped out of the bathroom and walked over to one of the walls which slid open to reveal a hidden closet containing a row of pressed uniforms on hangers. They used to be so important to her. She spent her whole life working towards the right to wear those uniforms. And now? What was the point? They meant nothing.

You're just full of self-pity today. Snap out of it, she thought.

Shaking her head she pulled the nearest uniform off the hanger and proceeded to get dressed. The uniforms were still important. They had to retain their structure. Without it there would be no order and everything would fall apart. She knew that. Cursing at herself for being so self-indulgent she finished dressing and headed for the door.

Turning before walking out she looked back at her bed and thought about her bunny. Why did she remember it so clearly? Even in her dreams in that smoke filled room she could make out every detail, yet she always saw her mother with a cloth on her face. Even when she dropped the cloth her face wasn't visible. Why?

There's that self-pity again. Forget the damned bunny.

If only it was that easy. She must have seen that bunny a million times in her dreams over the years. Maybe one day, after she had retired, she would go see a shrink and have them explain to her how the bunny represented the day the child in her died, or some bullshit like that. Maybe they'd tell her that it stood for her mother. If they were really ambitious they might convince her that it was some side of her personality.

Enough already. Get your shit together. Clenching her teeth she straightened her uniform, swept a hand over her hair, turned and walked out the door.

The corridors were busy as usual. The crew went about their duties as though nothing had changed. As far as they knew, that was the case. She was sure that none of them had considered the fact that they probably wouldn't see the Sol System again. They couldn't tell the crew that part. At least not yet, anyway.

Would they continue with their duties if they knew? Would they still wear their uniforms? They would have to if they wanted to stay on board the Hermes. Then again, it wasn't like they had much of a choice. They had no way of getting back home without the Hermes. No, the real fear was mutiny. She didn't think they would mutiny, but anything was possible. After a few years out here they may start getting all sorts of ideas. A bunch of treasonous officers in the brig might look pretty good to them. Perhaps they would free the Diakans and head back to Sol with their tails between their legs?

None of that mattered today, however. And she wasn't a fortune teller. The truth was nobody knew what would happen over the next week, never mind the next year, so there was no point worrying about it. The less the crew knew the better. The best thing for them was to focus on their duties, not to ponder 'what ifs'.

The most important part of her duties right now was to make sure the Hermes was ready for the next encounter with the Kemmar, so her first stop was Engineering. The visit wasn't entirely work related, though. She hadn't seen Raj since Sol, and missed him. With all that had happened, she needed to see his face.

When she arrived at Engineering she found Raj standing by one of the giant reactors reading a report. As usual, he was so immersed in what he was doing that he didn't even notice her approach.

"Good morning, Raj," she said.

Her voice startled him, making him jerk his head up from the report. He looked at her with wide eyes, which then settled once his mind registered who had spoken.

"Good morning, Lynda," he said.

She smiled at him, already feeling better about everything. He didn't return her smile. Instead a look of concern spread across his face.

"Is everything ok?" she said.

"No, I don't think everything is even close to being ok. Lynda, what is going on? Why did the Marines shoot and kill the Diakan Engineering Adviser?"

Wolfe frowned. She needed to bring Raj up to speed. "Can we discuss this in your office?"

"Yes, follow me." Raj led her to the back of Engineering. A door opened and they entered a cluttered room. There were a couple of chairs and a desk. The door closed behind them and Raj turned to face her, not bothering to sit down. "So what is going on?"

"The Diakans tried to take over the ship."

"What? Why?"

"They didn't like that the Captain picked a fight with the Kemmar."

"But they are only advisers. It is not their place to question command decisions."

"Apparently they were more than advisers. They produced a Space Force command chip which gave them mission oversight. It also gave them authority to take command of the Hermes if the mission was threatened."

"Their actions were legal?"

"No. They overreached their authority, and they took hostages to coerce the Captain into surrendering."

"I see. So the hostages weren't enough to convince the Captain?"

"Oh they were. They weren't enough to convince me."

"Oh no, what did you do Lynda?"

"My job. I'm responsible for the Captain's safety. The Captain had surrendered, but I refused to let them take him or the ship."

"But if he had surrendered?"

"The only way the Captain would surrender control of the ship would be under duress. Their actions were illegal, so I stopped them."

"And may I ask who they had taken hostage?"

"The Reiver woman and her daughter. They had Chief St. Clair as well."

"They took a mother and her child hostage?"

"Yes."

"You did the right thing. That was unacceptable, even for a Diakan. But why did they kill Boufos?"

"The Marines were going to arrest him, but he ran. We hadn't found the hostages yet and needed to prevent any contact with whoever had them. The Marines were authorized to use deadly force."

"I see. Did you recover the hostages?"

"Yes. They are safe."

"Good." Raj studied her with those analytical eyes. "You look tired, Lynda."

"I didn't sleep well."

"The nightmares again?"

"Yes."

Raj gave her a sympathetic look and shook his head. "So what happens now?"

"The Diakans are in the brig, where they'll stay, and we'll continue on with our mission."

"And Space Force? How will they see all this?"

"The Diakans acted illegally."

"Yes, but will Space Force agree?"

Lynda paused, unsure how much she should say. Raj looked at her and nodded.

"Space Force will side with the Diakans, won't they?"

Lynda looked into his eyes, trying to see how he felt about what he said, but found no clues. "Yes, Raj. We believe that Space Force will side with the Diakans."

Raj nodded. "So we will not return to Sol."

The way he said it stunned her. It wasn't a question. There was no emotion at all. Rather, it was like he had just solved a math problem.

He didn't wait for her to answer. "This must be devastating for you. Space Force has been your life for as long as I've known you."

"Don't worry about me. I'll be fine."

But she knew he saw right through her. He knew she was far from fine. And when he took a step closer and wrapped his arms around her she couldn't hold back any longer. All the emotions she had struggled to keep bottled up inside came pouring out.

CHAPTER 49

Jon was eager to get back into action. The repairs had taken longer than they should have and his worry for the Reivers intensified. His main concern was that the Hermes would be ready for battle, so he made repairs to the armor plating a priority. Still, reinforcing a damaged hull took time, even with the AI coordinating the repair bots. There was nothing they could do but sit and wait for the job to be finished. Now that the repairs were done, however, he wanted to get back to work.

"Sound general quarters," he said.

The general quarters announcement sounded throughout the ship telling everyone to man their stations and prepare for combat. The bridge and the rest of the ship illuminated with a distinct red hue, reinforcing the announcement.

Helm, initiate jump countdown."

"Initiating jump countdown," said Richards.

The computer started its countdown and everybody prepared for what was to come. Jon noticed that there was a marked difference in the crew's attitude. There was a bit of nervousness, as would be expected, but it was now accompanied by a steady resolve. They knew what to expect, and they knew the dangers. They showed no signs of panic, or exuberance. They were just determined to get the job done. He approved.

The crew had all been briefed on the plan. They were going to jump in some distance from the jump gate, take some quick scans, and jump out. This way they would know what they were dealing with before engaging the Kemmar. Then, depending on whether they were dealing with one large battleship, or several smaller ships, they would take the appropriate action.

"Jump complete."

The Hermes landed between one of the system's planets and its moon. This hopefully would allow them to take some scans without being noticed. They would only be there for a few moments, and if the battleship wasn't looking or scanning in their direction, they might not be detected. The sensor operator immediately began scanning and at the same time the jump countdown commenced. Within seconds they were back where they had started.

"Report."

"Scans are showing no contacts," said the sensor operator.

"Are you sure, Ensign?" said Jon.

"Yes, Sir," said the Ensign, still studying her console. "No contacts. Scans show no other ships in the system."

Jon looked over at Wolfe. "What do you think, Commander?"

"They might have gone back across the gate. Maybe they needed to go back for repairs?"

"Or maybe they're setting a trap for us. I guess we'll soon find out. Set coordinates to jump back in just outside the asteroid field, close to the coordinates of the Reiver colony."

Breeah had relented and given Jon the coordinates to the colony. Jon had made it clear he wasn't leaving the colonists, so there was no point in keeping the location a secret any longer. She had also given them the frequency that would deactivate the asteroid plasma cannons as well as the camouflage grid surrounding the colony and hiding it from view.

The Hermes landed back in the binary star system just outside its asteroid field. They scanned again, but still there was no sign of the Kemmar battleship. After recent events he fully expected to be in a full scale battle by now, but the system was quiet. Too quiet. Even the Kemmar drones were gone.

He shrugged. "Helm, take us into the asteroid field to the coordinates of the Reiver colony."

"Yes, Sir."

The Hermes slowly entered the familiar asteroid field. At the same time it was broadcasting on the necessary frequency which would tell the asteroid defenses that they were a friendly ship. While the broadcast would tell the colony that they were friendly, Jon knew that they might not actually believe it and take action against the Hermes. He hoped it would not come to that.

He knew that the colony had the ability to monitor recent events. They would have witnessed the battle with the Kemmar, but they also would have seen Jon destroy the two Reiver ships. As far as they knew the Hermes was a hostile vessel, and the battle with the Kemmar didn't necessarily change that. For this reason, Jon had Breeah add a message to the broadcast letting the colony know that the Hermes was not their enemy. Still, they might think that she was forced to do so.

So far, the plan seemed to be working. The plasma cannons didn't fire and there was no need for any stunt flying like before. Richards maneuvered around the large rocks easily, and the familiar sound of the small rocks rapping against the hull resonated throughout the ship.

Before long they had reached the coordinates for the Reiver colony. From what Breeah had told him, the colony actually used several large asteroids. There was one central asteroid which was where most of the population lived. The other neighboring asteroids were used for different functions. One of the large rocks, for example, served as a spaceport, and housed their ships. Another, was used for repairs and fabrication. Shuttles were used to ferry people and supplies between each rock.

A special camouflage grid was used to keep the whole operation hidden from scans. It consisted of multiple satellites surrounding the colony and disguised as asteroids themselves which then projected the camouflage grid around the Reivers' homes. Once the grid was in place, anybody looking or scanning in this direction would see nothing more than asteroids.

The technology had limits, however. If a ship approached the location and took a closer look they might be able to uncover the hidden colony. To avoid this the Reivers had installed the plasma cannon defenses throughout the field. They ensured there would be enough firepower to destroy, or at least discourage anyone from getting too close to discover them.

"Arriving at coordinates, Sir," said Richards.

"Full stop," said Jon.

"Reading full stop."

Jon and the rest of the bridge crew stared in horror at the viewscreen. Where there was supposed to be a grid of satellites protecting the colony, there was only debris. The Kemmar had found them.

"Helm, take us in for a closer look," said Jon, breaking the silence.

The Hermes moved past the satellite debris. Once inside, they crept up to the main asteroid where the colonists were supposed to live. The asteroid itself was large, roughly the size of a small moon. Domed structures connected by a complex web of transport tubes covered the surface. Jon knew from discussions with Breeah that some of those domes housed colonists, while others were responsible for power generation, food and water supplies, fabrication, education, and pretty much anything else required that the Reivers could produce.

It was supposed to all be humming with activity as people went about their daily routines. Instead, much of it was now in ruins and more debris floated around them like a celestial graveyard. There could be no doubt now, the Kemmar had attacked the colony. Looking at the wreckage Jon noticed that several domes were not damaged. If the Kemmar wanted to destroy the colony everything would have been turned to dust. Why were some structures still standing?

Jon opened a comm with Breeah. She should have a view of the wreckage from her window. "Breeah, are you seeing this?"

"Yes, Captain."

Jon was struck at how calm her voice was. She never stopped surprising him. "I'm seeing several structures still intact. The colony's computer systems might still be operational. I'd like to find out what happened here. Is there any way we can access them?"

"Yes there is. I can provide you with access instructions, but I do not have full clearance."

"Our AI can deal with that once we establish a connection. The important thing is to find out if there are any systems we can access first. Hopefully they weren't all destroyed."

"Yes, let's hope so. I will send you all the information needed to establish a connection."

"Thank you, Breeah. I will keep you updated."

Jon closed the comm and looked at Commander Wolfe. "Commander, when Breeah sends those codes have the AI take over the colony's network and access its security systems so we can find out what happened here."

"Yes, Sir."

Wolfe fed the data into the AI which then initiated its electronic assault.

"Pinging planetary computer system," said the AI. "Receiving response from system. Sending login information. Login accepted. Account privileges are restricted. Initiating takeover of planetary system."

The AI began a massive brute force attack of the colony's computer systems, which were woefully unprepared for its electronic warfare capabilities. In no time the AI was burrowing a path through the network, moving up the access hierarchy until it finally gained access to the security systems.

"Takeover complete," said the AI.

"Display information relating to Kemmar attack of the colony."

"There is video footage of this event. Would you prefer viewing the video, or the security logs?"

"Display video."

The viewscreen switched from its view of the colony wreckage, to the security video. The bridge watched as the video showed the Kemmar warships destroying the camouflage grid and approaching the colony. The Reivers resisted but were no match for Kemmar firepower which proceeded to lay waste to any Reiver defenses.

When the ships stopped firing, instead of completely destroying the colony, they launched dozens of shuttles, which proceeded to land on the asteroid. Kemmar soldiers then spilled out of the shuttles in full battle armor and poured into the colony's transport tubes. The Reivers tried to fight off the invaders but were no match for the armored Kemmar soldiers and were soon overcome.

But the Kemmar weren't killing the defenders. It appeared as though they were simply stunning them. The Kemmar quickly swept through the complex. Though not one Reiver surrendered and all fought with any weapon they had access to, in the end they had no chance.

Jon's stomach turned as he watched the Kemmar load the unconscious humans onto the shuttles. When the operation was concluded the shuttles returned to their ships and the Kemmar left the asteroid field. The video showed the Kemmar ships come together again and form a larger ship, although not as large as the one they first encountered. The battleship then headed for the jump gate and disappeared back into Kemmar space.

Jon leaned back into his chair and rubbed his chin with his thumb and finger. He stared at the viewscreen in silence. The Kemmar had taken them prisoner. From what Breeah had told him that meant slavery. He couldn't allow that to happen. He had to do something.

"Commander Wolfe, Chief St. Clair, meet me in my ready room."

CHAPTER 50

"AI, based on information gained from the captured Kemmar warship, can you speculate where the Kemmar would take the human prisoners?" said Jon.

Commander Wolfe and Chief St. Clair both sat across from him and Jon didn't need his heightened senses to tell that all the recent events had them both on edge.

"Non-Kemmar prisoners are taken to a planet known as Kerces. They are taken to an installation on the planet where they are reprogrammed so as to make them useful to the Kemmar Empire."

"You mean they are brainwashed and turned into Kemmar slaves," said Kevin.

"Yes, that is a reasonable interpretation of the data," said the AI. "The Kemmar Empire controls a vast galactic slave trade. The Empire itself is diverse and consists of thousands of different species. There are also multiple affiliate cultures that while friendly, are not members of the Empire. The slave trade is active throughout the Empire as well as within these affiliated systems. Conquest is used to expand territory and to supply inventory for this slave trade. If a slave is not controllable it cannot be sold. Kerces fulfills this need by reprogramming prisoners. Those who cannot be reprogrammed are considered useless and terminated."

A cold chill slowly crawled up Jon's back making him shudder. The Kemmar were slavers. No better than the Juttari. Perhaps even worse. The Juttari used captured populations for their own needs, whereas the Kemmar used them as products to be sold.

"Is Kerces the only planet used for this function?"

"No. There are many planets throughout the Empire serving this function. Kerces is the closest and therefore the logical destination."

"AI, display Kerces's location on viewscreen."

Wolfe and Kevin both swiveled their chairs around to see the viewscreen that appeared on the wall behind them. It flickered on and an image of a grayish blue planet appeared. Kerces looked to be an icy, desolate place, inhospitable for the development of any type of civilization. A great place to take prisoners. Even if they could escape from wherever they were held, where would they go?

"AI, display the flight path the Kemmar battleship would need to take from the jump gate to the planet Kerces."

The viewscreen zoomed out from the planet to display a wide swath of Kemmar space overlaid with a dotted yellow line indicating the logical flight path the battleship would likely travel to the planet."

Jon looked back to Kevin and Wolfe. "We could cross the gate and jump ahead of the battleship and lay an ambush for it."

Kevin and Wolfe swiveled back to face Jon. "Some well-placed gravity mines would help even the odds. We could mine their space lane and once the mines detonated we could jump in and finish the job," said Kevin.

"But then we would still have to board the battleship and rescue the Reivers," said Wolfe.

"True. We'd take heavy casualties boarding that ship," said Kevin.

"They could kill off the Reivers before we got close to them," said Jon. "Ok, so boarding the battleship is not a good option. How about the planet?"

"Depending on the planet's defenses a planetary assault might be a better option. The Hermes could provide orbital support for the strike teams making the job easier," said Kevin.

"AI, analyze the Kerces planetary defenses," said Jon.

The viewscreen showed an image of the icy planet once more and zoomed in closer revealing numerous orbiting satellites. "Kerces is defended by an orbital defense grid located at medium orbit. There is a restricted security perimeter around the planet. Unauthorized vessels entering this perimeter are fired on by the defense grid."

"Do we have enough information on Kerces to plot its precise coordinates into the jump system?"

"The seized Kemmar database has provided the coordinates for all planets within the Kemmar Empire."

"Do we have enough information to jump into low orbit around Kerces just inside the defense grid?"

"Yes, the coordinates are available for this task."

"Will the defense grid fire on us if we do?"

"The grid's purpose is to defend against attacking ships. It is assumed that those ships would be approaching the planet from outside the grid. As a precaution against the grid being used to attack the planet itself, the satellites were made to only point outward. Therefore, if the Hermes were to jump into low orbit within the defense grid, it would not be fired upon."

"What about the planet's gravitational pull? Is the jump system capable of landing the Hermes in low orbit without inadvertently causing us to enter the planet's atmosphere?"

"The Kemmar database provides enough data to calculate a precise landing into low orbit without causing any undue stress on the Hermes or its systems."

"Good. Do you have any information on the location where the prisoners will be taken?"

The viewscreen zoomed in further to reveal the planet's icy surface and magnified the planet's southern hemisphere. It sailed over frozen mountains, their glistening peaks like frigid claws gashing the sky, and then dropped into a wide valley and eventually zeroed in on a complex of buildings.

"Analyze installation's defenses."

"The defenses are limited. The installation was designed to keep prisoners in, rather than keeping invaders out. It was likely assumed that the orbital defense grid was protection enough. There are automated defense systems setup on the complex's perimeter." The viewscreen zoomed in again to show and array of weapon towers encircling the buildings. "They are intended to be used against escaping prisoners, but can also be used against an attacking force. Defense systems are primarily energy weapon based."

"Thank you, AI."

"You are welcome, Captain."

Wolfe and Kevin turned their chairs back to face Jon. Kevin spoke first. "I see where you're going with this, Sir. We jump into low orbit, take out the installation's defenses, and send down assault teams to liberate the prisoners."

"That sounds about right," said Jon

"What if that battleship is still there?" said Wolfe.

"AI, how long will it take for the Kemmar battleship to reach Kerces?"

"Traveling at its average speed, the battleship will arrive at Kerces in thirty-four days."

"I'm assuming the battleship won't stay much longer than what is required to drop off their prisoners. They'll need repairs among other things. Here is what I am thinking. We cross the gate and then jump to a remote location of Kemmar space to hold position there for as long as it would take for the battleship to arrive, unload the prisoners and get underway. We jump close enough to Kerces so we can have a look, but remain out of range of their defense grid. If everything is clear we jump into low orbit inside the defense grid and begin the rescue operations. Thoughts?"

"It's risky, but it can work," said Kevin. "I will personally lead the assault teams. We'll get the job done."

"I'm sure you will. I almost feel sorry for the Kemmar."

Kevin responded with a big toothy smile.

"Commander, what about you?"

"I don't know. We are working with a lot of 'ifs', and we don't know how accurate that data is."

"I agree, but it's the only intelligence we have."

"I suppose we'll have to make it work."

"Good. We can use the wait time to get everything to 100%. I want to be underway within the hour. No point sitting around here waiting for another Kemmar battleship to cross through the gate."

CHAPTER 51

The Hermes left the asteroid field headed for the jump gate. The two suns shot streams of light across the viewscreen. They both still grappled with each other, and they would continue to do so for millions of years until one finally emerged victorious.

Jon was happy to leave the two stars behind. He looked forward to crossing the gate into Kemmar space. While they still needed to rescue the colonists, they'd be in an unexplored region of the galaxy, far from Sol, Diakus, and the Juttari.

"Approaching jump gate coordinates," said Richards.

"Ping the gate," said Jon.

"Pinging gate."

Directly in front of the Hermes the jump gate began to appear. It started as a faint shimmer which transformed into a massive, circular translucent field.

"Set course to enter gate."

The Hermes entered the translucent field and disappeared, as did the gate once they had crossed. The Hermes exited through another translucent field and entered a previously unknown region of space. There were no nearby planets or stars, and Jon could see how the Reivers were able to cross through the gate for so long without being detected.

The Hermes would now jump one more time to a remote region of Kemmar space the AI had selected. There they would wait until the opportune time when they would initiate their assault of the Kerces complex.

CHAPTER 52

"Really Doctor, we're fine," said Breeah. Doctor Ellerbeck stared back at her from the display, the pitying look on her face making Breeah's jaw tighten.

"It's just that you've had several traumatic experiences lately, and now seeing your home destroyed, I'm worried about how it is affecting you," said Ellerbeck.

"It is nothing I cannot handle. I am a Reiver, Doctor."

"You are a human first. There is only so much trauma the human body can take."

"Hardship is part of the Reiver way of life. As you can see I have not been traumatized."

"Just because you can hide your emotions, doesn't mean they aren't there. How about Anki? How is she holding up?"

Breeah looked over at Anki happily playing with one of the toys the Captain had fabricated for her. "She is doing fine as well. You are looking for problems where none exist."

"Look, I'm just concerned about you. At least promise me that you won't hesitate to contact me if you…"

"Yes Doctor, I will come see you right away if anything changes. Now if you'll excuse me I have things to do." Breeah terminated the connection without waiting for Ellerbeck to respond. She liked Doctor

Ellerbeck, but her questions were offensive. She was not weak, and neither was her child. She looked back over at Anki who was now singing a song and making her toys dance. Her smile returned.

"Captain Pike requests entrance," said the computer.

"Enter," said Breeah, walking to the door. It opened and the Captain walked in. "Hello Captain, what brings you this way?"

"Hello Breeah, I wanted to see how you and Anki were holding up."

"Are you here to question our strength as well?" Breeah said with a scowl. "I assure you Captain you will find no weakness here."

"Hey, slow down, I'm not accusing you of anything."

"Really? Are you not concerned that I will fall apart? Lose my sanity?"

"No. Not at all. Where's all this coming from?"

Breeah exhaled and let her shoulders relax. The feeling surprised her. She hadn't realized how much tension she had been carrying. "I'm sorry Captain. I was just speaking with Doctor Ellerbeck who was very concerned about how all the recent events had been affecting us."

"She is just doing her job. You're a member of this crew now and your health is her responsibility."

"I know she meant well. Her questions just angered me. My father did not raise me to be weak."

"I can see that. Trust me Breeah, nobody on board this ship thinks you're weak."

"I am not. And neither is my daughter."

"Of course not. Still, seeing your home in ruins must be upsetting. It certainly upset me."

"We know the risks of our way of life. It would have been better had they not been taken prisoner, though. For a Reiver, slavery is worse than death."

"Well, I'm also here to tell you that we're going to rescue your people."

"What are you saying, Captain? My people are lost. There is no rescue for them."

"I think there is. We've got a pretty good idea where the Kemmar are taking them and we're going after them."

He was insane. Truly insane. What was this obsession he had with saving her people? "Captain, I have told you before, forget my people. They are lost. Save your crew. You do not need to put them in danger again. You have done enough already."

"The Kemmar are likely taking your people to a planet called Kerces. It is something of a prison planet. Once the battleship drops them off and leaves the system we will conduct a rescue operation and free them."

"Now you are going to attack a Kemmar planet? Was the battleship not enough?"

"Trust me Breeah, we can do this."

"If you succeed? What then? You do not know my people. They may not want to follow your orders."

"I know that they're human, and that's enough for me. If they don't want to stay on board I can drop them off somewhere, but I'm not going to stand by while the Kemmar turn them into mindless slaves."

He wasn't just insane. He was infuriating. And stubborn. He did not listen to reason. *Ancestors help us all.*

CHAPTER 53

Kevin ducked as Sergeant Henderson's fist grazed the top of his head. A split second later Kevin had his hands in front of his face deflecting a rather vicious looking knee strike. Other than Captain Pike, Sergeant Henderson was the only man he knew who could give him a good, honest workout and he was proving to be up to the task today.

Before Henderson could shift his balance Kevin stepped in and landed a powerful elbow into his ribs. The sparring suit registered the force of the blow and announced that three ribs were fractured with a possible punctured lung. While the force of the blow threw Henderson sideways a few feet, the sparring suit protected him from any injury.

The sparring suit was a versatile piece of equipment that accommodated training in a diverse range of conditions. It could simulate combat suit conditions, allowing one to move with the same agility and speed that a combat suit would bestow. It could also simulate unprotected combat, show the results of blows to unprotected parts of the body, and even restrict movement of that part of the body to simulate combat while injured. There were also settings for weapon simulations allowing for training with everything from blades to energy weapons. Short of real combat experience, the sparring suit was that best way to stay ready for battle.

"Ok Chief, how about we make this a little more interesting and get rid of the gravity?"

“Sounds like fun,” said Kevin, a big smile spreading across his face. “Initiate zero gravity conditions.”

The artificial gravity in the room was removed and the two men simultaneously pushed off the floor towards each other. Henderson was first to strike spinning around in the air and sending a hard heel kick towards Kevin’s sternum. Surprised by the speed of Henderson’s attack, Kevin didn’t have time to change his own offensive posture to a defensive one and was barely able to get an arm in front of his chest. The kick landed just above Kevin’s elbow and sent him spinning backward head over feet, the blow hard enough to register a fractured arm.

Henderson used the force of the strike to spin away. He pushed off the floor with his hands and sent his body sideways toward the nearest wall. When he reached it, he used his feet to shoot himself toward Kevin’s still flipping frame.

Kevin saw the Sergeant flying at him head first and tried tucking in his arms and legs to present a smaller target, but again the Sergeant was too fast. Once in range, Henderson came down hard with a powerful hammer fist strike and drove Kevin into the floor. While the suit protected him from the impact, it also registered massive injuries including a broken back. The fight was over.

“Computer, return gravity to normal conditions,” said Kevin. Both men maneuvered their bodies to land on their feet when the artificial gravity pulled them back down to the floor. Kevin walked over to Henderson and nodded. “Nice finish.”

“Thanks Chief,” said Henderson.

“One day I’m going to beat you in zero gravity.”

“Maybe. And one day I’m going to beat you in full gravity hand to hand.”

“Let’s not get carried away,” said Kevin laughing and slapped Henderson on the back.

CHAPTER 54

Jon studied the information on his display. They had ample time to prepare for the assault on Kerces and he took full advantage to learn as much about the Kemmar as possible. The database from the captured Kemmar ship proved to be an invaluable intelligence source.

Considering the size of the Kemmar Empire, he found it surprising that nobody had heard of them before. Their Empire seemed to occupy a galactic sweet spot which neither Juttari nor Diakan had explored. He wondered how many other undiscovered empires existed in the galaxy. The Kemmar had not known about jump technology until they found the gate, and the gate itself was in a remote area of Kemmar space. It was entirely possible that no other gates existed in their territory.

That in and of itself fascinated Jon. The Kemmar Empire was quite large. The fact that they controlled so much territory without gates was truly impressive. According to the database the Kemmar civilization began on a planet known simply as Kemm. Multiple races inhabited Kemm, but one race in particular rose to dominate the rest. This race called themselves Kemmar. They were aggressive and believed in their inherent right to rule all those around them. The Kemmar were superior in strength, and easily overwhelmed the other races. The Kemmar seized power early on and held it unopposed for millennia.

The result of this was a sense of inherent superiority. The other races existed for no other purpose than to be useful to the Kemmar. And they fell into line. It was like some bizarre pack mentality taken to an extreme end. The Kemmar were the alphas and the other races accepted this and remained permanently submissive. Where it suited the Kemmar they enslaved, and where it didn't they allowed them some measure of freedom. But there was no mistaking that any freedom enjoyed remained a Kemmar gift.

Eventually the Kemmar discovered space travel and took to the stars. Once equipped with FTL technology, they discovered other inhabited worlds and peoples of varying levels of advancement. When they made their first contact, they assumed that since they were the more technologically advanced race, that the inhabitants would simply accept Kemmar rule without argument. Some inhabitants had other ideas. They resisted and the Kemmar were outraged. They sent in warships and bombed the planet from orbit. The survivors were turned into Kemmar slaves. This was the moment the Kemmar officially became space slavers.

As they expanded their reach, each inhabited planet they found was given an ultimatum, submit to Kemmar rule or be enslaved. Sometimes the population was so far behind the Kemmar that they weren't even given an ultimatum. The Kemmar simply moved in and did as they pleased. Eventually they encountered other advanced races. Here they showed their diplomatic ability. Rather than challenge these races and spiral into a costly war, they chose to trade. They quickly found that slaves were easy to trade, and the intergalactic slave trade was established.

Jon realized that this was why they didn't initially attack the Hermes. They could see from the Hermes that they were easily as advanced as the Kemmar, and probably didn't want to start a conflict with another advanced race. The battleship had more firepower than the Hermes, so the Kemmar likely believed they could just intimidate them now and engage in diplomacy later. They never would have expected that the Hermes would fire on them first.

But the Hermes did fire on them, and now they were going to attack one of their planets. At the very least they had become fugitives in the Kemmar Empire as well. Worst case scenario they had started a war between Sol and the Kemmar. That didn't really concern Jon. There would be plenty of time before the Kemmar ran into more Sol ships, and even then the Kemmar had no hope against the combined force of the Galactic Accord. The wars fought between the Diakans and Juttari were of a scale the Kemmar had never seen. As large as the Kemmar Empire was, they were nothing compared to the Juttari or the Diakans.

Still, the Hermes only one ship and for them they were large enough. Hell, one of their battleships was large enough. He hoped he wouldn't have to tangle with another one anytime soon. The odds were not in his favor. Once they attacked Kerces the Kemmar would come after them with a vengeance. Getting through Kemmar space was not going to be easy. It didn't matter. These Kemmar were vile creatures. He would not let humans become their slaves.

Humans. Had the Kemmar encountered the lost colonies? He searched the database for any mention of them. There was nothing under the word human. Nothing under the word Earth. He brought up a list of advanced races the Kemmar encountered. Nothing. What about the other races? Did they provide any intelligence? There. One of the merchant races had an account of an encounter with a furtive race that refused all contact. It says they were technologically advanced and that they were bipeds, but there was no information on where they were located. Still it was something. The only way to find out more would be to contact the race that made the account. They were called Ottans and they were on the other side of Kemmar space. Once the Kerces assault was over they would head for Ottan space and find out what else they knew.

CHAPTER 55

Commander Wolfe made a point of walking every section of the Hermes. She didn't need to do this. She could monitor everything on the ship from the bridge well enough. But there was something about seeing things in person that ensured top performance. She also knew that letting the crew see her take a personal interest in their day to day duties improved morale. She didn't micromanage. Her officers were more than capable of managing their sections.She preferred that the crew saw her as human, rather than some unseen power on the bridge.

On this day she checked in on the crew responsible for the ship's energy weapons. Those responsibilities included the energy weapons themselves, but more importantly their targeting systems and power source. A medium sized reactor sat in the middle of the room like a large black egg. Rather than draw power from the ship's main reactors, the energy weapons relied on their own dedicated reactor. The ship's main reactors could then act as backup power if the dedicated reactor was taken out. Upon seeing her, the crew chief stood to attention and saluted, and Wolfe returned the salute.

"Are we ready for combat?" said Wolfe. She knew the answer but it gave the crew a chance to brag a bit, and take pride in their work.

"Yes, Sir!" The crew chief was younger, but proved himself to be highly competent. He waved a hand towards the big black egg and said, "We are running at full capacity."

"Good, we'll need all of that and then some for our next mission."

"We'll be ready."

Wolfe looked over at another member of the crew. She looked very young. Almost too young. Meeting her gaze the young woman spoke up as well. "If anyone tries to stop us they'll get glassed before they know what happened, Sir."

Wolfe smiled. "You'll get a chance to make good on that promise soon enough."

"Yes, Sir," said the woman, standing straighter than before. The rest of the crew smiled and many looked like they were ready to cheer, but weren't sure it would be appropriate.

The crew responsible for the rail gun batteries were no less proud of their pets. The primary responsibility of the rail gun systems was point defense, but they could also switch to offensive mode when needed. Their ability to destroy incoming missiles made them vital to any engagement. The seriousness in their eyes told her they knew it.

Like the energy weapons the rail guns used a sophisticated targeting system, but since they had to destroy incoming ordinance, targeting was the most important feature of these weapon systems. They were primarily projectile weapons they didn't need their own power source and relied on the ship's main reactors for power like everything else. The exploding shells used by the guns enveloped the ship in a fiery shield, blocking almost all missiles from getting through. So long as the rail guns could fire, the Hermes had a defensive barrier between it and attacking missiles.

Of course that was one of the jobs of enemy energy weapons. The rail gun point defense fire did not affect them, so their tactical role was often that of taking out rail gun batteries to punch a hole in the point defense shield. For that reason, ships without energy weapons were at a severe disadvantage against the Hermes. That also made this job especially dangerous. The rail guns were often a primary target and that meant that the rail gun crew were directly in the line of fire, making their job even more stressful.

She approached the crew who were busy loading ammunition into the rail gun feeders. "What is our status," she asked the rail gun crew chief.

The chief looked up at her but his hands continued working. "All batteries are online, Sir."

"How about ammunition?"

"We are reasonably prepared. We've been fabricating shells at a decent clip and will be ready for the mission."

"Good. I know you'll have all batteries at one hundred percent."

"Yes, Sir."

She turned her attention to one of the other crew. Another young face. "How are you holding up crewman?"

"I'm doing good, Sir," he responded, his face still grim, hands still moving.

"Good. Keep it up." She gave the young man an approving smile. This crew was all business. She admired their resolve. Unfortunately that resolve was going to be tested very soon.

CHAPTER 56

The Hermes initiated its first jump into the Kerces system, and landed behind a gas giant. Using the massive planet to shield it from detection the Hermes launched a small drone. The tiny craft used stealth technology to mask its heat signature. Any long range scans from Kerces or from ships still in the system would register nothing more than a cold rock drifting in space. Once clear of the giant planet the drone took a few quick scans and returned to the Hermes, which immediately jumped back out of the Kerces system.

"Report," said Jon.

"There are no signs of the Kemmar battleship, Sir," said Petrovic.

"Any other ships?"

"No, Sir. Reading all clear."

Jon nodded and took a deep breath. "Very well, sound general quarters. All hands prepare for planetary assault."

The general quarters alarm sounded throughout the ship and the lights took on the now familiar red hue. Jon looked over at Commander Wolfe whose face retained its tightness, her eyes asking an unspoken question.

"We're ready when you are, Sir," said Wolfe.

Jon nodded and opened a comm with Kevin in the hangar bay. "Chief, are your assault teams ready?"

"We're ready to launch, Sir," said Kevin.

"Good, we'll soften them up for you."

"Thank you, Sir. We'd appreciate that."

The corners of Jon's mouth turned up slightly as he closed the comm. "Helm, prepare to jump us into low orbit around Kerces."

"Yes, Sir."

"Initiate."

The Hermes landed just inside the defense grid. The planet lay before them like a giant ice cube. On the opposite side, floating several hundred kilometers away lay the defense grid, floating death to any approaching threat.

"Report."

"Orbital defense grid is not targeting us," said Petrovic.

"What about the planet surface?"

"I am not reading any threats, but something is interfering with the scans."

"Are we being jammed?"

"I do not have enough data to say for certain, but preliminary reports indicate it may be something in the atmosphere."

"Let's hope that's all it is. Helm bring us to an orbit directly above the Kemmar prison facility."

The viewscreen display changed perspective to show the frigid planet's surface. The Hermes maneuvered between the planet and its defense grid until it was just above the prison complex.

"Establishing synchronous orbit above Kemmar prison facility," said Richards.

"Target the facility's defensive towers."

"Sir, that same interference is disrupting the targeting array," said Petrovic. "We can't reliably target the towers. If we try we might hit the complex itself."

"Belay that order. We can't risk hitting the colonists."

Jon’s shoulders tightened as he considered this development. The plan was already changing and they hadn’t even started the attack yet. He shook his head and contacted Kevin again. “Chief we have a problem. We can’t target the installation’s defensive systems. You’re going to have to take them out yourself.”

“Understood. Leave it to us.”

CHAPTER 57

The Marines boarded the assault shuttles and the hanger bay echoed with the whirring sounds of their combat suits. Ten shuttles, ten Marines per shuttle. It should be enough, thought Kevin.

The shuttles had been specially designed for missions like this. They used Diakan stealth technology to hide from enemy scans. That and their speed allowed them to covertly insert a small force into enemy territory without being noticed. Which was great if things were going according to plan. But they weren't.

Kevin had hoped for some element of surprise when assaulting the installation. Even if the Hermes pounded them from orbit, they could still surprise the Kemmar with a stealthy ground assault. But that option was off the table now. They would have to use the shuttles to directly attack the installation's defenses. They did have enough firepower to pull it off.

Each shuttle was equipped with energy weapons and a complement of missiles. More than enough. The Kemmar would know they were coming, but what could they do about it? Kevin nodded to himself, confident in his Marines' abilities, and boarded his shuttle.

The shuttle thundered with the sound of heavy boots stomping on the metal floor as the troopers found their seats. When they sat down it sounded like multiple grenades exploding. Kevin dropped into his own seat at the front of the shuttle. There was a loud bang as the locking bolt on his combat suit secured him to the shuttle. He would not be moving from that seat until it was time to disembark. Nor were any of the other Marines, whether they liked it or not.

Once secured, his visor dropped down and sealed off his suit, protecting him from any loss of pressure inside the ship. The display on his visor instantly lit up and showed him the status of his men and the other shuttles. Everyone had boarded and were locked in. They were ready.

"Thirty seconds until launch," said the shuttle's computer, confirming the data on Kevin's visor. The ship began to tremble as its engines came online. Thankfully the suit blocked out much of the outside noise and he didn't have to endure the ship's roar.

Kevin wasn't a big fan of shuttle assaults. He preferred orbital drops as a method of troop insertion. With an orbital drop, the shuttles would take his troops to the edge of the planet's atmosphere and then everyone would jump and freefall until they reached a very low altitude and only then would they deploy their chutes. A HALO drop was more covert and made it harder for the enemy to kill his troopers, since they were each a tiny, fast moving target.

An assault shuttle, on the other hand, was designed to be a combination attack craft and troop transport. While the stealth technology and armor plating provided some protection, for each one of those shuttles the enemy destroyed, multiple troopers died. They needed the shuttles to transport the colonists back to the ship, so they had no choice. Sitting there, locked into his seat he couldn't shake the feeling that he was a metallic duck in a barrel.

One by one the assault shuttles rolled off their launch pads and left the Hermes hanger bay. Kevin switched his visor's display to give him a view of the shuttles and their status. The ships regrouped just above Kerces's atmosphere and fell into a V shaped formation. They sat floating for a few moments, turned as one, and flew down towards the planet.

While the stealth technology could hide them from scans, Kevin knew that nothing could hide the blazing torch each ship created as it entered the atmosphere. The entry was accompanied by the usual amount of shaking and bouncing. His team were all experienced veterans, but he almost wished he had a rookie on board. Atmospheric entry often terrified the rookies and their fear that the ship would break apart was always a comic way of relieving some tension.

No such luck on this trip. Each and every one of his men had done this before and they were all quiet and deadly serious. They knew what their jobs were and stayed focused.

He had lost some good men in their last battle with the Kemmar, and that was on the Hermes. Now they were attacking the Kemmar in their back yard. Still the group that boarded the Hermes would be the Kemmar version of the Special Forces. Highly trained and highly capable. He couldn't see the Kemmar sending anything other than their elite to board an alien warship. The prison guards would not be as skilled, of that he was certain.

The shuttles raced down from orbit and were now streaking across the sky hugging the angles of the endless ice covered mountains. Rather than dropping straight down onto the prison where they could be easily seen and targeted, the shuttles chose a more cautious option and approached from the far side of a mountain range.

Each shuttle stayed in perfect formation, the group moving together as one. The mountains below them were stunning in their starkness. There were no trees or vegetation. No wildlife. Nothing. Just ice. From its base to its peak each mountain was covered in glistening blue sheets.

The sight was mesmerizing. Kevin had never been on an ice planet before. They were too hostile and too cost prohibitive to develop. It truly was odd that the Kemmar chose to use one. He understood that it dissuaded escape, but there were plenty of other planets that could be used which could accomplish the same thing with less cost.

They crested one final mountaintop and the installation appeared in the valley below. His visor instantly identified the defensive towers and each shuttle immediately let loose a volley of missiles at their designated targets. The missiles streaked ahead of the squadron and then dispersed, each making a beeline for its designated kill.

As anticipated, there was no missile defense in place and they all slammed into the towers. The fireballs seemed strangely out of place amidst the desolate frozen landscape, but they were immensely satisfying. There were several "Oorahs" from the Marines as each tower blew apart. Kevin himself felt a tinge of satisfaction. These were slavers. Vile creatures. They would know human wrath before the day was done.

The shuttles reached the installation and broke formation. There was still defensive fire coming from the prison and the ships brought their energy weapons online to deal with the threats. They bobbed and weaved and buzzed around like a swarm of bees, cleaning up all remaining threats with bolts of blue fire.

Kevin saw on his visor that several ships had taken fire, but the heavy armor plating ensured only minimal damage. Below some Kemmar guards suited in full combat gear had ventured outside and were firing their handheld weapons at the shuttles. It seemed odd for prison guards to be wearing combat suits. It was probably an intimidation tactic. If you were a prisoner the last thing you would do is attack a guard wearing a combat suit. Either way their fire had no effect. The shuttles were designed to withstand heavy weapon fire and personal energy weapons were not powerful enough.

A couple of Kemmar soldiers turned into more serious threats, brandishing mobile missile launchers. They became an instant priority and the shuttles turned their attention to them. Within seconds the threat was eliminated, but not without a missile being fired. The rocket raced towards Kevin's shuttle, which in turn let loose a volley of countermeasure drones. Kevin held his breath.

Their low altitude made evasion much more difficult. But the missile was deceived by the drones and exploded just behind Kevin's shuttle. The concussion bounced the shuttle around with immense force making Kevin thankful for the locking bolt. After a few terrifying seconds the shuttle regained control and resumed the attack on the prison's defenders.

The shuttles streaked to and fro, strafing and hammering all threats. It took several minutes before most of the ground fire had been eradicated. The time had come.

Kevin opened a comm with the rest of his troops. "All hands, initiate ground assault."

CHAPTER 58

Successive bangs repeated throughout the shuttle as the locking bolts released the combat suits. In turn, each Marine stood and readied their weapons. The shuttle hovered above its insertion point and a hatch slid open.

"Alright. Single file. When you drop in secure your position and wait for the order to advance," said Sergeant Henderson.

He had a smaller team of thirty men, while Kevin had seventy. His team would attack the roof of the complex, and work their way down from there. Kevin's team attacked from the ground. They would likely meet stiffer resistance and needed more firepower. Henderson's team would rely more on speed, swooping down from above and moving rapidly through the complex.

Each Marine hit the roof and quickly moved to establish a perimeter. Above them three assault shuttles hovered, ready to provide supporting fire if needed. The sergeant's visor identified a service door as the best point of entry and he ordered his men to advance.

They surrounded the door and he stepped up and tried to open it without success.

"Stanis, get up here and blow a hole through this door."

"Yes, Sir." Private Stanis stepped up to the door and the other troopers moved out of the way. Stanis brandished a large shoulder held plasma cannon which he pointed at the door and pulled the trigger.

The cannon blew a large hole in the left side of the door and the door frame. Stanis then lowered the plasma rifle and slammed a heavy boot into what was left of the door. It buckled under the force of the Private's kick and fell to the side with a screech. Stanis stepped back and two troopers flanked each side pointing their rail guns at the entrance.

Henderson waited for resistance, but no enemy fire came. He carefully peered through the doorway and saw a flight of stairs leading to an opening on the lower level. They would be waiting there.

"Johns, we need eyes in there."

"Yes, Sir," said Private Johns. He stepped forward and accessed a compartment on his suit. It opened and a mosquito sized drone flew out. The drone hovered in front of the doorway, tiny in size, almost invisible to anyone who wasn't specifically looking for it. Johns took remote control of the drone through controls on the arm of his combat suit and sent it down into the opening.

As hoped, the drone entered a large room unnoticed and transmitted a video feed to the Marines' visors showing a group of Kemmar soldiers waiting to cut down anyone coming down the stairs.

The stairway was wide enough for two troopers to descend at a time. With the enemy waiting down there, they would open fire the moment they saw boots coming down the stairs. Kevin examined the opening at the bottom. There was enough room for two to leap in. They didn't need to use the stairs. Their combat suits could easily handle a jump from that height.

"Ok, we need to move in fast and hard. No stairs. We jump in two by two. The Kemmar will open fire once they see us but if we move fast enough we should overwhelm them. Patel, and Daniels, you go in first. Stanis and Krukov, you follow right behind them."

"Yes, Sir."

With any luck the Kemmar wouldn't react fast enough to stop them. Speed was vital.

The first two troopers jumped in and rolled as soon as they hit the ground. They immediately started taking fire. Seconds later two more troopers dropped in, and they continued to drop two by two. Each time the Marines rolled as soon as they hit the floor and opened fire while seeking cover.

Henderson watched on his visor as their combat suits took hits, but the defenders seemed confused by the tactic and kept changing targets, shifting fire from one attacker to another. The result was that no trooper took enough fire to cause more than some minor damage.

Patel was the first to take advantage of the confusion jumping out and running for a pillar in the middle of the floor. One of the Kemmar started firing at him but Daniels forced him to stop with his own deadly accurate covering fire. Once Patel took cover behind the pillar he opened fire on the Kemmar positions. Daniels jumped out and ran for a closer position behind some equipment. He took more fire than Patel but made it with only minor damage to his combat suit.

Then it was Stanis and Krukov, who each took turns advancing and gaining ground. Behind them troopers continued to drop in through the stairway. With each soldier's entry the rate of fire multiplied, offering more cover for the lead soldiers to advance, while more troopers leapfrogged forward.

Henderson hit the ground himself and rolled away to the left while his men continued to lay down covering fire. Red energy bursts still shot out from the defenders but it was more sporadic now as the Marines forced the defenders to keep their heads down.

They were in a relatively large room and from its layout it looked like it was used for large meetings, perhaps presentations, or training. The open room had several supporting columns, equipment and furniture which were now used as cover by his troops.

The defenders had created a makeshift barricade out of some large equipment and had been using it for cover, but the sustained Marine rail gun fire now began shredding it, creating gaps in their defenses.

There were only a handful of Kemmar and they didn't have enough firepower to defend against Henderson's Marines. They also didn't appear to be as well trained and couldn't exploit any of their early advantages. Soon the advancing troopers overwhelmed them.

As their defenses fell apart a Kemmar stood trying to return fire more effectively. The Marines shot him down so quickly that Henderson was sure he didn't even have enough time to realize his mistake.

Recognizing the hopelessness of their cause some tried to retreat, but were cut down while fleeing, the Marine rail guns perforating their backs. Surprisingly not one Kemmar surrendered. Death seemed preferable to capture. After the way they treated their prisoners it was no surprise that they expected the same in return.

Eventually all resistance was quashed and the Marines secured the room. There were no fatalities and only minor damage to some of the combat suits.

"Perimeter secured," said Daniels, who stood at front of the room. Ahead of him was a long corridor.

"Excellent work. Let's keep moving."

They raced down the corridor with Henderson leading the way until they reached a corner. There Henderson held up a fist telling everyone to stop.

"Johns, we need eyes around that bend."

"Coming right up Sarge."

Johns ordered the mosquito drone to round the corner. It transmitted its video feed to the Marine visors just as before. The video revealed a large energy weapon battery mounted on the ceiling. If any soldier turned that corner they would be cut down the moment they appeared.

Luckily, the gun's targeting systems didn't recognize the drone as a target.

"Can you take that gun out?" said Henderson.

"I think so Sarge," said Johns.

Private Johns carefully maneuvered the drone remotely and it flew closer and closer to the gun, until it landed right on top of it. Once in place the Private Johns sent a destruct command and the drone exploded, destroying the energy weapon right along with it.

The threat safely removed, the troopers turned the corner and raced down the adjoining corridor. This hallway was much tighter than the last and it made for slow going with barely enough room for two troopers at a time. This stretched the group out like a train with multiple cars being pulled down a track.

Henderson knew they had to rely on speed to get through, but his fears were realized when his display showed the troopers in the rear taking fire.

"What the hell is going on back there?" said Henderson.

"Some Kemmar got behind us, Sir," said Private Martinez from the rear.

"How many?"

"Looks like five, maybe six."

The team tried to turn around and lend support to the exposed soldiers but the tight corridor made a coordinated counterattack difficult.

From his position he couldn't even see the attackers let alone get a firing solution on them. He clenched a metal fist and cursed when Martinez disappeared from his display. He then watched in horror as Private Lee fell as well.

A quarter of his team in the rear had now stopped and were trying deal with the Kemmar threat from behind. He knew he couldn't help them and that the priority was to move fast. So he ordered the rest of his team to continue advancing.

Ahead they were reaching the end of the long hallway where there were another set of doors. As they approached the doors slid open and a group of Kemmar in combat suits rushed through.

The three troopers in front fell almost instantly and disappeared from Henderson's display as red lightning streaked over their heads hitting the troopers behind them. Henderson ducked and cursed. They were caught in a crossfire.

CHAPTER 59

Kevin's Marines dropped to the ground while the shuttles pounded the entrance to the building with heavy energy weapon fire. The onslaught had a dual purpose. It provided cover for the troopers hitting the ground, and it softened up the entrance so that they could advance without opposition.

The seven shuttles floated only a few meters off the ground, all of them firing as the Marines jumped off.

Kevin hit the ground and his combat suit immediately compensated for the icy surface. The ice under his feet was so hard that it didn't even give an inch under the weight of Kevin's combat suit. Above him the shuttles continued to pound the building, their blue bolts melding with the icy landscape and clear sky.

Many of his Marines had already hit the ice and the rest continued to drop from the shuttles above. With the heavy fire from the shuttles the troops did not meet any resistance and were able to all disembark without problem. Nonetheless, the troopers all spread out so as not to give the enemy an easy target.

"Ok, listen up. We do this by the book. No heroics. We move in, take the atrium, secure it and wait for further orders."

"Yes, Sir," said the rest of the Marines over his comm.

"Move out."

The shuttles were still pounding the front of the building. It was hard to imagine that anything could survive such a barrage. As they got closer Kevin could see that the front of the building had been turned into a mangled mess of melted steel and perforated mortar.

The shuttles had hollowed out the entrance, leaving no signs of resistance. No defenders could withstand such a powerful assault. When they got close enough the shuttles stopped firing, allowing the troops to move in. With the shuttles floating behind them, ready to destroy any new threats, the troopers flooded through the front of the building.

"Damn, what a mess," said Reynolds.

"That'll teach them not to mess with humans again," said Burke.

"Good thing we have our own air supply. Can you imagine smelling that shit?" said Patel.

Inside there were dozens of bodies, or at least what resembled bodies. The shuttles had obliterated everything leaving armor covered body parts strewn throughout. Kevin was also thankful that his combat suit shielded him from what he knew would be a repulsive smell.

The atrium was massive and the troopers fanned out establishing a perimeter and insuring there were no surprises. Kevin surveyed the room. It was connected to numerous hallways snaking out in a dizzying array of directions. It could take days before they found where the prisoners were held.

"We need access to their systems. Find me a way in," ordered Kevin.

"Got it, Chief. I've found an entry point to the prison's network," said Chen over the combat suit's comm. "It appears it hasn't been damaged by the attack."

"Good. Initiate a network takeover."

"Initiating," said Chen, attaching a device to a podium shaped unit with a clear, glass like top. "There's a problem, Sir. The device can't communicate with the Hermes AI."

"Must be that damned interference again. Is there a workaround?"

"Maybe. We can only transmit up to a certain range and then the signal loses strength. If we send one of the shuttles higher up in the atmosphere we can use it as a relay to amplify the signal. The device should then be able to link with the Hermes AI."

"Good. Hang tight while I get a shuttle in position."

On Kevin's orders one of the shuttles floating in front of the building broke formation and rocketed up into the sky. In a matter of minutes it reached an altitude where it could both communicate with the ground team and the Hermes. It then acted as a repeater allowing communication between both groups.

"It's working, Sir. We've linked up with the Hermes AI. Initiating takeover of enemy network."

The Hermes AI used the relay to attack the Kemmar network, unleashing a powerful electronic attack. The team waited as the AI broke through the myriad defenses setup to protect the prison systems from intrusion.

The AI's electronic warfare capabilities were unrivaled and Kevin knew it would soon take control of the prison's systems. They would then not only know where the prisoners were being held, but also where the Kemmar were hiding.

"Mayday, mayday, taking heavy weapon fire from multiple bogeys!" said the relay shuttle pilot over the comm. "Taking evasive action."

Thousands of meters above the prison Kemmar fighters swarmed the shuttle, painting its hull red with energy weapon fire.

CHAPTER 60

"Enemy system takeover terminated," announced the AI.

Jon watched with dismay as the Kemmar fighters destroyed the assault shuttle.

"Where did those fighters come from?"

"Uncertain. Preliminary data indicates they were stationed on the far side of the planet, Sir," said Petrovic.

"Why the hell didn't we see them?"

"The same interference that is disrupting our communications and targeting also concealed the fighters from our scans."

"Target fighters. Energy weapons only."

"We can't get a lock on the fighters, Sir."

"Then fire in their direction. Full spectrum array."

"The fighters are descending on the prison, Sir. If we fire we risk hitting our troops."

"Goddammit!"

CHAPTER 61

The assault shuttles hovering in front of the prison and above the roof turned and raced into the sky to meet the attacking Kemmar fighters. The fighters screamed downward racing for the prison.

The fighters were outnumbered, but their speed and agility made up the difference. Coming into range the shuttles let loose a round of missiles and the fighters scattered firing decoys behind them. When the last of the missiles exploded the Kemmar fighters were still in the sky and now coming around for a run at the shuttles.

The sky lit up in a blue and red laser show as both sides tried to gain the advantage. The Kemmar fighters danced and sidestepped around the blue bursts, but the shuttles were heavier and slower and took numerous hits.

The heavy armor plating protected the shuttles, allowing them to withstand more damage, but that protection had its limits. As the shuttles took more hits their armor plating weakened, and it seemed inevitable that it would eventually fail.

The Kemmar fighters changed tactics and now focused their attack on one shuttle. Acting like a pack of wolves they worked to isolate their target and separate it from the protection of the group. They hit it from all sides with sustained fire. The Kemmar energy weapons soon burned through the shuttle's plating and the sky lit up with the white flash of the exploding shuttle.

The shuttles regrouped and worked to counter the Kemmar strategy. The dog fights continued and the shuttles tried desperately to use their superior numbers to gain an advantage.

One Kemmar fighter flipped and swayed and raced in all directions imaginable trying to shake the two shuttles chasing it, the shuttle pilots displayed incredible skill and continued to give chase, yet the killing shot continued to elude them.

The reality was that there was only so much the shuttle pilots could do with the heavier and less maneuverable ships. Soon it became clear that the Kemmar fighters had the upper hand and that it was only a matter of time until the shuttles were wiped out. That conclusion became even more certain when the fighters painted the sky white for a second time.

CHAPTER 62

Sergeant Henderson dropped down on one knee and fired on the advancing Kemmar. The troopers beside him did the same, while the Marines behind him stayed standing. The combined rail gun fire sent a torrent of bullets ripping through the enemy, shredding their suits and stopping their advance.

To the rear his Marines were getting control of the situation and now coordinated their fire more effectively, forcing the Kemmar to retreat. As the Kemmar fell back the troopers followed, determined to terminate the threat. Their attack, however, served to stretch the team even further leaving them even more exposed.

The Kemmar had to be dealt with or they would continue to harass their rear flank. On the other hand they needed to keep pressing forward and couldn't afford to stop and wait. They also couldn't afford to lose more soldiers.

Sergeant Henderson had lost almost a third of his team in the crossfire. Nine troopers dead. And now five had gone after the Kemmar attackers behind them. If they advanced now, with the troopers on the rear giving chase, they would be down to a team of sixteen.

In the end, standing still was not an option. They had to press on and not lose any momentum. The troopers chasing the Kemmar would have to catch up.

"OK we're moving out. Krukov and Daniels, ready your grenade launchers and lob a few through that doorway. We charge and glass whatever's still alive behind those doors."

"Yes, Sir," said the two Marines.

The two Marines slid open the doors, let loose a volley of grenades into the adjoining room, and took cover again behind the wall. The ground shook from the force of the concussions.

The troopers again slid the doors open and they all charged into the room. They took fire the second they entered and each trooper scrambled to find cover. But there was none. The Kemmar defenders had a superior position and now unleashed a relentless barrage of energy weapon fire on the exposed Marines.

Some tried to charge the Kemmar position, but were slaughtered before getting close enough to do any harm. In the first frantic moments several troopers blinked off Henderson's display while the rest showed heavy damage to their combat suits. Left with no choice Henderson ordered the rest of his men to retreat back to the other side of the doors.

They continued to take heavy fire as they bunched up in front of the doorway trying desperately to get to safety. They tried returning fire to cover their retreat, but to no avail and more Marines died in the process.

Only eight Marines made it to the other side. The rest had simply vanished from Sergeant Henderson's visor. What was worse, he couldn't see the other five who had given chase to the other Kemmar soldiers. He assumed they were dead as well. He knew this was true when Kemmar soldiers rounded the corner behind them and opened fire.

The doors flew open in front of them and more Kemmar soldiers pushed into the corridor firing their energy weapons at the trapped group of Marines.

CHAPTER 63

Kevin's stomach hollowed out as he watched the last of Henderson's team blink off his visor. He stared at the blank display in disbelief, refusing to believe what he saw. Thirty Marines, gone. His friend, gone. He fought against the grief. Fought to keep his composure. There would be time for grief later.

Henderson had known the risks. He was a veteran. A lifer. He had accepted death long ago, and he was lucky enough to meet the reaper in the thick of battle. It was a warrior's death. A good death. He would have approved.

Kevin clenched an armored fist. He wouldn't let the Sergeant die in vain. He looked around at the different doorways. The shuttles were not doing well against the Kemmar fighters, so taking over the prison's systems wasn't an option. Neither was standing around and waiting. But searching blindly for the prisoners would take too long. That left only one option. They would have to split up.

"Listen up," he announced over the combat suit's comm. "It doesn't look like we're going to get access to the prison's network. So to improve our chances of finding the prisoners we are going to break up into five squads. Each squad will take a different route and we will search until we find those prisoners. Any Kemmar you come across is to be presumed hostile and shot on sight. We will take no prisoners. Is that understood?"

"Yes, Sir," said the rest of the Marines in unison.

"Good."

Kevin quickly organized the squads and assigned each a route. He gave the order for all squads to move out and they each entered their designated corridors. Kevin leveled his Gatling gun in front of him and led his team down their chosen path. He had managed to contain his grief for now, but a blind fury had taken hold in its place, and he couldn't wait to run into some more Kemmar.

CHAPTER 64

"Sir we've lost another shuttle," said Petrovic.

The air battle had turned for the worst, and they were now down to only four shuttles. If the shuttles originally had a numerical superiority, it was now lost. The Kemmar fighters were simply better equipped for aerial combat and would soon destroy the rest of the shuttles. Then what? Jon shuddered at the thought.

Orbital support had been vital to the mission's success. Without the interference the Hermes could easily eliminate all external opposition from orbit and also take over the prison's systems. Finding the prisoners would be simple and any Kemmar defenders could be dealt with easily. But none of that was possible and now they were all running blind.

"Helm, break orbit and enter the planet's atmosphere," said Jon, knowing now what he had to do.

"Yes, Sir," said Richards.

"Sir?" said Commander Wolfe.

"I know, but under the circumstances it's our only option."

"Yes, Sir," said Wolfe, nodding.

Jon sensed the rising tension on the bridge. A quick look around confirmed his feeling. Everyone focused on their work, but he saw the tightness in the neck and shoulders, the rapid glances at each other, the clenched jaws. The plan hadn't survived the opening shots and now drastic measures were underway.

The Hermes turned and began its descent towards Kerces. Entering a planet's atmosphere with a ship as large as the Hermes wasn't completely unheard of, but it was to be avoided. A ship like the Hermes was designed for space, not atmospheric travel. Once inside the planet's atmosphere the Hermes would be far less maneuverable. This made it more vulnerable, and they all knew it.

The Hermes approached the fringes of the Kerces atmosphere and positioned itself so that it would enter with its belly first, as that was the thicker section of the hull. It then began its descent. Flames licked at the underside of the ship and then turned into lashes. The Hermes continued its measured descent and on the viewscreen it looked like they were entering a giant fiery mouth. The flames were now wrapping around the sides of the ship, orange fangs pressing down hard, trying to crush the life out of their prey. But the Hermes persisted and soon broke free, with nothing but sky and ice ahead.

"Take us to within firing range of the Kemmar fighters," said Jon.

Ensign Richards dropped the Hermes to an altitude of thirty thousand feet.

"We have targeting back, Sir," said Petrovic.

"Glass every one of those damn fighters."

"Yes, Sir!"

A merciless stream of blue light erupted from the Hermes boring holes through two of the Kemmar fighters. Their flaming carcasses fell from the sky and crashed into the glacial mountains below. The rest of the fighters broke off their attack of the shuttles and turned their attention to the Hermes. They raced at high speed straight for the Hermes, too fast for the now regrouping assault shuttles to catch.

The Hermes continued firing destroying one more fighter, but the rest evaded the energy weapon onslaught and bridged the gap between them and the warship in blistering speed. In comparison, the Hermes sat motionless in the sky, too cumbersome to outmaneuver the agile fighters.

"They're trying to ram us. Bring rail guns online. Point defense mode."

Rail gun turrets sprang up across the Hermes hull and opened fire. The shells created their exploding barrier in front of the Kemmar fighters, blocking their access. But the Kemmar fighters were not missiles and did not fly straight into the barrage. Instead they scattered, looking for a gap. The Hermes continued to fire its energy weapons at the fighters and destroyed another attacker, but that left five more.

Two of the fighters focused their fire on one of the rail gun turrets, their energy weapons unhindered by the rail gun fire. The Hermes managed to destroy another fighter, but the concentrated fire succeeded in destroying the rail gun turret creating a hole in the point defense shield. In the blink of an eye the Kemmar fighter took advantage of the weakness and smashed into the Hermes hull.

The resulting explosion rocked the Hermes and breached the hull. In short order the other fighters changed direction and flew straight for the breach. The shuttles had made it to within range of the Hermes and were now firing on the Kemmar ships, but it proved futile. The Kemmar pilots were too determined, and their ships too fast to be denied.

There was a large flaming hole in the Hermes hull, and the remaining three Kemmar fighters slammed into it in rapid succession. The Hermes yawned as massive explosions rocked it threatening to snap the beleaguered ship in two.

The powerful concussions threw Commander Wolfe across the bridge, her head slamming into the unforgiving floor. She lay there in a heap, face down, her body crumpled and broken, the only movement a twitching foot.

Jon struggled to reach her, but the ship continued to lurch, and every movement caused him to lose his balance. He grabbed hold of a railing and gripped it with the power of a vise. Using it to steady himself he placed one foot after another until he finally reached Wolfe's body. Bending down he placed a hand on her neck feeling for a pulse. He found it. She was still alive. But he knew it wouldn't be for long.

He opened a comm with Doctor Ellerbeck. "Doctor, we have a medical emergency on the bridge. It's Commander Wolfe."

"Understood. I'll get someone up there as soon as possible."

Jon closed the comm and turned his attention back to the bridge. "Report!"

"We have sustained heavy damage, Sir," said Petrovic. "Inertial dampeners are offline, and there is a massive hull breach on the port side. We have multiple casualties and injuries and there are reports of fires raging throughout the ship."

Jon looked around him. Several of the bridge crew had also been thrown from their stations. Some picked themselves up off the floor, while others lay inert. Blood streamed from head wounds on two crew members who sat with a confused look in their eyes. Another stared in shock at the gruesome bone poking out of her broken forearm.

Smoke had started to creep in adding to the confusion and making the air thick. The foul smell of burning circuits combined with the smoke to make breathing difficult, causing multiple coughing fits. Jon found his way back to his chair, the smoke now stinging his eyes.

"We're losing altitude, Sir!" said Richards.

"Can you compensate?"

"Negative. I've only got thrusters. I can use them to slow our descent."

"Can you land her in the valley?"

"Yes, Sir."

Jon opened a comm with the rest of the ship. "All hands brace for impact. Emergency landing underway."

CHAPTER 65

Kevin and his team approached a double set of doors, which opened as they got closer. Ahead was a large open area, which looked like an indoor gymnasium of some sort.

"They must use this for the prisoners. We're getting close," said Kevin over his comm. He gestured for his team to enter in two groups, one taking the right flank and the other taking the left.

The Marines rushed through the doorway two by two, splitting up as they went, rail guns leveled in front of them and ready to fire. They moved so fast that it would be difficult for the enemy to target them. But there was no resistance. No firing. Kevin's group continued to advance.

They reached the far side of the large room with ease and regrouped at a far wall. There were openings at both ends of the wall.

"Listen up. There could be Kemmar on the other side of this wall waiting to ambush us. So we're splitting into two teams. Private Chen, you and your team are going to take the opening on the left."

"Yes, Sir."

"The rest come with me on the right. Nice and easy. We're not getting nailed by a Kemmar ambush. Move out."

The two teams split up and approached their designated openings, flanking them from both sides. Kevin looked back at Chen and held up a metal fist. He waved it forward and the two teams entered.

They moved in with fingers tight on their triggers, ready to take on an entrenched enemy. But what they found stopped their advance faster than any Kemmar energy burst could. From one end to the other were rows of naked humans hanging upside down from the ceiling on hooks.

None lived.

There were hundreds of them, both men and women, and all visibly tortured, their bodies riddled with cuts, welts and blisters. Their arms were not bound, but hung down instead, like some morbid human willow tree, making it impossible to walk through without the corpses touching you.

"What the hell is this?" said Chen.

"The Reivers," said Kevin. He looked ahead and saw a set of doors and it all began to make sense. "They make the rest of them walk through here, to get to the gymnasium."

"Those fuckers!" said Chen.

Several other Marines grunted in agreement.

Kevin knew they had to get through to the other side of the doorway. So with grim resolve he gave the order to advance.

Even with his combat suit on he swore he could feel every hand of every corpse touch him as he passed. He didn't want to look but couldn't help staring at the lifeless eyes of each Reiver he passed. He felt them all pressing against him, grabbing at him, trying to hold onto him. He knew it was all in his imagination, but he couldn't shake the feeling they were trying to hold him back. Trying to keep him from reaching the doorway and crossing through to the other side.

"I don't know if I'll be able to sleep after this one," said Reynolds.

"You and me both," said Burke.

"These Kemmar are some twisted motherfuckers," said Chen. "I've got something special planned for them."

"Ok, everybody stay focused. Keep your eye on the prize," said Kevin.

The Marines made it through the Reiver corpses and reached the doors on the other side with half the group flanking the left side and the other half flanking the right.

"Ok, same as before," said Kevin. "On three we go in, two by two."

"Yes, Sir," said the rest of the Marines.

"One, two…"

Just then the doors slid open and a round metal object flew through.

"Bomb," yelled Chen.

But before the Marines could get out of the way a blinding flash of light discharged from the device and the power drained from Kevin's combat suit. Where he was once a metal Goliath, he now collapsed under the dead weight of the unpowered body armor. He hit the ground hard and heard the rest of his Marines doing the same.

He tried to open a comm with the rest of his team, but to no avail. "Chen, Reynolds, Burke, respond." But there was no response. He tried to get up, but his combat suit wouldn't budge. Everything was dead. Then realization swept over him. The device was an EMP weapon. It fired a focused electromagnetic pulse at his team frying the power supply and all the circuits in their combat suits.

They were all trapped.

He heard the heavy stomping of more combat suits, but any hopes of rescue were dashed when Kevin looked up to see two armored Kemmar standing over him. Dread swept over him as they bent over and each grabbed one of his arms, lifted him up and dragged him through the doorway.

CHAPTER 66

The Hermes left a fiery trail as it fell from the sky. The remaining assault shuttles followed closely yet were almost invisible beside the wounded warship. Thrusters fired underneath the ship ensuring the fall was a controlled one, and the Hermes dropped its landing gear, hoping for an easy landing.

Ensign Richards manually controlled the fall, positioning the ship for a landing in the valley directly in front of the prison complex. On the viewscreen the ground came up fast. Mountain peaks and frozen cliffs rushed past as the Hermes dropped past them, like a giant skydiver, waiting until the last minute to let loose her parachute.

They were still falling too fast. Even with Richards's flying prowess, they were not slowing down enough for a soft landing. There simply wasn't enough power in the ship's thrusters. As alarms rang out, fires raged and smoke filled the bridge, Jon stared at the viewscreen. He stared at the crystal blue surface rushing up to meet him and wondered if this was it. Would he die here on this desolate frozen world? Would he finally be free?

I want to live.

He heard the words, or rather felt them, but wasn't sure where they came from. Was it him or the creature? He didn't know. Did it matter? With all that had happened did he still want to die? The answer was no. Why?

At that moment he thought of Breeah and Anki. For all his efforts to save the Reivers, for all his dreams of freeing humanity, at this moment the only thing that made him want to go on was Breeah and Anki.

Why them? Did he love Breeah, or was she a just a replacement for the wife he lost? What about little Anki? The little girl did bring out his paternal instincts. Was it because he missed his daughters so much? Did it matter? They needed him and he realized he needed them just as much. He wanted to protect them. And for whatever reason, that desire made him want to live again.

He looked back at the viewscreen. Richards had managed to slow the drop considerably. At their current speed the Hermes would be damaged by the impact, but shouldn't be destroyed.

He looked over at Commander Wolfe's still motionless body. A medic was crouched over trying to revive her. Jon yelled at the medic. "We're going to crash. Grab hold of something."

***

At first Commander Wolfe didn't know exactly where she was. She looked around at the mayhem surrounding her and was jolted back to reality. The battle. The Hermes had been hit. People were injured. She had to get up. The crew needed her. But something was wrong with her legs and she couldn't move them.

She looked down expecting to find them pinned under some piece of equipment, but there was nothing. She noticed the medic working on her. She had been injured, and from the looks of everything it was serious. Although the Hermes didn't look any better off.

Chaos reigned around her. People were injured, equipment was destroyed. They needed her to keep things under control. As she saw the viewscreen and the ground rushing up at them, she opened a comm link with Chief Engineer Singh.

"Yes, Lynda."

"Raj?"

"Yes, what is it?"

She heard the commotion in the background and knew things were no less chaotic down in Engineering than they were on the bridge.

"Lynda, I'm very busy down here, what do you need?"

"Raj…" Her throat exploded into a violent coughing fit and she struggled to catch her breath.

"Lynda? Are you alright?"

Tears were streaming down her cheeks and she knew they weren't only from the coughing. Everything around her seemed to slow down. They were going to hit the ground any second now. The medic who had been looking after her was lunging, trying to grab hold of a railing to brace against the impact. This was it.

"I'm sorry Raj."

The Hermes hit the ground.

***

The impact made the medic change directions in mid-air, and her body surged hopelessly into a bank of consoles, bouncing off of them and turning like a helicopter before landing on the ground in a broken heap.

Commander Wolfe's body didn't fare any better and flew yet again across the room into a nearby wall, the impact so strong that Jon doubted any bones remained intact. Her lifeless body fell to the floor.

Jon stared at his vibrant first officer's corpse in disbelief. So much talent. So much potential. She was the very last person who should have died. But she was dead. All because of him. She was not the only one. Reports were coming in fast from throughout the ship. The casualty rate was climbing.

The seated crew members fared much better. The threat of a crash landing forced them all to secure themselves with their seat restraints. The bridge's Marine sentries were also unscathed. They wore full combat suits which protected them from injury, so while they were bounced around a fair bit they got up and took their posts as if nothing had changed.

On the viewscreen the orientation had changed to show the prison complex on the far side of the icy valley. Regaining his focus Jon realized they hadn't heard from Kevin and his Marines.

"Do we have communications now?"

"Yes, Sir. The interference is gone," said the comm officer.

"Open a comm with Chief St. Clair, and see if you can bring up his combat suit's video feed."

"I am receiving no response, Sir."

"Ok try Sergeant Henderson."

"No response."

"Can you locate their combat suits?"

"No, Sir. I am not getting a response from any of the combat suits."

"I thought you said the interference was gone?"

"It is, Sir."

Jon slumped back into his chair as realization donned on him. No response from the combat suits could only mean that they were all destroyed. If the combat suits were destroyed, that meant the Marines were all dead. Could it be possible? Kevin? Henderson? The fleet's finest, dead?

"Captain, we are under attack," shouted Petrovic.

Petrovic's words pulled Jon back into the moment. On the viewscreen were dozens of Kemmar soldiers in combat suits charging the ship. There could be no doubt now. The ground assault had been defeated and the Kemmar were now coming for the Hermes.

The assault shuttles responded first and swooped in on the attackers opening fire immediately. Energy weapons and missiles lit up the icy landscape as the shuttles did their best to fend off the attackers. The Kemmar kept coming and fired missiles of their own at the shuttles buzzing above their heads.

The four remaining assault shuttles simply didn't have enough firepower to clear the battlefield and were eventually picked off by the Kemmar missiles, each disappearing from the sky in a flash of light.

"Ensign Petrovic, can you open fire on the enemy ground troops?" said Jon.

"Negative, Sir. Weapons are offline," said Petrovic.

Jon stared at the screen as the Kemmar soldiers came closer, and opened a ship wide comm. "All hands, arm yourselves and prepare to repel enemy boarders."

They had fought off a boarding party in their previous encounter with the Kemmar, but with a full detail of Marines. How could they fight them off now? What if they couldn't? The Kemmar would turn them into slaves and take the jump technology for themselves. A slaver race with a jump system.

They could grow to rival the Juttari and Diakans in no time. What's worse, they would be within striking distance of Sol. Under the terms of the Accord the Diakans would have to defend Sol against the Kemmar, but what would happen if the Kemmar became allied with the Juttari? They would be unstoppable.

Of course the chain of events might take another direction, but it didn't matter. Regardless of how Jon felt about the Diakans or the Juttari, Jon knew he couldn't let the jump system fall into Kemmar hands. He had only one option. He had to destroy the Hermes.

But what about the crew? What about Breeah and Anki? Should they all die because of his mistakes? He couldn't let that happen either. Still, where could they go? Kerces was a frigid wasteland. If they left the ship they couldn't hope to survive for long. If they could survive, the Kemmar would eventually find them and either kill them or enslave them. Not an option either.

"Ensign Richards, is the jump system still online?"

"Yes, Sir, but it has sustained some damage."

"Can we jump?"

"Sir?"

"You heard me Ensign."

"Uh, yes, Sir, but we're not supposed to attempt a jump while inside a planet's atmosphere, let alone while on the ground."

"But we can jump. How far?"

"The planet's gravity will drastically reduce our range."

"Can we get out of this system?"

"I think so."

Jon glanced at the viewscreen. The Kemmar were now pouring into the Hermes from the hull breach. It was now or never.

“Initiate jump.”

CHAPTER 67

Multiple explosions rocked the Hermes, as the strain of the jump caused the hull breach to grow even larger, flushing both human and Kemmar out into open space. Jon gripped his chair's armrests, bracing himself against the powerful convulsions. The bridge itself was a scene of devastation and chaos, the crew that was still alive struggling to remain at their posts. But that task proved impossible for some as their stations erupted in flames and smoke.

"Report," said Jon, trying to keep focused.

"We have landed in a neighboring Kemmar system three light years from our previous position. Reading two inhabited planets and multiple ships in orbit."

Jon had hoped they would land in an uninhabited region, but jumping from Kerces's surface gave them little control over their destination.

"What is our jump status?"

"Jump system is at zero percent. We are not jump ready."

"Are the Kemmar still on board?"

"Yes, Sir," said Petrovic. "Kemmar boarders are still on board. Reading multiple firefights between the Kemmar and the crew."

They were a good crew, but Jon knew they didn't stand a chance. They might hold the Kemmar off for a while but with most of the Marines gone they had little hope of prevailing.

"Sir, one of the ships is breaking orbit. They are on an intercept course."

Jon felt like he had been catching falling knives since the start of the rescue mission, and this was the final blade to fall. If the Kemmar boarders didn't succeed in taking the Hermes, the Kemmar ship approaching would.

"AI, initiate self-destruct sequence," said Jon.

The bridge crew turned almost in unison to look at Jon. He could tell from the confused look on their faces that they were too preoccupied with the battle to come to the same conclusion. He had to keep them calm. They needed to stay in control if they hoped to survive.

"We cannot allow the jump system technology to fall into Kemmar hands. You are all to arm yourselves and proceed to the lifeboats." Jon stood and turned to the two Marine sentries. "Marines, you will escort the bridge crew to the lifeboats. Kemmar boarders are to be shot on sight. Is that clear?"

"Yes, Sir," said the two Marines in unison, towering over Jon and the rest of the crew in their combat suits.

One of the Marines walked over to the bridge weapons locker and opened it. The bridge crew rose from their stations and walked to the Marine who handed out rail guns and grenades to each crew member. The only thing they lacked was combat suits, but they all had extensive combat training and Jon knew they could take care of themselves.

Jon geared up, taking as much hardware as he could comfortably carry, and ran for the exit. The corridor was bathed in red light and smoke, and the self-destruct klaxon boomed along with the AI's repeated instructions for all hands to head for the life boats. Jon raced down the corridor and opened a comm with Breeah.

"Captain, what is happening?"

"We are evacuating the ship. Are you and Anki still in your quarters?"

"Yes."

"Stay there. I'm on my way."

Jon ran through the corridors at an incredible speed. The crew had their orders. All that mattered now was that he save Breeah and Anki. In his hands he held two rail guns and it didn't take long for him to use them. Two Kemmar rounded a corner as he sped by and without breaking stride Jon opened up on both of them, shredding their visors with a simultaneous barrage of rail gun fire.

He kept running, the heavy sound of metal hitting the floor behind him confirmation enough that the soldiers were dead. All around him were signs of battle and calamity. The walls were covered with scorch marks from energy weapon fire, fires burned in seemingly random locations, dead bodies littered the floor, and the never ending smoke was everywhere.

Reaching Breeah's quarters he pounded on the door. His heart crashed against his ribs. His breaths were quick and shallow. His head kept turning from side to side in quick jerking movements expecting to see more Kemmar at any moment. The door slid open and Breeah rushed out holding Anki in her arms.

"Let me carry Anki. She won't slow me down as much."

Breeah paused, then held Anki out, who jumped into Jon's arms. Jon shifted the little girl to his left arm and handed Breeah one of his railguns.

"I'm assuming you know how to use one of these?" said Jon.

Breeah frowned at Jon, but didn't respond.

"Ok, let's go. We need to make it to the lifeboats. I've already run into two Kemmar so there's a good chance we might run into a few more before we get there."

With that they took off running back the way Jon had come. Jon matched his speed to Breeah's and Anki gripped his neck with all her strength, bracing herself for any move Jon might make. She learned fast, thought Jon.

Turning a corner they came upon a wounded crewman sitting against a bulkhead. Jon slowed down and approached the man. His uniform had scorch marks in the abdominal area and black blood oozed out with each breath. Jon bent down and locked eyes with the man.

"Kemmar… four of them."

"Take it easy son. Do you think you can make it to the life boats?"

The man shook his head no. Jon looked down at his wound again. Even if he could get him to the lifeboats there would be little anyone could do for him. Lying on the floor beside the man was his sidearm. Jon picked it up on placed it into the man's palm. The man wrapped his fingers around the gun and looked back at Jon and nodded. Jon returned the nod and stood up.

"Let's go," he said to Breeah. She looked at the man for a few moments longer, but her face remained hard and expressionless. She looked up, pointed her gun straight ahead and started walking. Jon quickly came up beside her and they picked up the pace, breaking into a brisk jog.

They made it to the lifeboats without further incident. Despite the chaos throughout the rest of the ship the scene at the lifeboat hanger was surprisingly controlled. Much of the crew had already arrived and had boarded their lifeboats, while the remaining crew members were finding their assigned docks. The hangar itself was a long metallic cylinder with a platform running up the middle and doors on both sides leading to each lifeboat.

The lifeboats themselves were like mini shuttles. They were designed to be compact and swift. As such, they were Spartan as far as accommodations went. Since they had to make a quick escape under extreme situations, each lifeboat was capable of creating its own FTL bubble. This feature wasn't lost on Jon and he was counting on it to get away from their Kemmar hunters.

Jon, Breeah and Anki ran down the corridor until they reached the command pod, the one designated for the Captain. When they approached the scanners recognized Jon and the doors opened for him. The doorway was narrow, only fitting one person at a time, and Breeah motioned to Jon to take Anki in first. Jon nodded in agreement and took the little girl inside.

As he stepped in he heard the sound of weapon fire behind him. He dropped Anki in a chair and whipped around, shouldering his weapon as he turned. Through the doorway he saw Breeah down on one knee firing her railgun. Coming from the other side was energy weapon fire, but the bolts shooting by were blue.

Jon rushed to the doorway and turned to face their attackers, but they were not Kemmar. On the far end of the hangar firing back at Jon and Breeah were the Diakans. Jon returned fire and dropped one of the Diakans instantly. The rest scattered and broke off their attack. Jon let loose a few more rounds to make sure they were gone and turned to enter the lifeboat again.

Breeah did not follow. She stayed on one knee, gun pointed forward, but her head was bent forward. Jon's stomach flipped and he was almost paralyzed with fear. He lunged and seized her by the armpits and pulled her into the lifeboat with one powerful movement.

The door closed behind him as he lay Breeah on her back.

"Mama!" screamed Anki.

The front of her shirt was scorched and steadily becoming drenched with blood. Anki lunged at her mother crying. Breeah reached out her arms and Anki fell into them sobbing into her shoulder. Breeah tried to calm her daughter down whispering into her ear and stroking her hair.

Jon knew he had to move fast. He retrieved a medical kit it and went to work dressing Breeah's wound, his hands moving with speed and precision. He applied a gel-like substance. As soon as it made contact with Breeah's skin it spread across her abdomen and flooded into the open wound causing Breeah to groan in pain. At the same time the lifeboat heaved and was discharged from the Hermes.

Jon finished the dressing, ensuring the gel was completely covered so that it could do its job. He tapped Anki on the shoulder. The little girl turned to him, eyes red and face wet.

"Anki, I need to give your mother some medicine to stop the pain."

Anki nodded and looked back at Breeah who reached up and wiped her daughter's tears. She cupped Anki's face into her palms and looked into her eyes.

"You need to be strong now. This is who we are. Promise me."

Anki shook her head no, her bottom lip quivering.

"Promise me."

Anki's eyes were locked with Breeah's and the firmness of her mother's tone made her gain some measure of control over herself.

"I promise," said Anki.

Breeah smiled. "That's my good girl."

"Anki, I need you to go back to your chair now and strap yourself in," said Jon.

Anki held her mother's gaze a bit longer and reached down and kissed her on the cheek before getting up and moving back to her chair.

"We don't have any biobots on board so we have to do things the old fashioned way. The gel I put on your wound will help it heal and prevent any infection from setting in. I'm going to give you a shot for the pain."

"I wish things could have been different, Captain."

"Everything is going to be fine. Call me Jon."

Breeah smiled. "If I die, promise me you will watch over Anki."

"You're not going to die."

Breeah's hand seized Jon's wrist with surprising strength. "Please Jon. I need to hear you say it."

"I promise."

Breeah nodded, released his wrist and lay her head back down on the floor.

"You need to rest, and I need to make sure we get away safely."

"See to your duties," said Breeah, her voice no more than a whisper.

Jon stood and went over to the pilot's chair and brought up a display.

"AI are you online?"

"Yes, Captain. I have transferred my core to your lifeboat's systems."

"Have all the lifeboats disembarked?"

"All lifeboats are clear of the Hermes, though still within the blast radius."

"How long until the Hermes self-destructs?"

"Hermes will self-destruct in three minutes."

"How long until the Kemmar intercept us?"

"At current speed the Kemmar ship will intercept in twenty minutes."

"Options?"

"The best course of action is for all the lifeboats to scatter while entering FTL velocity."

"Scatter?"

"If the lifeboats stay together the Kemmar ship will eventually overtake us and seize all the lifeboats. Scattering is the only way to ensure maximum survival rates. The Kemmar might be able to capture one lifeboat but the rest should escape."

"Makes sense. How will we regroup later?"

"We will not be able to regroup, Captain. Once the lifeboats enter FTL there will be no way to communicate with each other."

"So they'll all be on their own?"

"Yes, Captain."

"There must be another option."

"I'm afraid not, Captain. Under the circumstances this is the only option that maximizes the crew's survival rate."

Jon was stunned. How did it come to this? He knew he didn't have time to feel sorry for himself. He also knew the AI was right.

"Shall I proceed, Captain?" said the AI.

"Proceed."

The AI sent a message to all the lifeboats letting them know of the situation and initiated each lifeboat's FTL drive. For a few moments, all the little ships hung there motionless as FTL bubbles took shape around each craft. Shimmering in the darkness, they all looked like a swarm of fireflies for a few seconds, then shot out in hundreds of different directions. They broke the speed of light and hit FTL speeds in seconds.

A couple minutes later there was an explosion in the engineering room and the ship's massive reactors let loose their power and completely obliterated the rest of the ship leaving no trace of the Hermes behind, not even dust.

CHAPTER 68

"Captain, I've got something odd on my scans, just ahead."

"There's a surprise. Something odd in space. Who would have guessed? How about some more information so I know what the hell you're talking about?" said Captain Seiben, shaking his head. Why in the galaxy did he ever let his brother talk him into giving his kid a job?

"It looks like a small ship. Maybe a shuttle or an escape pod."

"Out here? Are there any larger ships nearby? Any wreckage?"

"Nothing. Just this little ship."

"Ok nephew, you were right, that is odd. What is its course?"

"It looks to be adrift."

"Just garbage then. Leave it for the next salvage scow that comes along."

"But Captain, there could be someone on board."

"Whoever is on board that thing is dead. They are not our concern."

"But they might be alive. They might need our help."

Captain Seiben brought his hand up and rubbed his eyes. "Do you think we are some kind of rescue ship now?"

"No."

"No we are not. Not a rescue ship. Not a salvage scow. You know why? I'll tell you why. Because we are a freighter. We carry freight. And we have to deliver that freight to get paid."

"Yes, Uncle. Um, I mean Captain. But if there is someone alive on that ship and we don't help them they will die. It wouldn't take us that long to check it out. There might be something of value on board."

"Goddammit, we're not a salvage scow."

"Yes, Captain. I'm sorry. I didn't mean it that way."

Captain Seiben settled back into his chair and rubbed the stubble on his chin. The damn kid was making him feel guilty. He was going to have to have a talk with his brother when they got home.

"Alter course to intercept the vessel."

"Yes, Captain. Thank you."

"Take that damn smile off your face. And tell the twins to get their asses over to the hangar bay. We're going to need their help getting into this hunk of space garbage."

"Yes, Uncle. I mean, Captain."

* * *

The hulking freighter lurched to a stop near the tiny lifeboat. From the ship's mid-section a large, slow moving craft appeared. It lumbered forward and as it drew close two mechanical arms stretched out and seized the lifeboat with a pair of giant metal pincers. The craft turned and headed back toward the freighter with the lifeboat in tow.

Inside the hangar bay Captain Seiben watched the operation from a safe distance high above on a metal catwalk. Once the lifeboat was safely on board and the hangar bay doors were closed Captain Seiben and his nephew rode a lift down to the main floor. On the main level he was joined by two burly identical twins.

The four men walked up to the lifeboat and quietly circled it.

"You see those markings?" said Captain Seiben. "This is a military craft."

"Do you recognize them?" said the nephew.

"No. Never seen them before. Whoever they are they're a long way from home." Seiben walked up to one side of the vessel and pointed to a rectangular outline in the hull. "This looks like it's the hatch. Probably the easiest way to get inside. Bring the jaws over and we'll pry it open."

The twins turned and walked to a corner where there was an assortment of tools, work tables and spare parts scattered around. They picked up a very large piece of equipment and carried it over, each twin holding a huge handle. The Captain gestured for them to get started and they positioned the tool on the side of the lifeboat's hull. The tool attached itself to the lifeboat with powerful magnets. Massive blades and levers then went to work on the hatch, cutting into the seal and prying back the edges.

When enough of the hatch was freed, the levers opened up and the door creaked open. The four men peered at the opening but could see only darkness.

"Can you see anything uncle?"

"No. Space garbage, just like I said."

Seiben frowned at his nephew and stepped forward to get a closer look. Approaching the dark opening he hesitated for a moment, then shrugged and walked the rest of the way in. He tried to make things out in the darkness. But he didn't need to see to know what the cold metal that suddenly pressed against his forehead was.

Responding to the pressure on his forehead he slowly backed out of the lifeboat's hatch, hands high above his head. Once outside a large intimidating man appeared wearing a blood stained military uniform. He pressed one weapon to Seiben's head and his other hand held a second weapon which now pointed at his nephew and the twins. The three men followed their Captain's lead and raised their hands in the air.

The military man looked the four of them over, his face riddled with confusion. He scanned the room, taking in everything at once, and returned to the four men. He silently looked from one to the other, as if trying to make a decision. Then, to Seiben's relief, the man lowered his weapons.

The man looked Seiben in the eyes and then spoke, his voice barely hiding his astonishment.

"You're human."

Thank You for reading Sol Shall Rise.

Stay tuned for Book 2 of The Pike Chronicles coming this winter.

To join my email list and be notified of new releases go to http://bit.ly/1sryzwQ

Please feel free to email me with any questions at gphudsonwrites@gmail.com

I answer all reader emails

Made in the USA
Columbia, SC
09 September 2020